CW00496391

DEBUTANTE MURDER PLOT

A 1920S HISTORICAL COZY MYSTERY - AN EVIE
PARKER MYSTERY BOOK 17

SONIA PARIN

Debutante Murder Plot Copyright © 2023 Sonia Parin

No part of this publication may be reproduced in any form or by any means, without the prior written permission of the author, except in the case of brief quotations embodied in critical articles and reviews. This is a work of fiction. Names, characters, places and incidents are the product of the author's imagination or are used fictitiously. Any resemblance to actual persons, living or dead, organizations, events or locales is entirely coincidental.

ISBN: 9798386262587

CHAPTER 1

"There are few hours in life more agreeable than the hour
dedicated to the ceremony known as afternoon tea."
Henry James

The Ritz, 1922

*E*vie tried to maintain a calm and matter-of-fact
tone when she said, "Henrietta hasn't spoken to
me in days."

Lotte Mannering did not look at all surprised. The
lady detective gave a knowing shake of her head. "You
could never have anticipated the outcome of your investigation. Is she actually holding you responsible?"

"She most certainly is. In Henrietta's opinion, I should
have discovered the identity of the blackmailer and

turned a blind eye to her friend's indiscretion." The very indiscretion which had led Lady Montague to produce an illegitimate heir, thereby providing the opportunity for blackmail, Evie thought.

"So what were you supposed to do when you found the incriminating letters in the maid's possession?" Lotte asked.

At the time, Evie hadn't given it much thought because there had only been one course of action. However, she had not considered other people's expectations.

"In Henrietta's opinion, I should have used the information to put a stop to the blackmail. Then, I should have discredited the maid and, finally, I should have destroyed the evidence." Instead, she had returned the letters to Lady Montague, the rightful owner.

The haughty septuagenarian had dismissed it all as nonsense, declaring the letters were nothing more than the product of someone's wicked imagination.

"Lady Montague should have taken care of it by destroying the evidence herself," Lotte declared. "You shouldn't blame yourself. You were not to know her daughter-in-law would discover the letters and use them to exile her to their country estate."

Yes, if only she knew then what she knew now. "Exiled to their country estate which happens to be in a windswept island off the Scottish coast, only accessible by boat and only at certain times of the day."

Sitting at a center stage table in The Ritz's Palm Court, Evie cast her eyes over the gilded trellis and widely spaced marble columns framed by archways and deep steps, finally landing on a central niche where a sculptured female figure in gilded lead stood, flanked by floor to ceiling mirrors, both enhancing and enlarging the popular meeting place.

She had only recently read an article describing the famous venue and now realized the article had described the setting but had omitted any mention of the atmosphere.

She and Lotte Mannering had come under scrutiny, right from the moment they had made their entrance and even as they sat, sipping their tea.

The edge of Evie's lip lifted as she acknowledged the fact she had recognized everyone currently enjoying their afternoon tea, including two recently married ladies flaunting their paramours—the new *de rigueur* fashion accessory employed by the most daring of ladies.

What extraordinary times we live in, Evie thought as, these days, it seemed more fashionable to put oneself on display for entirely the wrong reasons...

The sumptuous room buzzed with speculation.

Who was doing what with whom?

"We might need to think again about me taking on society cases," Evie mused.

"Nonsense." Lotte set her teacup down and cast a discerning eye over the selection of delectable tidbits on offer. "Don't fixate over it. You'll find plenty of distractions, especially in town. There are the seasonal scandals to contend with. The salacious bits of gossip swarming around. Mark my word, intuition will serve you well. You only need to learn to trust it."

Evie knew Lotte was referring to another case which had brought her abilities into question. If only she hadn't noticed a single mourner at a funeral... "My intuition won't necessarily pay the bills." After all, during that particular investigation, no one had actually engaged her services. Of course, she didn't need to earn a living but she had gone into business with the lady detective and that meant providing a service for a fee.

Shrugging, Lotte helped herself to another piece of lemon cake. "You noticed something unusual and you followed a trail. I really don't see what the problem is."

Evie knew she had to be practical. Otherwise, she would be paying her share of expenses out of her own pocket.

"Is that all that's worrying you?" Lotte asked.

She had layers of concerns, Evie admitted. "My problem might have something to do with the criminal mind. Honestly, I have reached the point where I cannot look at a person without wondering what malicious intentions they might be hiding behind their polite smile." Evie tilted her head and subjected Lotte to a careful scrutiny. Something about her looked different and it had definitely caught her attention.

Was it her hair or her clothes?

Both were quite stylish—a sharp contrast to some of her previous disguises.

Her jawline appeared to be more defined. She knew Lotte often used enhancements to change her physical appearance but Evie couldn't quite work out how the lady detective would make her face look thinner.

Heavens! Had she slimmed down? The last time they'd met in town, she had been playing the role of a wealthy widow and Lotte had expressed a desire to dabble in something risqué…

Shaking her head, Lotte gave the edge of her lip a dainty dab with her serviette and said, "There's something else bothering you and there's no use denying it." Lowering her voice, the lady detective asked, "Is it Tom? Is he giving you trouble?"

Evie wished she hadn't reached for her teacup just then. The fine porcelain cup slipped off her finger, rattled onto its saucer, spilling half the contents on the table and, in the process, alerted a waiter who swung toward her at the same time as a lady at the next table extended her hand to draw his attention. In that split second, the lady's large diamond ring snagged the waiter's sleeve, causing him to lose his hold on the tray he held, thereby spilling the contents of a carafe onto the lady's lap.

"*Armand,*" the lady yelped.

The waiter offered his profuse apologies while a swarm of waiters appeared on the scene and within minutes managed to restore calm and order.

The least amount of fuss was employed to deal with the spillage on Evie's table, with the distraction giving her the opportunity to change the subject.

Everyone who had turned to look resumed their conversations, casting discreet glances their way, just in case they could be provided with more fodder for gossip.

Leaning forward, Evie diverted Lotte's attention to the reason for their meeting. "What is our client's name?"

"Parsody Jane Buchanan. She's in town for the presentation."

"Parsody? What sort of name is that?"

"It's the sort of name you give your daughter when you know she's going to grow up to be the wealthiest debutante of the season. Her parents perished with the *Titanic.* Now she has come of age and her guardian has engaged us to keep Parsody safe and away from the clutches of greedy fortune hunters."

Evie took a sip of her fresh cup of tea. "It's strange to still be talking about the season. Life has changed so much in such a short time and yet, as Henrietta would say, everything that really matters remains intact and unsullied by the wheels of progress."

Lotte snorted. "Everything that matters to the wealthy. I suppose it makes sense. They still need to marry and, in order to do that, they need to meet the right people." Lotte searched her handbag and retrieved a small notebook. "Mr. Jameson, that's the name of the guardian. He has taken a house in Grosvenor Square." Lotte snorted again. "This is straight out of Jane Austen.

"She must be terribly wealthy," Evie said.

"Terribly?" Lotte scoffed. "What a strange way to describe obscene wealth."

"Does she have any other family?" Evie imagined they lived too far away to offer support.

"No. Her arrival was a surprise and it happened late in her parents' lives. They'd both been in their early forties. What few relatives they had seem to have died in the last few years."

"I suppose that explains the guardian." That seemed almost too sad to contemplate. "Do we know the name of her close friends?"

"She doesn't have any."

That certainly surprised her. "What?"

Lotte skimmed through a page in her notebook and turned it. "Here it is. She is a solitary girl who enjoys spending endless hours in the library and in the potting shed. Apparently, she is a keen botanist and collector of plants. Although, her guardian hopes she will eventually outgrow that. This is her first time in town. She has spent the last eight years traipsing through the Continent. She spent the war years safely ensconced in Switzerland and lately she'd been living in France."

"She must be fluent in several languages," Evie suggested.

"Most likely. However, despite all her traveling, she lacks worldly experience. And that's where we come in."

"Did you say this is her first time in town?"

"Yes."

"Heavens, she must really enjoy her own company."

"I have the feeling Mr. Jameson might be trying to change that. Either that, or he is preempting the unavoidable. She is bound to want to marry and there is no better time or place. If she misses her chance here, he'll have to put in more effort and make the rounds of house parties and whatnot."

"And, of course, he wants to make sure she marries someone suitable." Evie wondered how that would work out for him. When wealth was involved, people's intentions could become hazy and easily misconstrued. "This sounds like the ideal job for a chaperone." Or a matchmaker, she thought.

Lotte nodded. "Or a horde of chaperones."

"Is there such a thing as a gaggle of chaperones?" Evie wondered.

Lotte smiled. "You must be thinking of your nearest and dearest family members and their antics."

Yes, and they were all in town for Caro's presentation. As the new Lady Evans, she was expected to be presented to the monarchs. The days leading up to the event would be taken up with numerous functions, all attended by Henrietta, Sara and, of course, Toodles.

Parties, dinners and the presentation itself, followed by more parties and dinners.

Henrietta would never miss attending the presentation. Even if she tried, she could not avoid keeping Henrietta in the dark about their client. However, that might work in her favor. Henrietta would never be able to resist assisting them with a case, something that would require her to set aside her grievances and talk to her again.

"If you're not interested…"

"Heavens, whatever gave you that idea? When do we start?"

"We are due to meet Miss Parsody Jane Buchanan tomorrow afternoon. We have been invited to tea."

Evie's eyebrows drew down.

"Is there a problem?"

"Caro is due to arrive tomorrow. The Evans' house in town is still undergoing renovations so she and Henry will be staying with us. Remember, she's still the new Lady Evans and is here to be presented. This is not something she is looking forward to. While she managed to avoid it last year, there's no escaping it this year."

Evie realized she might have been too hasty in expressing her interest in Lotte's new case. Thinking about the days ahead, she knew she would be extraordinarily busy.

Taking a pensive sip of her tea, she murmured, "Considering Caro's lack of enthusiasm for the whole idea of meeting the monarchs, this might help take her mind off it all. Yes… I should ask for her assistance."

"That sounds good to me. The more, the merrier.

Until we actually meet Miss Parsody Jane Buchanan, I am going to assume she is a female wolf hiding in sheep's clothing."

That struck Evie as curious. "Why?"

"I cannot believe someone with a vast fortune is content to spend her days hiding away in the country while the rest of the world, from London to Buenos Aires, continues to celebrate life to make up for the misery endured during the war years."

"She might be an eccentric," Evie suggested. "Surely you cannot be suspicious of someone merely because they choose to be different."

Lotte smiled. "That is the very definition of being suspicious. We notice things because they stand out and are different from the usual."

"Of course, you are right. Do we know if she's to be presented?"

Lotte nodded. "Yes and I have no idea how she feels about it."

This would be the first full dress court presentation held at Buckingham Palace since 1914. The previous year, there had been a presentation but with so many people still picking up the pieces of their shattered lives, it had lacked the usual spark.

Lost in those thoughts, Evie took a sip of her tea and stared into space.

Lotte helped herself to another slice of cake. Glancing at Evie, she said, "Please tell me you're not still dwelling over giving away your services for free."

"Not really…" Evie dismissed the concerns she'd been entertaining. She wanted to confide in Lotte, especially as she had already asked if Tom had been giving her trouble.

However, she suspected Lotte would only laugh at her dilemma.

Soon enough, Tom would find out what she had been doing behind his back and she had no idea how he would react. "Oh!" she exclaimed.

"What?"

"Don't look now," Evie whispered. "It's the new Lady Amelia Stuart. She's with the man she's flaunting as her paramour."

"What of it?" Lotte asked, her accent changing from cultured to something that wouldn't be out of place in the East End.

"I just noticed his hand gestures. They are astonishingly effeminate."

Lotte smiled. "And therein lies your answer."

Evie's eyebrows curved up. "They are not lovers?"

Lotte nodded.

"But why is she flaunting him?"

"Because it's fashionable and, despite being newly married, Lord Stuart barely spares his new wife the time of day. He'd rather attend a parliamentary debate and spend his evenings at any one of his clubs than take his wife out to lunch or dinner."

Shaking her head, Evie murmured, "Appearances can be deceiving."

"Indeed." Lotte leaned forward and lowered her voice. "Now, are you going to tell me about Tom?"

CHAPTER 2

"You ou missed a productive luncheon with Lotte," Evie said as she reached Tom who had commandeered a prime spot for his motor car outside the hotel.

"As if I had a choice…" Tom held the motor car door open for Evie. "I'm sure you'll tell me all about it."

Evie had expected to find Tom in a foul temper. To his credit, he had welcomed her with a warm smile. If he didn't volunteer information about his experience that afternoon, she would have to prod, but the way Tom had been carrying on over the last few days, she knew it would be safer to poke a bear with a sore head. "I'll do my best to remember the pertinent details." She waited for Tom to settle at the driver's seat before saying, "I lost count of the number of cakes Lotte ate."

"I fail to see why that's pertinent," he said, driving past a long line of taxicabs waiting to claim his spot.

Evie grinned. "It sets the scene."

Tom glanced at her, his eyes narrowed with suspicion. "I'm already familiar with the Ritz's Palm Court."

"If not the scene, then, the mood." She proceeded to mention all the ladies she had recognized.

Tom looked into the distance. "Give me a moment to picture it all in my mind."

Despite the note of sarcasm in his voice, Evie complied and spent a few moments wallowing in guilt and reconsidering her actions. She had no idea how Tom would react to her secret undertakings. Only time would tell. Belatedly, she wished she had discussed it all with Lotte. Secrets could become such a burden, she thought.

Glancing at Tom, she asked, "Would it help if I described their attire?"

Tom growled. "No. I believe I have had enough talk of attires for one day..." His voice hitched, "*One lifetime.*"

Evie hid her smile and decided the risk of poking a bear would be well worth it. "Really? And here I was hoping you would tell me all about it."

Tom tipped his hat back and scowled at Evie. "Countess, are you trying to provoke me?"

"Tom, surely, it wasn't so bad." Anticipating his visit to the Savile Row tailor, Tom had spent the last few days muttering and growling under his breath and trying to think of every conceivable excuse to bow out of the appointment, all to no avail as he'd finally succumbed to the inevitable need to acquire the correct outfit for Caro's presentation at court.

Rules were rules.

Tom pushed out a hard breath. Employing a nasal tone and doing his best to imitate Edgar, the butler, he said, "According to Edgar, full dress uniform is invariably worn by all gentlemen entitled to wear it." Tom shook his head and growled, "The information seems to be ingrained in every male's head because the tailor, Mr. Strutford, imparted the same instructions. Despite my obvious accent, he wished to know if I had been a Scottish officer because, if I had been, then I would have been expected to wear a kilt."

"I think you would look dashing in a kilt," Evie chirped. "What else did the tailor have to say?"

Tom spoke through gritted teeth. "Gentlemen who do not wear uniform may wear either velvet Court dress *new style*, velvet Court dress *old style* or cloth Court dress."

"That all sounds rather glamorous!"

"Countess," Tom snapped.

Smiling, Evie purred, "Yes, Tom?"

"*Breeches!* Did I mention the knee breeches?"

Evie sank a little in her seat. In a small voice, she asked, "Breeches?"

"Yes, Countess. *Breeches.* I am a grown man and I will be required to wear silk knee breeches and silk hose. *Hose, Countess. Hose.*" As he continued, the words shot out of him, "Patent leather shoes with steel buckles. A white bow tie… White gloves. Countess… *White gloves.*"

It was difficult to tell which he considered the most objectionable. "Tom, Caro will certainly appreciate your efforts. I believe she's secretly looking forward to the event. Perhaps, you might also—"

"No. There is absolutely no chance of me changing my mind about being forced to wear silk knee breeches."

"Are you sure? I sometimes find myself dreading a certain event only to end up enjoying it."

To his credit, he gave it some thought only to reiterate his opinion. "Breeches, Countess. *Knee breeches*."

"Tom, I was referring to the event."

Tom conceded the point. "I'm sure it will be a happy occasion... *for some*."

Mimicking his exasperation, Evie said, "If it's any consolation, I will be required to wear ostrich feathers. Not one ostrich feather, but three, Tom. Can you believe it? Think of all those poor ostriches being plucked just to satisfy the whims of a monarch who no longer sits on the throne. I don't know what Queen Charlotte was thinking. Even Caro will be wearing three ostrich feathers, Tom. Three instead of two because she's married. Had she not been married, she would have been required to only wear two ostrich feathers, but since she is married she must wear three, Tom. Three."

He tilted his head in thought. After a moment, he said, "No, you won't get any sympathy from me. Ostrich feathers do not trump silk knee breeches."

Evie hid her smile. "What about the poor ostriches?"

"Yes, I suppose they do deserve compassion."

"Well, at least that's something. I wouldn't want to think you didn't care about the plight of the poor ostriches." Evie glanced at him and measured his tolerance to more prodding. Deciding to give him a respite, she asked, "Where's Edgar?"

Tom grumbled. "And that's something else. I know you told him to accompany me just so he could make sure I kept my appointment. I'm beginning to think you don't trust me."

"Be honest, Tom, you were going to find any excuse under the sun to avoid going. I was almost tempted to wait and see what happened if you were left to your own devices, but you know how important this event is. Caro is going to be presented and we must all do our best to make sure this is a memorable occasion and that includes dressing accordingly."

Tom rolled his eyes. "She's only doing it to appease her mother. She told me so herself."

"When did you two speak?"

"What? The traffic, Countess. I can't hear a thing."

Yet a moment ago, he'd had no trouble hearing her or making himself heard.

Evie was suddenly struck by a bout of suspicion. "I cannot believe this. You and Caro have been in cahoots." Evie knew Henry Evans' mother, the free-spirited Lady Louisa Evans, wouldn't care one way or the other about the presentation. But to Caro's mother this would mean the world. The little village where she lived would no doubt mark the occasion with a great deal of fanfare, celebrating Caro's elevation from lady's maid to titled lady.

However, Caro had been reluctant from the start, saying she had no business being presented to the monarchs because she might put a foot wrong and then open her mouth and utter some sort of nonsense to the wrong person or to the most significant people in the room. All those present would never let her live it down and her husband's reputation would forever be tarnished by her abysmal and uncouth behavior. "I hope you weren't trying to talk her out of attending her presentation."

"Countess... *Knee breeches!*"

Yes, indeed. Evie decided she'd been right to ask Edgar to accompany Tom because he would have done anything and everything in his power to get out of an event which required him to wear such an objectionable garment.

Tilting her head, she gave him a coy smile. "Will you be absent tomorrow afternoon again? We are to meet Miss Buchanan for afternoon tea. Her guardian, Mr. Jameson, has engaged us to keep an eye on her. She's a wealthy heiress in need of assistance navigating the treacherous waters of society. Our job will be to ward off any unsavory characters."

Shifting, Tom drew in a deep breath and glanced at her. "I see what you're doing."

"What?" she asked innocently.

"I'm not sure what but you are doing it and it involves your feminine wiles. I'm sure it does. Yes, indeed. You are trying to persuade me into doing something I clearly don't wish to do. Admittedly, it is unavoidable." He gave a determined nod. "Although, I'm sure I could start a new trend. It's time to get all the men attending the presentation out of childish breeches and into long trousers."

"Tom, surely you don't mean to take on the establishment."

"Countess, I am sorely tempted. Please, do not test me."

He looked straight ahead but Evie could see the edge of his mouth had lifted in amusement.

Tom gave a decisive nod. "With any luck, someone will be murdered and we won't have to attend the function."

Evie drew in a breath and released a long sigh. "You don't really mean that. What if we hear about the murder right in the middle of the presentation? We'll have to launch an investigation with you still wearing your knee breeches. That's sure to turn a few heads."

His lips parted. After a moment, he glanced at her, his eyebrows drawn down. "You had absolutely no trouble picturing that scenario. Admit it, you are enjoying this."

Evie's eyes sparkled with amusement. "Yes, I can just picture us giving chase and you insisting we stop by Woodridge House so you can change out of your little boy breeches."

Sounding affronted, he said, "So you admit they are little boy breeches."

"Tom, be sensible. The Duke of Wellington wore them and he won the Battle of Waterloo. As for the strictness of the rules, on one occasion, he was turned away from *Almacks* for wearing long trousers."

"You're talking about someone who died decades ago." Shaking his head, he tapped the steering wheel and then wagged a finger at her. "You owe me, even if I'm doing this as a special favor to Caro."

Evie would have given anything to see his face when the tailor showed him a sample of the clothes worn for special occasions at the palace. "Did you say you'll be wearing a bow tie? Yes, I think you did. Well, take comfort, several years back, you would have been required to wear a lace jabot."

"*A what?*"

"It's a frilly tie with flounces. Like the ties worn in the 1700s. So, you see, you should always look on the bright side." As they approached Woodridge House, Evie smiled. "Here we are. By the way, you didn't tell me where Edgar is."

"He had a special errand to run. I believe he is looking for a ring."

"A ring!" Evie swung toward him. "What sort of ring?"

"I didn't ask."

"Why not? What if it's an engagement ring for Millicent?"

"Then, I'm sure she will tell us all about it."

"Tom. Think hard. What did Edgar say? This is important."

"Why? If it's an engagement ring, then he means to surprise Millicent with an official proposal."

"Millicent doesn't like surprises."

"I'm sorry, Countess. My mind was occupied on other matters."

Of course, Evie knew they shouldn't meddle. She only hoped Millicent would be happy about this particular surprise.

He steered the motor car into a vacant spot in front of Woodridge House and sat back.

"You always do that," she mused.

"What?"

"Take a few moments before climbing out."

He gave her a knowing smile. "Before we venture inside and are met with who knows what, I like to savor the moment of being alone with you."

"That's very sweet, Tom, but we have a lot to do. Caro arrives tomorrow and tonight we have a soiree to attend. Also, Millicent will want to go through the schedule for the week…"

"Say no more." He hopped out of the motor car and came around to open the passenger door for her.

Evie looked at him with curiosity. "Now I'm confused. You're whistling and you look quite happy."

"That's because now I'm thinking about what awaits us on the other side of that door."

"Tom, I never thought I'd say this about you." She took his hand and climbed out. Standing almost toe to toe with him, she smiled, "Tom Winchester, you are an enigma."

As they walked up the steps to the front door, Tom asked, "Do you think today will be the day Henrietta finally speaks to you again?"

"You're enjoying this."

"I have to admit, it has been entertaining and quite a novelty to see Henrietta giving you the silent treatment."

They both smiled at the footman who opened the door for them.

Evie waited for him to withdraw before lifting her chin and saying, "You should prepare to be disappointed. Henrietta still hasn't forgiven me for betraying her friend, Lady Montague, and I doubt she will anytime soon. I believe, in this instance, she is determined to extract an apology, including a full admission of guilt from me."

"And will you comply with her wishes and apologize?" Tom asked as he helped her out of her coat.

Evie snorted and made her way to the drawing room, saying over her shoulder, "Not on your life," even as she silently admitted she would eventually have to concede defeat and do everything within her power in order to keep the peace.

Tom was about to laugh in response when he heard the distinct sound of Henrietta's clipped tone. Reaching for Evie's hand, he drew her back and pressed his finger to his lips.

In their silence, they heard Henrietta, the Dowager Countess of Woodridge, say, "My dear, we face the gravity of our internal difficulties and conflicts and grapple with the riddles and uncertainties of a world in constant flux but this I know with absolute certainty."

Oh, dear.

What did Henrietta know with such absolute certainty?

Tom appeared to be just as curious. He nudged her forward only to be pulled back by a tug from Evie.

"What? Don't you want to hear the rest?" he whispered.

Evie looked toward the drawing room and then looked over her shoulder at the front door. They'd only heard the tail end of a conversation. They couldn't possibly piece it together.

"Countess, there's only one way to find out what they're talking about. We can only hear so much out here..."

The next remark they heard had them both tiptoeing closer to the drawing room.

"Oh! I just remembered what my question was... Are you going to tell Birdie?"

"Toodles, my dear, you needn't worry about Evangeline. She will, no doubt, find out in due course."

Evie straightened and took a decisive step back earning herself a roll of the eyes from Tom.

"Countess, this is your house," he whispered.

Hearing Henrietta again, Evie pressed her finger to her lips.

"There are ways of revealing a suitor's true character. Trust me, I know what I'm talking about. In such cases, the woman believes that her suitor wants her only for herself. My process allows the woman to be dissuaded of the notion."

Evie and Tom strained to hear Toodles' response.

"Did you make that out?" Evie whispered.

Tom shook his head.

The next voice they heard belonged to Sara who must have entered from the other door. "Is Henrietta still going on about suitors?" Toodles must have nodded because Sara then asked, "Has she told you what makes a good suitor?"

"Sara, don't be so dismissive," Henrietta said. "In the past, there has been no quality more reliable than Hanoverian simplicity. Someone resplendently plain."

"Henrietta, you seem to need reminding. The current monarchs have changed their family name from the German sounding Saxe-Coburg-Gotha to the more British sounding Windsor. I doubt any of them will be seeking to increase their Hanoverian links. Everyone is now looking north to Scotland for grooms and brides."

"Sara, I am merely talking about the character trait."

"Speaking of character trait," Sara said, "you'll find women these days marrying for love."

"You mean, they are blinded by it." Henrietta snorted. "I believe I can prevent that from happening. Or, at the very least, circumvent that inconvenient trait."

Evie grabbed hold of Tom and pulled him back.

"They are discussing us," he said.

"We don't know that for sure." Evie gave a firm nod. "We… we should walk in and pretend we didn't hear any of that… nonsense."

At the sound of someone clearing their throat, Evie and Tom swung around.

Evie's butler, Edgar, stood at attention, while Evie's

little French pug, Holmes, sat beside him, his little head tilting from side to side.

"Edgar!" Evie exclaimed.

"My lady. Mr. Winchester." He inclined his head.

To his credit, Edgar refrained from expressing his opinion about finding the lady of the house eavesdropping on the dowagers and Toodles.

"We were just on our way to the drawing room and... I was going to ring for tea. Yes, tea would be perfect."

"I will organize it, my lady."

"Wonderful." She gave him a coy smile. "Do you know if the others have returned from their outing?"

"I believe they have, my lady. You will find them in the drawing room."

"Thank you, Edgar. By the way, did you take care of your business? Tom was telling me about you hunting for a ring."

Edgar's cheeks flooded with a burst of crimson red. "I... Yes, thank you, my lady." Eager to avoid fully engaging Evie's curiosity, he swung on his heels and rushed off.

"Take the hint, Countess. Edgar doesn't wish to discuss it any further." Turning toward the drawing room, Tom murmured, "Deep breath, Countess. We are about to enter the lioness' den."

CHAPTER 3

Eavesdroppers never hear any good of themselves

The drawing room
Woodridge House, Mayfair

*W*ith an encouraging push from Tom, Evie walked in and sent a glance skating around the drawing room.

"Henrietta, look. Here's Birdie and Tom is with her." Evie's granny, Toodles, sat back and smiled at her, eyes brimming with amusement. It seemed she was eager for some entertainment.

At least, one person found the awkward situation amusing, Evie thought.

"Grans." Evie then looked at her mother-in-law. "Sara."

Finally, she offered Henrietta a smile that mirrored Henrietta's reserved look. "Henrietta. I trust you have all enjoyed your day so far."

Henrietta lifted her chin and looked askance, while Sara and Toodles both gave vigorous nods.

"It's been an educational day, Birdie. Henrietta has a new hobby horse."

"A what?"

Henrietta lifted her chin even higher and pursed her lips as if to suggest she would not be sharing information about the subject, certainly not with the likes of the treacherous Evangeline, the Countess of Woodridge, who had been personally responsible for exiling her dearest friend to a remote island.

Making herself comfortable next to Toodles, Evie watched Tom as he moved to his favorite spot by the fireplace, which provided him with the perfect view of the scene in the drawing room.

"Henrietta's new hobby," Evie's grandmother repeated.

When Toodles didn't offer any further explanations, Evie said, "I hope we are not interrupting."

"Not at all, Birdie. Henrietta was just telling us—"

Henrietta interrupted by declaring, "Herbert Williams-Stoker."

Evie wasn't familiar with the name. She sat back and waited for Henrietta to continue in the hope that whatever she said would offer some clarity about Herbert Williams-Stoker.

Giving a firm nod, Henrietta continued, "Unless someone leads him to the altar, he risks becoming a perpetual bachelor."

Evie knew that while most people had made the

journey from their country estates to their houses in town for the purpose of attending the annual presentation, some had come with the express purpose of finding a suitable husband or wife.

"He's an extremely good catch," Henrietta declared. "His stables are quite impressive and his hunters are the envy of the county."

Tom mirrored Evie's slight lift of her eyebrows.

"Stoker," Sara shuddered. "Makes me think of Bram Stoker, that author of gothic horror stories. Is he related?"

"I'm sure it's not relevant, Sara. I'm only saying he is a perfect catch and any woman would be lucky to have him." Henrietta slid her eyes over to Evie. "There is an ideal candidate for him out there... not far away. This is the perfect time and place for someone and they mustn't miss the opportunity."

"I hear marrying for love is becoming quite fashionable," Toodles echoed Sara's earlier remark.

Henrietta nodded. "Regardless of the reasons for marrying, it pays to consider mutual interests..."

"Alice Howitts," Sara chirped. "She's an accomplished horsewoman. They would be perfect together. She came out a couple of years ago and she's still available. I'm sure she'll be in town. She has a younger sister who will, I'm sure, be presented this year."

"And what do you think are the chances Herbert Williams-Stoker will meet Alice Howitts at the same function?" Henrietta asked.

Sara narrowed her eyes. "You're up to something. I know that tone of voice. It reeks of confidence. For your information, two people don't need to be in the same room to meet. They can hear about each other from second parties."

Henrietta smiled.

"Aha! I know what you're planning. A whisper here, a word there, followed by a surprise rendezvous."

Henrietta took a sip of her tea. "I do not care to share my tactics. You have yours and I have mine."

Were they playing matchmaker? Looking around the drawing room, Evie caught Henrietta stealing measuring glances at her.

If she tried to interpret Henrietta's look, she might come to believe Henrietta was trying to find her a suitable husband. The subject hadn't come up, certainly not since Tom had made his intentions... more or less clear. She knew Henrietta would prefer she marry someone with a title, something which, to everyone's surprise, Tom had managed to acquire. Although, it had recently encountered a slight stumbling block...

"No," Evie whispered. Henrietta couldn't possibly be trying to play matchmaker with her. However...

She wouldn't be surprised if Henrietta had decided to employ subtle tactics. Yes, indeed. Evie decided Henrietta was working on a ploy to encourage Tom to pick up the pace and make a decisive move, sooner rather than later.

Looking over her shoulder, Henrietta asked, "Did you catch all that, Millicent?"

Evie swung around and saw Millicent, her secretary, sitting near a window with a notebook in hand. She appeared to be taking notes. Her pen flew across the page suggesting she was putting her newly acquired shorthand skills to good use.

Lowering her pen, Millicent looked up and nodded. When she saw Evie, she grinned and waved.

"I believe Matthew St. John is searching for a wife," Sara offered. "He's no saint but he is now the heir to his father's earldom. That makes him the catch of the season. He was at *Quaglino* last night and that reminds me." Sara reached for a newspaper and waved it. "That was the Prince of Wales I saw there last night. It's been reported in black and white."

"My dear, you can't believe everything you read." Henrietta looked up in thought. "St. John. Does he have a title? People might be marrying for love now but a title remains quite a carrot to dangle." Henrietta helped herself to a piece of cake. "Do we know anyone in search of a titled husband?"

When Edgar entered and set a fresh pot of tea on the table, Toodles stood up and helped herself to some tea. "I do have other granddaughters. Perhaps I should suggest they pay us a visit."

Tom joined her at the table and poured a cup of tea. When he handed it to Evie, he winked. She had no idea if he'd been following the conversation. If he had, then he had to be wondering if there was any rhyme or reason to it all.

"Henrietta, you're obsessed with the sound of your own voice. I just told you Matthew St. John is heir to his father's title," Sara said. "Meanwhile, he is Viscount Lindsey."

Henrietta tapped her finger on the teacup. "Yes, yes, of course. The Earl of Glastonbury's son. A handsome man. I'd been thinking of another St. John." Henrietta smiled at

Toodles. "As for your granddaughters, my dear Toodles, the Earl of Glastonbury will insist his son marry a lady."

Toodles huffed. "Are you suggesting my granddaughters are hoydens?"

"I would never dream of casting aspersions on your family." Henrietta gave Evie a pointed look. "I am merely suggesting he will want someone who has been brought up to understand our way of doing things. You see, not everyone has the ability to adapt to our ways and that can create all sorts of problems."

Toodles' voice hitched. "Your way?"

Recognizing her granny's effort to disguise her incensed tone, Evie shifted to the edge of her seat, just in case she needed to come between them.

"Toodles, my dear. Don't take offence. The Earl of Glastonbury is set in his ways. In fact, I'm sure he will insist his son should look for someone from within their immediate social circle."

Toodles smiled. "My granddaughters stand to inherit a substantial fortune. It will be his loss."

Before Henrietta could respond, Sara interjected, "Actually, alliances between peers' sons and commoners are no longer considered out of the question." Sara shrugged. "As long as a family is well-connected, no one really minds. The Duke of Devonshire's daughter married a commoner. Her new husband's family is well-to-do now but his great-grandfather was a tenant farmer."

Henrietta and Sara looked at each other and Evie would have sworn they held a silent conversation. As if by mutual agreement, the topic of conversation was set back on track.

Evie looked at Tom and they both shrugged.

"The Cleghorn family's estate is near the Earl of Glastonbury's estate and they have two daughters. Although, one is already married," Sara said. Looking up, she went through a list of names until she hit upon the right one. "Mariah Cleghorn."

"Good heavens, Sara. It took three seasons to marry off her sister. It's that guttural laugh that runs in the family. Very unbecoming. Of course, her settlement will be significant so there's no danger of her being left on the shelf. But it will take some doing..."

"Sometimes I forget we are living in 1922," Toodles said. "The way you two carry on, anyone could be forgiven for thinking it was 1822."

Evie glanced at her granny and tried to gage her mood. Her attention remained fixed on Henrietta. Either she had forgotten Henrietta's dismissal of her other granddaughters or she was biding her time to deliver a biting retort.

"Lucian Ellery is another eligible one with a solid pedigree." Once again, Henrietta's gaze landed on Evie. "Any woman would be lucky to have him."

Evie hoped Henrietta's plans didn't include finding her a suitable husband.

"He has political aspirations," Henrietta mused.

"I heard a rumor about him and Elinor West," Sara said. "She happens to be one of mine."

One of hers?

This seemed to amuse Henrietta. "The poor girl has inherited her mother's flightiness and Elinor has made it worse by being accident prone. He couldn't possibly be serious about her."

Sara gave a determined nod. "I'll accept the challenge."

Henrietta scoffed at the idea.

Lifting her chin, Sara declared, "As the saying goes, fortune favors the brave."

The remark amused Henrietta. Laughing, she asked, "Brave? How will you ever manage that?"

"I will be bold." Sara tilted her head. "I can't help but notice you only have men on your list."

"That is my secret weapon, my dear." Henrietta took a sip of her tea. "Although, I'm keen to find out about the Buchanan girl everyone has been talking about."

The remark caught Evie's attention. She tried to disguise her interest by standing up and helping herself to another cup of tea. Returning to her seat, she gave them her full attention.

Unfortunately, the discussion came to an end when the dressing gong echoed throughout the house.

All three stood up with Henrietta saying, "Two of my candidates will be attending Lady Horace's soiree tonight. I believe that will give me a head start. I don't seem to recall seeing any of your young women on the guest list."

"You've seen the guest list?" Sara demanded.

Henrietta laughed. "I told you I have my secret weapons."

Evie turned to say something to Millicent but she had already slipped out of the drawing room.

As soon as the others left the drawing room, Tom went to sit next to Evie. "Any idea what that was about?"

"Matchmaking. It's the season for it." Evie brushed the tip of her finger along her chin. "But there seems to be more to it than meets the eye. I believe they have turned this into some sort of competitive game."

Tom reached for Evie's hand, holding it almost as if he

needed to anchor himself. "For a wild moment, I thought they might have been looking to replace me."

"I'm thinking we should elope."

"Henrietta will never forgive you."

"This could be the perfect time to do it," Evie suggested. "She's already not talking to me."

"I thought we were on a case. We can't disappear now."

"Heavens, of course, you're right. I guess we'll have to put off eloping for another day."

"Are we attending Lady Horace's soiree?" Tom asked. "It would be interesting to see what they do."

"I agree, but we are expected elsewhere. I should go look for Millicent. We still have that schedule to run through."

Tom held on tight to her hand. "Henrietta is curious about Miss Buchanan. I wonder what she would do if she found out about the afternoon tea you're attending tomorrow?" Tom asked. "Do you realize how much power you could potentially hold over Henrietta?"

"Yes, but I promise not to let it go to my head. Tom, may I please have my hand back?"

He looked toward the door and then released his hold. "I suppose it's safe to remain here alone."

Moments later, Evie entered her bedroom and found Millicent standing in front of the wardrobe.

"Millicent, here you are. I looked for you in the study and the library..."

"I went to the library, milady, and then I remembered I had to bring out your evening gown."

"I do wish you hadn't insisted on taking on both roles, Millicent. One of the other maids could step in. I'm sure they'd appreciate the opportunity. You're my secretary now… although, I seem to have temporarily loaned you to Henrietta."

"Oh dear, about that…"

"Yes?"

"They needed a record of their conversation. My shorthand is coming along nicely so I offered to take notes."

"May I ask what this is about? Tom and I have had a couple of guesses but we might be quite wrong. Are they playing matchmaker?"

"Yes, at the start, that's what they were doing but now things have changed. Toodles suggested they needed to make it more interesting."

"Heavens, whatever do you mean?"

"Well, they have each set their sights on available candidates and they intend finding partners for them. However, they can't use each other's candidates and… while Lady Sara stepped out of the drawing room, Henrietta said it might be interesting to also try to dissuade each other's candidates."

"You mean Henrietta wants to employ sabotage?"

Millicent sighed. "I don't seem to recall her exact words. Unfortunately, she asked me to exclude that tidbit. Otherwise, I'd refer to my notes. Let me think… Yes, stealth was mentioned as well as sabotage."

"Heavens."

Millicent nodded. "She means to employ underhanded tactics, milady."

"And she doesn't wish Sara to know this? That hardly seems fair."

"That's what I thought. Then again, she was confiding in Toodles."

"And you think Toodles will tell Sara?"

"I'm sure she will. Although, Lady Henrietta referred to her tactic as her secret weapon. So... there might be something else up her sleeve."

"What makes her think Toodles will keep the information to herself?" Evie put her hand up. "You don't need to answer that, Millicent. I was just thinking aloud."

Millicent looked relieved. She opened her notebook and searched for the page she wanted. "You asked me to remind you of a few activities. Edgar has assured me all the arrangements for Lady Evans' presentation ball are in place. Also, everyone who has been invited has already replied with an affirmative. I have personally seen to the flower arrangements. They will be delivered on the morning of the ball. You have received three more invitations to parties." Millicent rolled her eyes. "They require an answer but, if you ask me, the people responsible for sending them waited until the very last minute."

Evie smiled. "And do you think I should be offended?"

"Yes, absolutely. Would you like me to decline on your behalf?"

Evie laughed. "My dance card is already full, Millicent. Yes, I do think we should decline."

Satisfied, Millicent continued, "Lady Evans arrives tomorrow and Lady Henrietta offered to teach Lady Evans to curtsy."

Evie smiled at Millicent's formal tone when referring to Caro. They had been in service together but, in Millicent's eyes, Caro had now been elevated and deserved the acknowledgement and deference. "Millicent, you know Caro would feel uncomfortable with you calling her Lady Evans."

33

"I can't imagine why. After all, that is her title. Anyhow… Lady Henrietta…" Millicent's cheeks acquired a delicate tint. Her shoulders rose and fell as she pushed out the words, "Lady Henrietta suggested you might want to join in because you might have forgotten how to curtsy to the monarchs."

"She said that?" Heaven only knew what Henrietta had planned for her. Would she bring out her riding crop?

Millicent went through her list and finished by saying, "I thought you might be interested in this." Millicent drew out a folded piece of paper which turned out to be a newspaper cutting. Handing it to Evie, she said, "Two days ago, a body was fished out of the Thames."

Reading the article, Evie said, "And he's been identified. His name is Mr. Benjamin Hammonds. Am I supposed to recognize the name?" She read on. "I see. The police are treating the death as suspicious."

Millicent nodded. "I thought you might be interested in looking into it."

Evie handed the press cutting back. "Lotte and I are working a case. Well, it's not really a case. We are chaperoning a young debutante."

"The young man's family might reach out to you and ask you to look into it, milady. Or, if you like, I could organize to send them your card."

"That would be a novel idea. Quite enterprising, in fact. Well done, Millicent. However, I'm sure Lotte and I will have our hands full."

Sitting down at her dresser, she removed her earrings and told Millicent about Parsody Jane Buchanan. "See what you can find out about her. We'll be meeting her tomorrow. Her guardian provided some basic information but I'd like to know if we have reason to worry."

"What do you mean, milady?"

"The guardian's request is rather odd. Granted, her inheritance is vast but she appears to have rather staid interests." Evie shrugged. "He painted a picture of naivety. I'd just like to know if she is harboring a rebellious nature. I wouldn't want to be given the runaround. In fact, now that I think about it, I wish I'd turned Lotte down. This trip to town is about Caro. She'll need all our support."

"And she will get it, milady. I think she will also appreciate having something to take her mind off... you know... not wanting to be presented."

Hence the newspaper cutting about the young man fished out of the river? Had Millicent been searching for something intriguing for Caro's entertainment?

"I'm glad to hear you say so, Millicent. I had a similar thought." With all the reservations she had been entertaining, Caro might decide at the last minute to change her mind about the whole presentation and flee.

Evie stood up. "Now, what will I be wearing tonight?"

After she finished preparing for the evening, Millicent asked, "Would you like me to find out what I can about Mr. Hammonds?"

It took a moment for Evie to remember he was the poor soul who'd drowned.

"Yes, if you like. Although, I don't see how or why his death would concern us." She and Tom had only ever become involved in investigations when the victims had been in one way or another involved with them.

Dabbing on some fragrance, Evie looked over her

shoulder. "Millicent? How exactly are you going to search for information?"

"I can't promise anything, milady. However… I believe I know someone who knows someone."

"And?"

"Well, that is all I'm comfortable saying at the moment. For all I know, I might end up having a nice cup of tea and a chat and get nothing else out of… my contacts."

Smiling, Evie assumed Millicent meant to contact everyone she knew working in service. "Millicent, you are a gem."

Picking up the newspaper article, Evie read it again and memorized the name.

Benjamin Hammonds.

She didn't really expect to hear talk about the incident during the evening but it might come in handy to keep her ears to the ground.

CHAPTER 4

That evening, at the stroke of midnight
North Audley Street, Mayfair

om brought the motor car to a stop outside Woodridge House and sat back.

"Countess, you've been unusually quiet. Did the evening wear you out?" Leaning in, he brushed a finger along her cheek. "You're smiling and I'm not sure how to interpret that."

Evie laughed. She'd spent the drive back to Woodridge House smiling because she'd been thinking about the evening's entertainment.

Sitting up, she exclaimed, "Listen. There's that tune we danced to. I must say, I rather enjoyed our evening. I could have danced all night."

He looked over his shoulder and tuned in to the music wafting from somewhere nearby. "Yes, someone is still having a jolly good time, but that didn't quite answer my question."

"They must have a live band. I'm sure it's coming from Grosvenor Square... or perhaps Upper Brook." Catching his blank stare, Evie sighed. "I've been quiet because, as you drove us home, I was entertaining an amusing thought."

"Are you going to share?"

"I'm not sure I can," Evie admitted. "You see, if I do, I risk ending the evening on a bad note."

"Does it involve me?"

"Well, as a matter of fact... yes, it does."

"In that case, I'm sure you know me well enough to realize I would not allow the evening to end on a bad note."

Evie straightened. "Very well, I'll tell you."

Tom shifted in his seat and gave her his full attention.

"Earlier," Evie began, "I was chatting with the hostess and you excused yourself."

He nodded. "I hope you don't feel I abandoned you."

"Not at all. After that, I tried to circulate but I found the other guests coming to me so I didn't have to move. Anyhow, Brigadier Peterson-Monkwell... do you know him?"

"No, the name doesn't ring any bells."

"You spoke with him tonight." Evie chortled. "It was really quite amusing. He sidled up to me and said..." Evie cleared her throat and, deepening her voice, did her best to impersonate the Brigadier, "Lady Woodridge, that young man of yours..."

"He referred to me as your young man?"

Evie nodded. "The Brigadier is rather old. To him,

everyone looks young. Anyhow, he said you were mounting a campaign. I searched the room and, when I located you, I saw you talking to several gentlemen. They all appeared to be listening to you with great interest."

Tom dropped his gaze and smiled. "What else did the Brigadier say?"

"He was quite amused by your enthusiasm. Before I could ask him for details, another gentleman joined us."

Tom nodded. "Yes, it's always a risk when I leave you alone. You're bound to attract people to you. I wouldn't be surprised if someone tries to sweettalk you away from me."

Evie hummed under her breath.

"Shall we go in?" Tom asked.

Reaching for his arm, she stopped him. "No, not just yet. You see, there's more to the story. The Brigadier eventually told me about your campaign."

"He did?"

"Yes. He said you were trying to rally the troops into a rebellion to protest against knee breeches."

"Oh, that…"

"Care to explain yourself?"

"Countess, you must admit a man has the right to at least try to retain a semblance of masculinity."

"Tom! What were you thinking?"

He grinned. "I was thinking there is strength in numbers. I thought that if I could get enough people interested, we could all—"

"No, Tom. You mustn't. Remember, we might reside in this country but we are still foreigners. We mustn't interfere with the order of things."

"But, Countess…"

"No, Tom. Do please promise me you will abandon all subversive attempts to interfere with the local customs." She couldn't believe he had tried to test the waters by getting other men's opinions on the subject and perhaps even their support.

What if he decided to go ahead and stage some sort of protest or take a stand by wearing long trousers instead of the required knee breeches to the presentation?

At worst, Evie thought, he would be denied entry to the palace. He knew what their presence there meant to Caro so she trusted him to behave. But what if his opposition to wearing knee breeches overwhelmed his common sense?

Laughing, Tom climbed out of the motor and walked around to open the passenger door. "Fine, I'll rein in my burning desire to take a stand and make a statement. But you can't blame me for wanting to know how others feel."

"Thank you, Tom." As Evie took his hand and they headed toward the front door, she noticed the music had ended and the streets had fallen silent. She found that odd. At any given time, a motor car could be heard or seen driving by and, late at night, people could be heard returning to their homes.

She was about to mention this when a scream pierced the otherwise silent night.

Several lights came on at Woodridge House. They both turned and looked toward the street corner.

"That sounded alarming," Evie murmured.

They saw more lights coming on in several buildings. A door opened in a nearby house and someone stepped out. A motor car drove by, the driver oblivious to the disturbance.

In the next few seconds the street fell silent again, only to be disrupted by a confusion of footsteps and loud, clamoring voices.

"I don't know about you, but I'm curious to see what that is all about," Evie said.

They hurried toward the corner of the street and stopped to see which way they should turn. Tom gestured to the right.

People were spilling out of a house and hovering by the door.

"That must be the house." Evie wished someone would burst out laughing and break the tension she felt in the air. Mostly, she hoped they'd been mistaken in assuming the scream had been filled with the shock of discovering something quite distressing.

This was too close to home. "Maybe someone collapsed."

"Do you know who lives there?" Tom asked.

Evie searched her mind. "I think that might be Bernard Mulberry's house. He rarely stays in town. In fact, I wouldn't be surprised if he's let the place. He's an affable gentleman who spends his time trout fishing."

Instead of hurrying, they moved toward the scene with caution.

"What do you think we should do?" Tom asked.

Evie signaled to a man standing slightly apart from the other people who'd emerged from the house. "Perhaps we can approach him."

"He looks anxious," Tom said.

The man stood facing the street and was trying to light a cigarette without success.

Tom took the initiative. Approaching him, he offered the man a light.

Giving Tom the opportunity to see what he could find out, Evie stood back and observed the other people who'd come out of the house.

They were all dressed in their best finery and were either holding whispered conversations or standing quite still and in silence.

Some were looking toward the end of the street, almost as if they were on the lookout for someone's arrival.

Others stood looking back toward the entrance to the house. Evie tried to put herself in their shoes and imagine what thoughts they might be entertaining but she came up with nothing.

Something had happened inside and these people had chosen to distance themselves from the incident. Although, they were not quite willing to leave the scene entirely.

What had made someone scream? Had there been a disturbance or, perhaps, a brawl?

Evie tried to remember if she had ever screamed. No, not even all those years ago when Bertie Somers had put a lizard in her basket. She remembered accusing him of being a vile creature but she had definitely not screamed. In fact, she had remained calm, even as her unsuspecting fingers had wrapped around the lizard.

A scream was a strong response. Any number of things could have happened to prompt it. Even someone toppling over a valuable vase.

She saw Tom hailing a taxicab but it continued on its way. Evie saw it drive around Grosvenor Square, onto the next corner, turning and stopping, most likely to drop off a passenger. Moments later, the taxicab drove by and, this time, stopped.

Tom held the passenger door open for the man he'd been talking with. When the taxicab set off, Evie hurried to his side.

"Well? Did he know anything?"

Tom nodded. "A man fell down the stairs."

"Heavens. Is he badly injured?"

Tom held her gaze for a moment before saying, "He did not survive the fall."

"He's dead?"

"Yes. It explains the scream we heard. The man I just spoke with was in a bad way." He dug inside his pocket and produced a card. "Stuart White. He was quite shaken by the sight."

"Death can be gruesome," Evie murmured.

Tom nodded. "Yes, although... He's seen worse."

"What do you mean?"

"He was babbling and... he told me he'd been at the Somme."

"He told you that?"

Again, Tom nodded.

Evie didn't need to ask for an explanation. Shuddering, she recalled hearing second-hand accounts of ghastly battle scenes endured for days on end.

"He didn't find it gruesome." Tom cupped her elbow. "He was struck by the silence that followed the scream and the gasps. When you're in the middle of a battle, you're too busy trying to save your own neck, you don't have time to scream and there is definitely no silence."

"Did he know the man?"

Tom shook his head. "Mr. and Mrs. Chapell have leased the house for their daughter's presentation. There seems to be an open invitation to all eligible bachelors. He knew a few people but not everyone."

"I assume someone telephoned for assistance. They should be arriving soon." Evie looked around the street but did not see any cars rushing toward them.

They had attended enough crime scenes to know the police would eventually make an appearance and would want to ask questions, even if it was an accidental death.

When Tom tugged her along, she did not protest.

Walking up the front steps to the house, no one stopped them, so they continued on.

At the threshold, they saw people milling about the hall. There was a central staircase, with rooms at either side. Some people stood by the drawing room doorway, others were leaning out of the opposite room, with no one making even the slightest effort to leave the house.

The tableau in front of them gave the impression of people waiting to see what would happen next.

No one spoke.

They all stood still.

Evie didn't see a single person shifting or fidgeting.

Moving further inside the house, they craned their necks and looked above people's heads and between their shoulders until they both caught sight of the body at the foot of the stairs.

The man's arms were spread out, his blank expression stared up at the ceiling and one of his legs was twisted at an awkward angle.

Why had no one thought to cover him?

Evie leaned in and whispered, "Did the man you spoke

44

with see what happened?"

"Stuart White? No. He was in the drawing room when he heard the scream. He thought someone had spilled a drink on a woman's gown or, worse, ripped it."

"What a strange assumption," Evie mused and glanced around. "Then again, everyone is dressed splendidly."

"Meaning, they are dressed expensively?"

"Yes. If someone damaged my gown, I'm sure I would be upset."

"I doubt you would scream."

"I might..." Edging closer, Evie noticed something protruding from the dead man's dinner jacket. It looked like a flask, suggesting he might have been drinking. Looking around, she could see people holding glasses and more drinks were being served, probably as a way to keep everyone calm. Evie thought he might have been drinking more than the average person. If he'd been inebriated, it would be easy to miss a step, stumble, and fall.

Then she noticed his shoes. They looked quite new. From experience, she knew soles needed to be roughened slightly. Her nanny had always recommended sanding them. Otherwise, they could be slippery. Had he been careless and slipped? Or had he been drinking excessively and missed a step?

"Countess?"

Evie drew him back. "Do you think he hit his head?"

"He might have broken his neck." Tom looked up. "There's a landing."

Yes, and the stairs wound down, with the last steps directly below the landing.

Around her, she noticed everyone's attention still fixed on the dead body. One woman wearing a black and burgundy beaded gown shifted her gaze from the body to the front door and then back to the body, almost as if intent on not missing the next step in the proceedings, which would, no doubt, come with the arrival of the police and an ambulance to take the body away.

"How many people do you think are here?" Tom asked.

"More than forty, I'm sure. Are you any good at remembering faces?"

He gave it some thought and then gestured to the drawing room. "You take that side, I'll take the other. One of us might recognize someone."

Evie watched him sidle over to the parlor opposite the drawing room. Turning, she moved toward the entrance to the drawing room.

Studying people's faces, she realized she didn't recognize anyone, either because she was not familiar with the people present or because she couldn't connect them to this scene.

She was about to walk further inside the drawing room when she heard someone rushing inside the house to say the police were approaching and would arrive at any moment.

Evie's heart punched against her chest.

How would she and Tom explain their presence? They were not guests so they would have to admit to being curious.

She turned and saw Tom making a beeline for her.

When he reached her, he whispered, "We should leave."

Outside, they walked a few paces away from the house. Stopping, they turned to look at the motor cars approaching the house. The police stopped directly in front of the entrance. Several uniformed police officers emerged from the second vehicle. Then, two men in suits climbed out of the first car. Detectives, Evie assumed. They both looked at everyone standing on the sidewalk. After a brief exchange, one of the detectives signaled to a police officer as if giving an order.

"It looks like we're being corralled," Tom murmured.

"Not us, Tom. We were simply taking a midnight stroll before heading home."

"And now we are thoroughly intrigued?"

"Yes, of course." She gave his sleeve a tug and stepped back only to stop. "I suppose it's rather cowardly. Perhaps we should wait and see what happens. In any case, we heard the scream and thought to…"

"Lend our support?" Tom suggested.

"Yes. Saying anything else would involve lying and I'm not entirely comfortable with that."

One of the policemen had a brief chat with each person hovering outside the house. He moved from one person to the next and appeared to only be writing down names and addresses.

As she didn't see anyone leaving, Evie wondered if there would be further questioning.

Meanwhile, the detectives had entered the house.

"I'm beginning to feel uneasy about this," Evie murmured. "Where's the ambulance?"

The police constable approached them and Tom provided him with their names.

Looking up from his notebook, the police constable asked, "Lady Woodridge?"

Evie nodded. "That's correct."

"Wait here a moment, please." The constable headed

inside the house. Moments later, he came out and was followed by one of the detectives.

"Oh, dear." Evie gasped. "They're headed our way."

"I think you're right."

"Why are they coming toward us?"

"Do you really need to ask?"

"Yes, I do. I can't believe the policeman has heard of me and, even if he has, I don't understand why my name should prompt him to alert his superior."

Tom snorted. "They probably have a photograph of you pinned up on a board warning everyone to be on the lookout for the meddling Countess of Woodridge."

"Tom, I am not amused. Do you think he's going to warn us to mind our own business?" Evie murmured.

The detective walked toward them, his hands inside his pockets, his hat tipped down. He stopped a few steps away from them, shook his head and then took the few remaining steps and looked up. "Lady Woodridge." He looked at Tom.

"This is Tom Winchester," Evie said.

"I'm Detective Inspector Rawlinson. Were you guests here tonight?"

"No, we were drawn here by the scream we heard," Evie admitted. "We live nearby and, as you can imagine, we were concerned." To Evie, it sounded like a perfectly good explanation.

"Where exactly do you live?" the detective asked.

She signaled to the street behind them. When raised an eyebrow, she provided him with the house number.

"As you approached the corner, did you notice anyone walking away from the house?"

The question struck Evie as odd. Looking at Tom, she said, "We were intent on making our way here. I don't recall seeing anyone."

"A motor car drove by," Tom said. Before the detective could ask for more detailed information, he added, "It came from the opposite direction and didn't appear to be in a hurry."

That seemed to satisfy the detective. "If anything else comes to mind, do please contact us. And, in case we have further questions, will you be available?"

"Yes, of course," Evie assured him. "We'll be in town for several days."

As he turned away, Evie breathed a sigh of relief only to tense at the sound of a familiar voice.

"It might be negligent of us, I agree, but I fail to see why we should remain there."

Henrietta?

"Lower your voice. Do you wish to be hauled to prison for escaping the scene of a crime?"

Sara.

"We didn't escape. We vamoosed," Henrietta corrected.

"What on earth is the difference?" Sara demanded.

"It's merely a more interesting way of saying we left in rather a hurry."

"Different word, same meaning. I doubt it would stand up in a court of law," Sara argued.

"Very well. You can scurry home while I will opt to walk briskly."

"Scurry? You make me sound like a rodent. I'm sure that was your intention."

"Different word, same meaning, Sara. Now, come along…"

CHAPTER 5

An unexpected encounter

*E*vie clutched Tom's arm. "It's Henrietta, Sara, and Toodles. Did you see them inside?"

"No."

"They were supposed to attend Lady Horace's soiree." Evie's tone suggested she couldn't understand their presence.

"They must have heard about the throng of bachelors here." Tom drew in a breath and pushed it out. "This is going to be a long night."

All three were deep in conversation and almost walked right past them. Toodles saw them first. "Look, there's Birdie."

Sara and Toodles steered Henrietta toward them.

"Grans, what are you doing here?"

Toodles looked at Henrietta and Sara. They whispered

among themselves and then Toodles replied, "We are making our way home."

Taking a more direct approach, Evie asked, "Were you inside that house?"

"Which house?"

"The one with all the lights on."

Toodles turned to study the façade of the building. "You're right. All the lights are on."

"Grans! Have the police spoken with you?"

Toodles gave her an impish smile. "Yes, that was rather fun. We all made a point of telling the detective we are related to you and could not possibly be responsible for any wrongdoing. He seemed to know you."

Yes, and Tom's joke about a photograph of her circulating around might not be a joke.

Henrietta lifted her chin and spoke in a haughty tone. "I don't recall making such a claim."

Sara nudged her with her elbow. "I heard you loud and clear. You claimed to know Evie right before you shot to your feet and said you were leaving."

"I do not shoot to my feet ever and you could not possibly have heard me when everyone was talking at once."

"What were you all doing there?" Evie asked. She didn't expect Henrietta to answer so she looked at Sara and Toodles for a response.

Sara scowled at Henrietta. "According to someone who shall remain nameless, I was busy plotting to kill one of her bachelors."

"Are you saying you know the deceased man?"

Sara rolled her eyes. "The moment he walked in, Henrietta made a point of claiming him as her bachelor."

That didn't answer her question.

"Henrietta claims I tried to steal him away because I happened to excuse myself and followed him out of the room. I mean… I didn't follow him. Rather, I happened to make my exit at the same time."

"Do you know his name?" Tom asked.

"No, I lost sight of him and the next time I saw him, there was a young woman standing over his body screaming."

"Do you know the young woman's name?" Evie asked.

"She's one of my debutantes. Lauren Gladstone," Sara declared with a worried look. "I hope she hasn't been scarred by the experience."

Henrietta tilted her head. "How odd that your debutante should find my bachelor."

"Henrietta! Are you about to accuse me of enlisting my debutante to bump off your bachelor? That would defeat the purpose."

The purpose?

Despite Millicent's explanation about Henrietta and Sara's matchmaking game, Evie remained in the dark. She only knew they were competing for some sort of matchmaking triumph.

Sara and Henrietta's exchange had attracted attention to them so Evie suggested they all return to Woodridge House.

"But we haven't seen the body being taken away," Sara complained.

"You wish to make sure he is quite dead?" Henrietta shuddered. "Isn't it enough that I am now one bachelor short? You should relinquish one of your debutantes to even the numbers. Now that I think about it, Lauren

Gladstone should not count because Millicent wasn't here to bear witness. Remember, everything has to be written down."

"You should both be ashamed of yourselves," Toodles muttered. "Have you no pity for that poor young man?"

"My dear, I'm sure he was a firm believer in heaven and is therefore enjoying an angelic welcome."

"How convenient it is to always have a bright side to look upon," Toodles remarked.

Evie knew better than to join in the conversation. In fact, she and Tom walked a couple of paces behind them, keeping their opinions to themselves.

When they reached Woodridge House, Tom hurried ahead to open the front door but it opened before he reached it.

Edgar stepped out and Evie could see several servants standing in the hall.

"My lady. We heard a scream and one of the footmen saw your motor car. We thought it best to remain inside," Edgar said. "The street has been eerily quiet this evening. A footman saw you and Mr. Winchester hurry down the street. We all stood by the windows keeping a lookout for your return."

Before stepping inside the house, Evie looked over her shoulder. The most prominent families lived in Mayfair. Most of them would have come to town for the season. Edgar was right. The street was quiet, unusually so for this time of year, but it wouldn't last.

She and Tom had attended a dinner near Kensington Palace and had then stopped off at the Criterion for some dancing. Along the way, they had seen evidence of many parties taking place.

Soon enough, there would be balls and dinners, enticing the most eligible bachelors.

"We're home safe now, Edgar." She gave him a brief account of events and encouraged everyone to turn in for the night. "I think we all just want this evening to be over." She hoped the others would take it as a cue to retire for the night, although Evie suspected they might want to talk about the incident that had taken place.

Henrietta leaned in and whispered something in Sara's ear.

"You want me to say I'm still in shock and in need of a drink?" Sara asked.

Henrietta rolled her eyes and whispered in Toodles' ear.

"I'll say yes to the drink but I'm not in shock," Toodles said and walked toward the drawing room.

Sara followed, with Henrietta saying to no one in particular, "I suppose I will keep you both company."

Evie looked toward the stairs and then toward the drawing room.

"Choose wisely, Countess," Tom murmured.

"We don't really have a choice." Evie squared her shoulders and headed to the drawing room.

Following her, Tom said, "Just as I thought. It's going to be a long night."

Henrietta did not miss their entrance because she'd been keeping an eye out for them. However, when her eyes met Evie's, she made a point of lifting her chin and looking away.

"I wouldn't be surprised if you're on speaking terms by the end of the week," Tom whispered.

Toodles poured the drinks and handed them around. "Birdie? Tom?"

They both declined the offer.

Evie sat on the edge of a chair while Tom walked over to the fireplace and made a point of studying the landscape painting hanging over it.

Sara took a sip of her brandy and shuddered.

Nodding, Henrietta said, "I saw the body when we made our way out of the house. While it was only a glimpse, I wonder if it will be enough to give me nightmares?"

Sara stared into her glass. "I don't understand how he fell."

"Birdie? Did you and Tom see the body?"

Evie nodded. "Only briefly."

"Did you come up with any theories?"

Evie was about to shake her head when a thought wove through her mind. She looked up and saw Tom studying her.

"What is it?" Tom asked.

"His feet were facing the wrong way."

Tom strolled over to the chair opposite her and sat down. "What do you mean?"

"His feet were facing the street." Evie closed her eyes and focused on the image taking shape in her mind. Nodding, she said, "If you're walking down the stairs and you trip, I imagine your first instinct would be to grab hold of something to stop yourself from falling or you might use your hands to break the fall. The stairs wound down." Evie stood up. "If he tripped at the top of the stairs, the curve of the stairs would have slowed him down. In any case, if he'd fallen…" She stretched her arms out. "He would have fallen facing the street."

Tom nodded. "There's only one way his feet would have ended up facing the street."

"Yes," Evie agreed.

Henrietta leaned over and murmured something to Sara who said, "You both seem to know what you're talking about but we're not quite following any of it."

"We're talking about the position of the body," Tom said. "We think he must have fallen from the landing."

"How could he miss a step there?" Toodles asked.

"Oh," Sara exclaimed. "Do you think he went over the banister?"

Evie shrugged. "He might have been leaning against it. I noticed a flask. It's possible he'd been drinking excessively." Or, Evie thought, someone pushed him.

In her mind, she pictured him standing with his back against the banister. She held her hand out and tipped it back and pictured a somersault…

Was it possible for someone to lean against the banister and fall back?

After some thought, she decided against the idea.

Had someone pushed him?

She considered the possibility. If someone pushed him, she thought, it would have taken a great deal of effort and determination.

"How did you all end up at that party?" Tom asked.

Sara told them about their evening and how they had been chasing their bachelors, moving from one party to another, only to end up at a party where someone died. When she finished her tale, Sara looked at Evie. "We didn't see you there. Were you in the other room?"

"No, Tom and I arrived after the incident took place."

Henrietta finished her drink and set the glass down. "This will definitely give me nightmares." She looked at Sara and then at Toodles. "Do please help me up."

Snorting, Sara said, "You're just trying to pretend you can't spring to your feet."

"You seem to forget my *seniority*."

"No, never. Your cantankerous nature reminds us of your old age every day."

Henrietta sputtered, "I am not the least bit cantankerous."

Sara took hold of her hand and pulled. "Are you resisting?"

"What nonsense. Just put your back into it."

Sara wound her arm around Henrietta and signaled for Toodles to do the same. "You're making yourself heavier."

"Heavier than what?" Henrietta demanded.

"Heavier than what you are."

"I'll have to think about that but I'm sure you mean to imply I am usually light."

Evie and Tom watched them leave and were able to follow their progress by the sound of their fading banter.

When silence settled in the house, Evie stretched and yawned. "I think I'm ready to follow them." She looked up and found Tom looking at her with a lifted eyebrow. "What?"

"I thought you'd be eager to discuss what we just talked about."

"The body facing the wrong way?" Evie shrugged. "It's an interesting observation. He did not fall. He was pushed. That's my conclusion. I can't see it happening any other way. What do we do about it? Telephone Scotland Yard?" She laughed. "I'm sure Detective Inspector... what was his name?"

"Rawlinson."

"I'm sure he has everything under control. He must have reached the same conclusion and far quicker than we did."

"The flask," Tom mused. "Did you notice it?"

Evie nodded. "What about it?"

"I'm surprised you haven't suggested it might have been placed at a strategic angle to make it look as though it had just slipped out of the pocket."

"Why would I suggest that?"

Tom shrugged. "Because you're always curious and question everything you see and because it would raise questions about the death. Who would want to make sure the death was treated as an accident?"

"Are we looking for a culprit?" Evie shook her head. "I shouldn't sound so surprised. However, I'd prefer not to jump to conclusions."

It was Tom's turn to look surprised. "What about the feet facing the wrong way?"

That observation raised too many questions, Evie mused.

"The police will have identified him by now. Then, by tomorrow, they will have a full picture of his life and know everything there is to know about him. If his fall was deliberate, they will track down the person responsible. He wasn't old enough to have an extensive past. It shouldn't take the police long."

"Countess, your mind is racing."

Evie smiled. "You mean, my butterfly mind that's flitting about the place. To be perfectly honest, I'm actually in shock. This is almost too close to home and the timing could not be worse. Caro is arriving tomorrow. Merrin is away and Millicent insists on being my lady's maid and Caro refuses to engage a lady's maid so Millicent will have to divide her time…" Evie closed her eyes for a moment. "Let's not forget we actually have a job to do and it starts tomorrow afternoon when we meet Parsody Jane Buchanan." That, Evie knew, would require some juggling.

"Anything can happen between now and tomorrow," Tom murmured.

"I am happy to end the night on that distracting note."

Tom gave her a whimsical smile. "So… not a long night after all. I suppose I should get some sleep. Tomorrow morning, you're bound to wake up with a head full of theories."

"Is that good or bad?" she asked as they made their way upstairs.

"Neither. It just means I should get a good night's sleep because I'll have my work cut out for me trying to keep up with you tomorrow."

CHAPTER 6

The next morning...

"I wondered what the commotion was about," Millicent said when Evie mentioned the previous night's events.

Surprised by Millicent's nonchalance, Evie asked, "So you didn't hear the scream?"

"I thought I did," Millicent mused in a pensive tone. "But I couldn't be sure because I'd been reading a penny dreadful novel and there was screaming on every other page."

"Screaming?"

Millicent nodded. "When I read, I like to hear the voices in my head. It's possible the real scream got mixed up with the screams in the story."

Evie wasn't entirely sure what Millicent meant by that. "You hear screams in your head?"

"It's the voice, milady. You know… I give each character in the story a voice. As I'm so used to doing it when I read aloud, when I read in silence the voices just crop up in my head."

"And when one of the characters screams, you scream?" Evie asked.

Millicent smiled. "I pretend to scream. Otherwise, the entire household would be in an upheaval every night. Even though I pretend, I still hear the scream in my head." She set a skirt down on the bed and walked to the wardrobe to hunt around for a blouse.

"When you went down to breakfast, did anyone say anything about the commotion?" Evie asked.

"If they had, I would not have been surprised when you mentioned it." Millicent held the blouse against the skirt. "In any case, I didn't go down. Instead, I had breakfast brought up. It's not something I do often but I was pressed for time because Lady Henrietta wanted me to type the notes I took yesterday. Now that I think about it, the maid who brought the breakfast up didn't say anything about the commotion. At least, I don't think she did. She's a bit of a chatter box and I was focused on the work I needed to do so I didn't pay much attention to what she said. Anyhow, did something dreadful happen?"

Evie told her about the young man who'd died from a fall.

Millicent gasped. "Dear me. That's just around the corner. Will you be investigating, milady?"

"I can't see how we would manage it, what with Caro's presentation and keeping an eye on Miss Buchanan. By the way, have the ostrich feathers been delivered?"

"No, milady. They should arrive today in time for the dress rehearsal with Lady Henrietta."

"I almost feel sorry for Caro. I still remember Henrietta putting me through my paces. She took great delight in wearing her riding costume and waving her riding crop at me. Just as well she no longer rides."

"You've had years of practice, milady. I'm sure she will be impressed."

It took a moment for Evie to understand what Millicent had said. "Henrietta will be overseeing Caro's curtsy."

Millicent hummed under her breath. "But you will accompany Lady Evans, and Lady Henrietta said you could do with more practice."

"She said that? When?"

"I would have to look through my notes. I'm sure she mentioned it during her argument about one of the bachelors. She accused Lady Sara of trying to steal him away." Millicent dug inside her pocket and produced a little notebook. "Yes, here it is. *Teach the treacherous Evangeline how to curtsy properly.*" Millicent's cheeks colored. "Did I say that aloud?"

Evie smiled. "You sounded just like Henrietta." As Evie slipped on her blouse and skirt, she remembered Millicent saying something about Henrietta wanting her to join in because she might have forgotten how to curtsy to the monarchs. "Henrietta is rather busy with her matchmaking scheme. I'm sure she will forget all about teaching me how to curtsy properly."

"I wouldn't be so sure," Millicent whispered.

Evie continued, "In any case, Henrietta is still not talking to me. How will she convey her instructions?"

Millicent smiled. "Through me, of course."

Sitting down at her dressing table, Evie looked over her shoulder. "Millicent, you will let me know if it's all too much. It's very cheeky of Henrietta to ask you to take notes." Although, Evie admitted, it helped to know what Henrietta was getting up to. "I suppose there's no point in asking if you've seen this morning's newspapers."

Millicent shook her head.

"Never mind. Tom will be poring through them as we speak. If there is any mention of last night's incident, he'll find it."

Millicent stepped back from arranging Evie's hair and drew out her notebook again. "I should make a note of it and remind myself to look into that young man who was fished out of the Thames. Did you hear anyone mention it last night?"

"No and I doubt Tom heard anything. He was busy trying to recruit likeminded people for his cause. An uprising in the making." While Millicent finished arranging her hair, Evie told her about Tom's efforts to find a way out of wearing knee breeches. "He says he'll go along with it all, but I suspect he is still quite determined and waiting for a window of opportunity."

Millicent hummed. "Edgar told me he'd never seen him looking so morose."

"I'm not surprised, Millicent. I'm afraid this has brought out the worst in Tom."

Standing up, Evie inspected herself in the mirror.

"I'll bring out the pale green ensemble for you to wear this afternoon, milady. Will you need me to accompany you?"

"No, Lotte Mannering will be there. Between us, we should be able to remember all the details required for this task. I doubt it will take up too much of our time." Looking over her shoulder, she saw Millicent's relief.

Moments later, Evie entered the dining room and found Tom holding up a newspaper.

"There's only a brief mention of last night," Tom said. "Most of the article is dedicated to the gowns worn by the guests."

"That hardly seems fair," Evie mused. "To the ladies present and to the poor soul who lost his life." Evie helped herself to some eggs and toast and sat down. "Is there any mention of a young man being fished out of the Thames?"

"No, I haven't come across anything." He set the newspaper aside.

Before he could ask, Evie said, "I only know what Millicent told me. The young man's name is Benjamin Hammonds."

"What sort of clothes was he wearing?"

"I don't know." Evie picked up her coffee cup only to lower it. "I see. Yes, you make a valid point or, rather, you were about to. *Clothes maketh the man.*"

Tom snorted. "Those would not have been my choice of words. Certainly not in this current climate."

However, the quality of the suit would tell them a great deal about the man, she thought. "Anyhow, Millicent showed me a newspaper cutting but the article didn't mention any details. It happened two... three days ago now. You must have missed it what with your thoughts being so preoccupied with other matters."

Tom set the newspaper aside and turned his attention

to his breakfast. Stabbing a piece of bacon, he said, "The tailor sent a note to say the clothes will be ready for a fitting tomorrow. You will have to excuse me."

"Of course. I wouldn't dream of standing in the way of your fitting. Would you like to come with us to visit Miss Buchanan?"

"I'll think about it."

Smiling to herself, Evie took a sip of her coffee. Lowering the cup, she frowned. Why hadn't she thought of it before. She knew she'd noticed the man's clothes. She should have made the connection. "Clothes."

"Please, Countess, no more talk of clothes," Tom grumbled.

"No... I mean... The dinner jacket. Last night..." While the thought took shape in her mind, she could barely string the words together. "He wore a dinner jacket. I noticed it when I saw something protruding from his pocket. Don't you see? All the men wore tailcoats. Who wears dinner jackets?"

Understanding her meaning, Tom gave a slow nod. "Young bucks wishing to make fashion statements. Eventually, I'm sure it will be embraced and adopted as the new *de rigueur* fashion." He grinned. "Then, *everyone* will need to visit their tailor..." He hummed under his breath. "It's actually not so unusual to see people wearing them back home in America."

"Yes." Evie looked up at the clock. Caro and Henry would be arriving soon. On the one hand, she wanted to welcome them without being weighed down by the burden of worry. However, Henry Evans had connections...

Tom must have entertained a similar thought. "Henry might be able to find out more."

"Yes, if he's willing to be sidetracked." Thinking about her schedule, she knew she shouldn't devote any time to the incident they had witnessed the night before.

"How invested is he in this presentation?" Tom asked.

"He will want to do his duty. However, it's worth a try. I'm sure it would only take one telephone call to a colleague and I feel it's not something we can keep to ourselves. We can't assume Detective Inspector Rawlinson will notice everything." Evie took a quick sip of her coffee, followed by a bite of her egg. She continued eating with barely disguised impatience.

"Countess, you'll give yourself indigestion."

"I'm thinking." And, she admitted to herself, letting frustration get the better of her.

"Are you sure you can wait until Caro and Henry arrive? I suspect you're feeling impatient and I'm afraid you'll do yourself harm."

"I want answers, Tom. It's the only way I'll be able to function for the rest of the day. As it is, I have no trouble picturing myself meeting Miss Buchanan and fretting about the identity of the man who died last night and, in the process, paying Miss Buchanan little to no attention."

"Perhaps a walk to clear your head?"

"That sounds like a marvelous idea. However, I doubt I'll be able to shake off this feeling. I can't even define it."

"Something else might be affecting you," Tom suggested. "I know you like an orderly house and I'm sure Henrietta's silence is not helping."

Evie laughed. "I'll admit to being uneasy. But there are

other layers to my concerns. Yesterday, I complained to Lotte about my growing lack of trust in people. If that young man was indeed pushed, the killer might have been right there in the house, watching us."

"You know the police will look into everyone's background. If there is a connection to the young man, they will find it," Tom assured her. "However…"

When he didn't continue, Evie said, "Yes, however. The police don't always see everything and, worse, you know very well they can fixate on the obvious." And they could easily dismiss the incident as an accidental death, she thought. Shaking her head, Evie sat back. "We have our priorities."

"Yes, of course." Tom looked heavenward. "Caro's presentation."

The footman removed Evie's plate. Thanking him, she finished her coffee. They had a long day ahead of them and she found herself agreeing with Tom's idea. A walk would do her good.

Rising to her feet, she walked to the sideboard and helped herself to eggs and toast. Setting the plate down, she settled down to her breakfast.

"Countess?"

Evie broke off a piece of the egg and looked up.

"You never have seconds," Tom said.

Frowning, Evie looked down. "Oh. Oh, dear. My mind must have been wandering…"

The sound of hurried footsteps approaching caught her attention.

Millicent stopped at the door and peered in. "Begging your pardon, milady. Is… is the coast clear?" She stepped inside and, seeing Tom and Evie were alone, she lowered her shoulders and appeared to relax. "Thank goodness."

Apologizing for the intrusion, Millicent walked to the opposite door but stopped when Evie said, "Millicent? Whatever is the matter?"

"A slight kerfuffle, milady."

Evie and Tom mouthed, "Kerfuffle?"

"Nothing serious, milady. Only... I find myself in the middle of something and it would be best for me to... to become invisible and avoid certain people." She turned to the door but stopped when Evie spoke up.

"Millicent! You can't possibly leave without explaining."

Millicent drew in a deep breath and turned. "It's the Prince of Wales, milady."

"Heavens! What about him?"

Millicent's cheeks colored. "Lady Sara could not possibly have seen him at the restaurant."

"What restaurant?"

"I forget the name, milady. Lady Henrietta has been accusing Lady Sara of being obsessed with seeing the Prince of Wales wherever she turns, and she's not wrong about that. Lady Sara has been seeing him in various places."

"And?"

"I shouldn't really say because... Well, it's not my place to tell tales."

Tom leaned forward and murmured, "Countess, perhaps we shouldn't interfere."

Evie looked at Millicent who appeared to be quite distraught. "I'm afraid I must insist, Millicent. Please tell me what is going on."

"It's a ruse, milady. If Lady Henrietta knew I'd figured it out, she would be cross with me and then she wouldn't ask me to sit in on their discussions and I wouldn't be able to take notes and then tell you what they were up to…"

"A ruse?"

Lowering her voice, Millicent said, "Lady Henrietta, milady, has been seeding suggestions. Only… Lady Sara hasn't noticed yet."

Evie found herself at a loss for words so she could only parrot Millicent's words. "Seeding suggestions?"

Millicent gave a brisk nod. "She's very tricky. Right in the middle of an argument, she'll narrow her eyes and whisper something about someone looking like the Prince of Wales, prompting Lady Sara to instantly crane her neck and begin searching for him."

Evie rubbed her temple.

Smiling, Tom shook his head. "I warned you, Countess."

"Millicent. Tell me more about this ruse. How sure are you this is what Henrietta is doing?"

Millicent's eyes widened in surprise. "I thought everyone knew, milady."

"Knew what?"

"The Prince of Wales is not even in England. He left last October on a tour of India and Japan. I believe he is due to return soon."

Yes, of course. Evie suddenly recalled reading about the prince's departure months ago. She had clearly not been paying attention to Sara when she'd told Henrietta about the newspaper article. "Wait a minute. How did Sara come to read about it?"

Millicent rolled her eyes. "Lady Henrietta asked one of

the maids to insert a page from an old newspaper inside yesterday's newspaper. She's quite cunning and even thought of tearing off a corner of the page which showed the date."

Puzzled, Evie asked, "Why do you think Henrietta is doing that?"

Before Millicent could answer or find some excuse not to answer, Edgar walked in and announced, "Lady Evans."

Caro walked in, her back straight, her head held high, her expression a perfect imitation of Henrietta's imperious aloofness. "Good morning, I do hope I am not interrupting."

Surprised by the manner of her entrance, Evie's eyes widened. "Caro?"

Caro kept her aloof expression in place for a full second before breaking into a bright smile and laughing. "No, this won't do at all. I'm afraid I will be a dismal failure," she declared as she walked in and greeted Evie and Tom. "And here you are, going to all this trouble."

Tom cleared his throat. "No trouble at all, Caro. However, if you don't wish to go through with the presentation, we will understand."

"Tom," Evie chastised. Out of the corner of her eye, she saw Millicent bob a curtsy and scurry out of the dining room.

"I do seem to have interrupted something."

Tom shot to his feet and drew out a chair for Caro. "Not at all. We always welcome interruptions, especially timely ones."

"Was that Millicent going out the door?" Caro asked.

"Yes," Tom answered. "She's dealing with a kerfuffle."

"A kerfuffle?"

"Yes, a kerfuffle and that was our exact response," Tom said. "Where's Henry?"

"He sent me on ahead to test the waters." Caro stopped and gave her a brisk smile. "I actually meant to say he stopped by his club and will be arriving later on."

Evie smiled. Not long ago, Caro had been her lady's maid and, like Millicent, Caro had been in the habit of saying precisely what she thought or what she wasn't supposed to say. "Caro? Why would he send you on ahead?"

"I'm sorry. You weren't supposed to hear that part."

If she had to guess, she'd say Henry wanted to avoid arriving during one of their awkward moments of pandemonium. "I'm afraid I did hear it."

"Well…" Caro looked around and lowered her voice. "Since you asked… He didn't want to arrive in the middle of something. You must admit, there's always some sort of drama in the making and… Is there?"

Tom prompted Evie's response with a raised eyebrow.

While Evie wanted to offer a swift assurance, her mind flooded with images of the last few minutes and the day before.

"There really is something going on. Is that why Millicent hurried out?"

"Caro, you mustn't concern yourself. Right now, we are all focused on your presentation. Tom has made a special effort to outfit himself with the appropriate clothes and Henrietta is eager to help you get that curtsy right. So, you see, you have nothing to concern yourself with. It is all taken care of and you will have a most splendid day."

Evie's assurances were drowned out by Henrietta's determined steps as she approached the dining room.

"Where is that girl?" Henrietta demanded as she entered. Coming to an abrupt stop, she spoke over Evie's head. "Is Millicent hiding in here?"

Tom spoke up. "No, but the Prince of Wales just went out the other door."

CHAPTER 7

*M*uttering something about Millicent constantly disappearing into thin air, Henrietta turned and saw Caro. "Lady Evans! What a delightful distraction."

Delightful distraction?

She really needed to stop being surprised and parroting what she heard because she was at a loss for words.

"My goodness, Caro. You must be thrilled," Henrietta continued. "At last, you will be presented. Have you tried on the gown?"

"Gown?" Caro asked.

Heavens. Caro had caught her affliction.

"I... Yes..." Caro nodded.

"Yes, of course," Henrietta smiled. "You have obviously tried it on during the fitting, but you haven't tried the gown on with the feathers." Henrietta clapped her hands. "What better way to perfect your curtsy than by doing so while wearing the gown and the feathers. We have no time to waste. Come along."

Henrietta herded Caro out of the dining room and began delivering her instructions, "It shouldn't be too difficult to master. You begin by sweeping one foot behind you, then bend your other knee and bow your head, all without losing your feathers, of course. The trick will be to make it all look as if you'd been born to perform a curtsy."

As Henrietta's voice faded, Tom leaned forward and murmured, "Countess, you need to breathe. She's gone now and your trick of sitting perfectly still seems to have worked. Henrietta forgot about you."

Evie straightened and gave him a tight smile. "I was not trying to make myself invisible."

"Did I say you were?" He gave her a brisk smile.

"Well, I'm still not out of the woods. A timely interruption would be highly appreciated."

They both glanced toward the door with Tom leaning slightly to look beyond the door and into the hall.

"No, I don't see any sign of an interruption, but I do believe we are dutybound to report your observations to the detective. He needs to know about the jacket, as well as the positioning of the body," Tom suggested.

Struggling with the idea of abandoning Caro, Evie shook her head. "I couldn't possibly."

"Countess, you shouldn't feel you are undermining the detective's abilities. As you said, it's possible he might miss vital clues."

"Caro might need my support and I'm sure the young man's identity has already been established. As for the dinner jacket..." It might reveal something or nothing,

Evie thought. Or, it could be another puzzle. Especially if the young man was British and not American.

When she shared her thoughts with Tom, he said, "Interesting. Yes, that might tell us he is eager to adopt new styles, not something readily accepted by the establishment here. They are rather fond of their tailcoats."

"Too many paths to follow, Tom."

"Yes, and that could be entertaining." Tom shrugged. "He might have borrowed the dinner jacket."

Evie looked at him without blinking. "Meaning, he might have been pretending to be someone of good social standing in order to attend the party?"

Shrugging, Tom said, "Yes, and the poor fellow didn't realize a dinner jacket would give him away."

"Not necessarily," Evie mused. "While everyone at the party wore tailcoats, someone wearing a dinner jacket might still be perceived as a catch."

"As you said, too many paths to follow."

They remained in the dining room long after the footmen had cleared all the breakfast serving trays and the table.

More than an hour later, a footman entered and stopped at the door.

Noticing him, Evie crossed her fingers and hoped he was about to announce the detective's arrival. Their conversation the previous night had been brief. If he was at all serious about investigating the matter, Evie felt the detective should have another chat with them.

The footman cleared his throat. "Lady Henrietta has requested your presence in the drawing room, my lady."

Resigned to her fate, Evie stood up.

"I suppose I should offer you my moral support," Tom murmured.

"Yes, you should, Tom."

"Very well." Tom stood up. "Lead the way."

Crossing the hall, she found Millicent standing outside the drawing room holding what looked like a hat box.

"It's the ostrich feathers, milady."

Thinking Millicent was still trying to avoid Henrietta, Evie offered to take the box in with her.

"Thank you, but you'll still need me to adjust them on you."

"Millicent, I'm sure I'll manage," Evie assured her.

"It wouldn't be right, milady." Millicent lifted her chin. "I must be grown-up about this." She eased the door to the drawing room open and slipped inside.

Evie was about to follow when they heard a knock at the front door.

Tom and Evie swung around.

Edgar appeared and walked across the hall, his back straight, his chin lifted. Before reaching the front door, he slowed down, cleared his throat and gave his shirt sleeves a tug, adjusting them so they would both only show a sliver of white over the coat sleeve.

Satisfied, he drew in a breath and opened the door.

Tom shook his head and whispered, "Do they teach that at butler school or is that his personal trait?"

"I'm sure it's a tradition handed down from butler to butler," Evie whispered back.

After a brief exchange, Edgar stepped back and gestured to the library.

"It's a man," Evie whispered. She could only see his

back and her view was limited because, for some reason, Edgar walked behind him.

They reached the library and, as the library door stood open, Edgar stepped inside. Most likely to see if anyone was in there. He then gestured to the man to follow him inside.

"I've lost him now," Tom whispered. "Did you recognize him?"

"No." She saw Edgar take the man's hat and watched to see what would happen next.

"The suspense, Countess. Is that something else they hand down from butler to butler?"

Edgar set the hat down on a table, straightened his sleeves again and looked up toward the staircase and then along the hall.

"Should we wave and let him know we are right here?" Tom whispered.

"Hush," Evie said. "Let him do his job. He won't like us interfering."

"Remind me to ask you to explain that to me, please." Tom slipped his hands inside his pockets and whispered, "He appears to be working out the odds of you being upstairs. Now he's looking toward the dining room door. Perhaps a footman told him about your second helping of breakfast and Edgar is now wondering if you're tackling your third helping of breakfast. Aha, he's about to turn toward us. No... wait. Something else has caught his attention..."

The sound of tiny feet scurrying along the hall grew louder and Holmes announced his presence with a bark.

Edgar wagged his finger at him, prompting Holmes to stop in his tracks.

"My money's on Holmes," Tom whispered.

"Doing what?"

"I don't know but, whatever he does, he'll get the better of Edgar."

Edgar's finger, now pointed at Holmes, lowered.

Tom chortled. "Yes, this should be interesting."

Responding to Edgar's prompt, Holmes lowered his head only to change his mind. Straightening, he barked.

Edgar admonished him with a wag of his finger again. Once he had Holmes' attention, he lowered his finger.

Holmes reacted by sitting down. This seemed to satisfy Edgar. He tugged his sleeves and turned toward the drawing room. The moment he took a step, Holmes jumped to his feet and raced toward the drawing room. Not to be outdone, Edgar harrumphed and picked up his pace. Neither Edgar nor Holmes had noticed Evie and Tom. When they did, they both came to an abrupt stop.

"My lady."

Holmes barked, wagged his tail and jumped forward, only to change his mind and scurry away as quickly as his little legs could carry him.

"Smart dog. He's beating a hasty retreat, leaving Edgar to face the music," Tom mused.

Edgar growled under his breath. A second later, he cleared his throat and regained his composure. "My lady, Detective Inspector Rawlinson wishes to speak with you and Mr. Winchester." He glanced over his shoulder and, no doubt, saw Holmes peering from around a corner. Turning back to Evie, he inclined his head slightly. "I should apologize for that display. I can assure you it will never happen again."

Tom grinned. "Edgar, don't be too hard on Holmes or yourself. There's no harm in a bit of mischief."

Edgar spluttered, "Mischief?"

Tom glanced at Evie. "I've just realized Edgar is the third person I've heard echoing words today. Is there something I should know?"

"Tom, you're not making sense and we shouldn't keep the detective waiting."

"Especially not when the detective's arrival just saved you from Henrietta's clutches," Tom murmured and followed her to the library.

"Detective," Evie swept in, her tone carrying the relief she felt. She hoped he had come to share information with them.

The detective turned away from the painting he had been studying. "Lady Woodridge. I hope this is not an inconvenient moment."

"Not at all. In fact, Tom and I had just been talking about last night…" Evie turned to Edgar. "I think the detective might welcome some coffee." She turned to the detective. "Or would you prefer tea?"

"Neither, thank you. I'm afraid I am pressed for time."

Oh, dear. She'd hoped he would stay for a good while.

Turning back to Edgar, she smiled. "Thank you, Edgar."

"Perhaps some tea for yourself and Mr. Winchester," Edgar suggested.

Evie was about to say no when she noticed Edgar's look of eager expectation. It seemed he wished to have the opportunity to return to the room.

"Very well, yes, thank you." Turning to the detective, she invited him to take a seat. "How can we help you?" She assumed he had more questions for them. Although, she still hoped he wanted to share information with them.

As she settled down opposite him, she hoped he hadn't come to issue a warning about meddling in police business.

"We have identified the victim." He reached inside his coat pocket and produced a small notebook. "James Clementine."

"Was he American?" As she asked the burning question, she looked up at Tom. If he thought it was a bad idea to share that information with the detective, he did not show it.

The detective shifted and sat forward. "It's interesting that you should ask. As a matter of fact, yes, he was. May I ask how you happen to know that?"

"I didn't exactly know it. The clothes he wore suggested he might not have been British."

"The clothes?"

Really? He'd only just arrived and he was already affected by the affliction.

Evie nodded. "His dinner jacket suggested it. Everyone wears tailcoats. I'm tempted to say dinner jackets are fashionable in America but I know for a fact tailcoats are still *de rigueur*. The younger set, however, are fond of introducing new trends."

He studied her for a moment. "Lady Woodridge, I should make something clear to you. The police are not overly fond of a member of the public taking an interest in police investigations. However, you do have a reputation for displaying keen observation skills. As well as…"

He appeared to struggle with the definition of whatever else she seemed to excel at.

"You have what some refer to as outlandish theories."

Evie hid her smile by looking down at her hands. She refrained from commenting, mostly because she was usually the first to argue against entertaining those so-called outlandish theories.

"As crazy as some of those theories might sound," Tom said, "they always provide leads for the police to follow."

Crazy?

Evie frowned. "Tom, I always thought you found them entertaining."

"I do."

And? she silently prompted him, but he did not offer to clarify the statement.

The detective cleared his throat and drew their attention back to him. "Your methods might be unorthodox. However, I am not entirely averse to the idea of you providing some sort of input. Are you likely to take an interest in this case?"

Evie ran through her busy schedule, tossing around every little task she needed to perform over the coming days, including the afternoon tea with Miss Parsody Jane Buchanan. Instead of answering, she asked, "What did you say his name was?"

"James Clementine. Are you familiar with the name?"

"No, but I'm curious to know how you happened to know it."

"He was identified by Lauren Gladstone. She's the young woman who found him at the bottom of the stairs. She met him at an afternoon tea several days ago. Also, he carried some documents, including a passport. As you know, anyone traveling now is required to have one."

"And he had it on him?" she asked.

The detective nodded. "He hailed from Boston and had been traveling around the continent for several months." The detective went on to mention the cities.

"Have the police contacted his family?"

"We've tried but we haven't met with any success. Our colleagues in Boston are looking into it."

"Where was he staying?" Evie asked.

The detective shook his head. "We haven't been able to establish that. We know he had been traveling around Europe so we assume he was staying in hotels."

"He might have been a guest in someone's house," Evie suggested.

To her surprise, the detective made a note of her suggestion.

He looked up from his notebook and studied Evie for a moment before saying, "I'm not sure that will yield anything. We've spoken with everyone who attended the party and no one mentioned hosting him. In fact, Lauren Gladstone was the only one acquainted with him."

The only one willing to acknowledge it, Evie thought. She studied her hands and remembered telling Lotte about her diminishing trust in people. What if someone had simply not owned up to knowing him?

"Tom? What was the name of that man you spoke with?" She turned to the detective. "There was a young man who'd found the scene quite distressing."

"Stuart White," Tom said. "He was shaking like a leaf. I put him in a taxicab but I'm afraid I can't recall the address he gave." He dug inside his pocket and produced the calling card Stuart White had given him. Flipping it over, he shook his head. "No, no address."

The door to the library opened and Edgar walked in

carrying a tray. Setting it down near Evie, he stepped back and Evie noticed he did not leave the room.

Evie stood up and walked to the table, all the while wondering how they could find out where James Clementine had been residing whilst in London.

Tom joined Evie by the table. "I'm sure I heard Stuart White give the taxicab driver directions to his house. Perhaps if I sift through my mind the information will surface."

The detective nodded. "We might be able to trace the driver. Did Stuart White give you the impression he actually knew James Clementine?"

Tom shook his head. "Hard to say. I don't really remember him saying anything specific but, at the time, we hadn't seen the scene inside."

Meaning, Stuart White might have said something but Tom hadn't made the connection or put the information into some sort of perspective. Evie poured a cup of tea for Tom and one for herself. As she headed back to her seat, she stopped.

Seeing this, Tom asked, "What? Have you thought of something?"

"The shoes." Evie looked at Tom and could almost see his mind at work, trying to interpret what she'd said. "I remember noticing how new they looked. I also noticed the soles and thought they might have been slippery."

"And you think he had the shoes made in London?" Tom turned to the detective. "That might be a way to find out where he was staying."

It seemed like a minor detail. Again, the detective made a note of the information.

"You said Lauren Gladstone had met him at an afternoon tea party. Have you spoken with the hostess?"

He nodded. "She couldn't remember him."

Taking a sip of her tea, Evie remembered the article she had read about the man who'd been fished out of the river. Hoping the detective would know more about it, she mentioned it.

"I heard about the incident but I'm afraid I don't know the details. Another detective is handling the case. Why do you ask?"

Shrugging, Evie told him about Millicent showing her the newspaper article. In reality, she was trying to delay the detective's departure because when he left she would be at Henrietta's disposal. "My secretary thought I might want to look into it."

"Despite it looking like a suspicious death, he might have decided to take his own life."

The detective's suggestion made Evie shudder. She couldn't imagine why anyone would wish to do that. As if to mock her naivety, she thought of the obvious reason. The war had changed people and some who had experienced it first-hand were still traumatized by the experience.

Lost in thought, she was startled when the detective stood up to leave. She looked around for a place to set her teacup down and was rescued by Edgar who took it from her.

"Detective, I've just remembered something. The newspaper article mentioned the police were treating the death as suspicious." Belatedly, she realized he had already mentioned that.

The detective shook his head. "As I said, I'm afraid I don't know anything about it."

Evie searched her mind for something else that might delay his departure. "I almost forgot to ask about the cause of death. Did James Clementine die from the fall?"

The detective's expression froze for a moment, suggesting he had been caught by surprise.

"Tom and I discussed the fall last night. The position of the body struck us as odd."

"Indeed."

Evie realized she would have to be more direct. "Is that what caused his death?"

"It would appear so, my lady."

The detective checked his pockets. Evie didn't think he was actually looking for something. Rather, he was using some sort of distraction to change the subject.

"Did you find the position of the body odd?"

"Odd?" the detective asked.

"Yes, it appeared to be facing the wrong way. At least, to my way of thinking. Although, I must admit, I have no experience falling."

When the detective didn't respond, Evie added, "It just seemed odd. You see, if he fell down the stairs, his head should have been facing the street. Instead, his feet were facing the street. Almost as if he'd performed some sort of acrobatic jump."

The detective blinked. Once again, he searched his pockets. Evie now imagined him wanting to produce some sort of prop to divert her attention.

Almost as a last resort, he looked at his watch. "I'm afraid I really must get on now. Thank you for your time. I hope it wasn't too much of an imposition."

"Not at all, detective. You're welcome at any time." Evie watched him leave and felt a knot of tension work its way around her shoulders. Sighing, she turned to Tom. "What did you make of that?"

Tom set his cup of tea down and shrugged. "We've only just met him. It's hard to say what he thinks."

Puzzled by his response, Evie asked, "What does that mean? Are you saying you can't tell if he revealed everything he knows to us and that he is, in fact, hiding something or, at the very least, withholding information?"

Smiling, Tom nodded.

"And you expected me to guess all that?"

"But you did. Anyway, I thought you could read me like an open book."

"Since when?"

Tom laughed. "Since you always know which buttons to push."

"I see. You are trying to lighten the mood."

"Admit it. You're quaking in your boots because you have no idea what Henrietta has planned for you."

CHAPTER 8

*a*s Evie walked across the hall, she smiled and thought she could always rely on Tom to lighten the mood for her.

"Ready for battle, Countess?" Tom asked just before he eased the door open to the drawing room.

"As ready as I will ever be, even though I have no idea what Henrietta has planned for me." She wanted to believe the Dowager Countess of Woodridge would use the opportunity to break the ice and, perhaps, make a few concessions so they could finally move on from the stalemate position they both found themselves in. Although, Evie acknowledged her responsibility. As the head of the house, she really needed to take the first step. In reality, she knew it didn't matter what she did or said, Henrietta would stick to her guns.

"That's the spirit. Remember, I'm right behind you," Tom assured her.

Evie laughed. "That's a good place to be if you want to be ready for a swift retreat."

They found the drawing room completely transformed. All the chairs had been pushed back and a path cleared for Caro to practice walking the full length without any obstructions to hinder her progress.

Dressed in her presentation gown with her three white ostrich feathers in place, Caro performed her curtsy, straightened and walked backward without turning her back to the monarchs, in this instance, represented by Henrietta who sat on a high-backed chair and appeared to be shrouded in an air of haughty imperiousness.

Caro yelped. Losing her balance, she wailed, "How am I supposed to see where I'm going? I don't have eyes on the back of my head." Caro wailed, stomped her foot and, in the process, dislodged her feathers.

Henrietta assured her, "My dear, the way will be cleared for you."

Millicent rushed up to Caro and adjusted the ostrich feathers while murmuring reassurances.

Evie waited for Henrietta to notice her but the dowager seemed intent on maintaining her aloofness.

Leaning toward Tom, she whispered, "Do you think the detective told us everything he knows?"

"I doubt it. In fact, I'm beginning to think he is employing an unfamiliar tactic. I'm sure you were just as surprised as I was to see him this morning and to hear him acknowledge your talents."

"You mean, my questionable tactics?"

Tom grinned. "Yes, those. Anyhow, I'm sure his visit had more to do with what he could learn from you than what he was willing to divulge about the case."

"Milady." Millicent rushed up to her. "You're here."

Evie laughed under her breath. Where else would she be? After all, she had been summoned.

Tom laughed. "You almost got away with pretending to be invisible again."

"You're not wearing your court dress," Millicent said.

"I'm afraid this will have to do, Millicent. It's nearly time for luncheon and I'm going out straight after that."

Millicent glanced over her shoulder.

To Evie's surprise, she appeared to be seeking Henrietta's approval to proceed. Something she received when Henrietta gave her a small nod.

"Right… Well, I have your ostrich feathers. We'll have to make do with that." Millicent walked to a table and reached inside the hat box she had carried in earlier.

"Deep breath, Countess. This will soon be over."

Millicent removed the paper wrapping and exclaimed, "My goodness. They've made a mistake."

Henrietta stood up and, her eyes wide with curiosity, walked over to where Millicent stood. When she saw what Millicent had revealed, Henrietta pushed out a breath.

"What is it, Millicent?" Evie asked.

"They've sent the wrong feathers, milady."

Henrietta shook her head but didn't say anything.

"What do you mean?" Evie imagined three pink flamingo feathers and knew that would not go down well with those in charge of ensuring everyone adhered to the strict dress code. "Did they only send two? Is that the problem, Millicent?" They hadn't made a mistake with Caro's feathers. Debutantes wore two but Caro was married, so she was required to wear three feathers.

"That's not it, milady."

"Then, what is it?" Maybe Millicent had really found pink flamingo feathers...

"The feathers, milady, are the wrong color. They're black."

For a split second, she wondered if the rules had changed.

As far as she knew, black ostrich feathers were never to be worn, under no circumstance. Except, of course, for those in deep mourning. And that exception did not apply to her because she had been a widow for a number of years now.

It had to be a mistake, but surely the milliner would know...

A lump formed in Evie's throat. Her eyes lowered and she covered her left hand with her right. Softening her tone, she said, "Perhaps it's not a mistake, Millicent."

Had they missed a court circular announcing the change?

"But milady, they're black and they're supposed to be white ostrich feathers. You'll stick out. They might not even allow you inside."

Giving her a small smile, Evie said, "You seem to forget, Millicent... I'm a widow." Yes, they must have changed the rules. Indeed, change appeared to be a trend these days.

Millicent's cheeks flooded with splashes of red. "Oh, dear. I'm so sorry."

Caro stepped forward, her eyes filled with concern. "This is all my fault."

"Heavens, Caro. Why would you say that?" Evie chuckled and tried to make light of the situation. "They're only feathers."

"Yes, but it's a reminder." Caro reached for her feathers, clearly with the intention of removing them but they swayed out of her reach so she ended up swiping at them several times, all to no avail.

Resigned to her fate, Evie said, "It's actually perfect." She gestured for Millicent to bring them. "I attended my presentation as Nicholas' wife, and was presented as the new Countess of Woodridge. It's almost fitting that I should attend the function again as his widow. In fact, it's almost poetic." She closed her eyes for a moment and whispered, "Yes, it's really quite right that I should wear black feathers." In her heart, she felt this would give her something she had never really sought. A form of closure, of coming full circle.

She opened her eyes and looked at Tom.

This would be the symbolic ending she needed in order to have a new beginning.

Henrietta muttered something under her breath. Taking a deep swallow, she lifted her chin, swung toward Tom and glowered at him before sweeping past him and out of the drawing room, saying, "This is your fault."

Tom gaped at her. A full minute later, he said, "Me? What did I do?"

"Tom, don't pay any attention to that."

"But what did Henrietta mean? How is this my fault? Wait a minute. I see. Yes, Henrietta is quite right." Giving a firm nod, he swung away and walked out of the drawing room.

Oh, dear.

Looking at a complete loss, Caro's eyes widened. "What just happened?"

Evie took the feathers from Millicent. "I'm afraid Tom has accepted responsibility for this."

"But why?"

Millicent rolled her eyes and gave Caro an elbow jab as she whispered, "Because he still hasn't walked her down the aisle."

"But that's hardly his fault. I mean… is it?"

"Never mind whose fault it is." Evie shook her head. "In fact, no one is at fault. As I said, it's quite right that I should attend the function wearing black ostrich feathers." She studied the feathers and added, "However, just to be on the safe side, could you please contact the milliner?"

"Certainly, milady, and if he's made a mistake, I'll give him a piece of my mind and then some."

Evie twirled one around. It had to be a mistake. Shaking her head, she handed them back to Millicent. "I should go after Tom and make sure he doesn't do something silly like… Well, I have no idea." She only hoped he didn't confront Henrietta.

Crossing the hall, she headed straight for the library but didn't find Tom there.

As she walked out, she encountered Edgar and asked him if he had seen Tom.

Edgar bowed his head slightly. "He stepped out for a moment, my lady."

"Stepped out?"

Edgar nodded and signaled toward the front door as if to confirm the fact Tom had indeed walked out of the house.

"Did he say where he was going?" She didn't actually blame Tom for wanting to distance himself by stepping out of the house for some fresh air.

Edgar shook his head. Clearing his throat, he held out a salver. "This arrived a moment ago, my lady."

Evie took the envelope and immediately recognized the name of the sender.

Why had she set this in motion?

Yet another complication.

Belatedly, she wished she had not interfered in something that was entirely Tom's business. Although, in reality, she'd had little to do with Tom being awarded a title.

"Thank you, Edgar." She slit open the envelope and read the contents. "Good heavens…"

There was nothing she could do about this now.

This was a *fait accompli.*

Like it or not, Tom's destiny was now set in stone.

The idea had cropped up in her mind and she'd acted before thinking it through properly. "Edgar, please make sure Tom's morning suit is presentable." The formal attire would be required. Like it or not, Evie thought…

Before she could even finish the thought, she shook her head. Folding the piece of paper, she returned it to the envelope and pushed all thought of it to the back of her mind.

Nodding, Edgar swung away and made his way up the stairs, presumably to check on Tom's morning suit.

That left Evie standing alone. Once Edgar reached the next floor and his footsteps receded along the hallway, it took her a moment to realize she was surrounded by silence. Quite hollow, she thought. Almost, echoing, she silently added. Her lips moved as she formed the words but she didn't dare speak up because she didn't want to disturb the serenity that settled around her.

Evie couldn't remember the last time she'd found the

house in such complete stillness, with no one talking or coming and going. Although, she knew if she listened carefully she'd hear Holmes skittering about the place.

Standing still, she looked around the hall with its marble tiles and ancestral paintings that had witnessed more than she could ever imagine.

The last few days had been a whirlwind of activities. It seemed like an eternity since she'd sat with Lotte to discuss Parsody Jane Buchanan and, even then, there had been a torrent of other concerns flooding her mind.

The year before, they'd avoided attending the social season. Although, that didn't necessarily mean they had sailed through calm waters. Evie knew they must have been caught up in some sort of incident or another.

Suddenly, she realized she should enjoy the moment while she could. Her lips parted again and she breathed out, "Ah, the blessed peace and quiet."

Just then, the front door opened and Toddles and Sara swept in, filling the hall with their lively chatter and laughter.

"Birdie, there you are. Sara and I have just enjoyed the most marvelous stroll and now we're famished. I hope we've arrived in time for luncheon. And, look, we found Lotte Mannering loitering outside. She's quite cross with us because we foiled her attempts to conceal herself in plain sight."

Evie turned toward the hall fireplace and looked at the clock on the mantle. The morning had slipped away and she knew she would struggle to recall everything she'd done and said.

"Birdie? You're a million miles away."

Sara and Toodles walked toward her with Lotte only a

couple of steps behind them. From out of nowhere, Holmes shot out, barking at some imaginary prey and disappeared along the hall.

"Strictly speaking," Lotte said, "I wasn't loitering. Grosvenor Square happens to be—"

"Luncheon. Yes, you're all just in time," Evie said before Lotte could reveal her reason for being near Grosvenor Square. She made eye contact with Lotte who had no trouble interpreting her interruption.

Out of the corner of her eye, Evie saw Toodles and Sara exchange a knowing look. Sometimes, Evie thought, she forgot how perceptive others could be.

Evie looked toward the drawing room and decided she couldn't deal with Caro's guilt. Gesturing toward the library, she said, "There's still some time before luncheon."

Sara and Toodles excused themselves saying they wished to freshen up. That gave Evie the advantage of having a private word with Lotte.

"I haven't told them about meeting Parsody Jane Buchanan and I'd prefer to keep it that way," Evie admitted. "They've heard of the heiress and have expressed a desire to meet her."

"I thought you wanted the extra pairs of eyes."

"I did but that was before I found out about their matchmaking game." Taking a seat, Evie added, "Henrietta went off in a huff so I don't know if she'll be joining us and Tom has disappeared." Evie didn't explain why. "My morning has been like a tornado caught inside a whirlwind." She looked over her shoulder and then leaned in to say, "I'm glad you came early. Did you hear about the young man falling down the stairs?"

Lotte nodded. "I read about it in the newspaper this

morning so I decided to come early and wander around the area in case I could learn anything of interest. When I bumped into Toodles and Sara they insisted I join them."

"The newspapers didn't mention anything about the death being suspicious."

"That's right and that's precisely what piqued my curiosity." Lotte admitted. "On the surface it looks like an unfortunate accident."

Evie nodded. "Yes, you're right. There might be more than meets the eye." She surprised Lotte by telling her she and Tom had actually been present at the scene. "It all happened just as we arrived from an evening out. We were about to walk inside when we heard a scream. The detective in charge called on us this morning. We think he's withholding information."

"Anything specific?" Lotte asked.

"Yes, the precise cause of death."

"That says a great deal."

"Perhaps." Evie frowned. "At this point, I don't know if he wishes to encourage me or dissuade me from poking around. If he thinks there has been foul play, he did not share the information." Evie filled her in on the observation she had made. "If the detective finds this was no accident, he will have his work cut out for him. There were quite a few people present at the party." Evie searched her mind. "I just remembered something else. The young man's name was James Clementine and he hailed from Boston."

That surprised Lotte. "A compatriot?"

"Yes, the police are trying to contact his family and…" Evie tapped her chin. "There was something else that struck me as odd. Lauren Gladstone, she's the young woman who found him at the bottom of the stairs and she's the only one who was acquainted with him."

"So, he was from Boston and he'd been traveling around," Lotte said.

"Yes. For several months." To Evie's surprise, Lotte drew out a small notebook and made a note of the information.

"Do you think the detective will keep you informed?"

"Tom thinks he's keen to see what information he can get from us so he might wish to keep the lines of communication open."

While they waited for the others, Evie told her about the article Millicent had drawn her attention to.

"Fished out of the Thames? I must have missed that." Lotte smiled. "Is Millicent trying to drum up business for us?"

"Yes, she is to be commended. Anyhow, I have a copy of the article. It's only a brief mention. Remind me to show it to you."

They spent some time discussing the incident. Looking at the clock on the mantle, Evie glanced toward the door and wondered how long they should wait for Tom. "I have no idea where the others are."

As she turned back to Lotte, she heard someone approaching in haste.

It didn't surprise her to see Millicent who hurried in and leaned in to whisper, "Milady, Lady Sara and Toodles have dozed off, they were that tired from their walk."

"But they said they were famished... Oh, well, that's two less for lunch."

Millicent straightened. "And..."

"And?" Evie could not have sounded more surprised.

Millicent appeared to measure her words. "Lady Henrietta has asked for a tray to be taken up to her room."

"Did she seem upset?" Evie asked.

"It's difficult to say, milady. The maid attending her rushed out to look for me and dragged me in because she couldn't understand what Lady Henrietta was saying."

Alarmed, Evie asked, "What do you mean?"

"She was murmuring a great deal and she sounded quite cross."

Cross with someone or with the incident with the black feathers they had experienced in the drawing room?

Millicent continued, "She only stopped long enough to say she would be eating alone and could I organize a tray."

Evie considered going up to see if she could do something to help Henrietta overcome her concerns but decided against it. She knew only too well Henrietta would dismiss her assistance as a mere platitude because, according to her, she always needed to reason with herself and that always took time.

"As for Caro... I mean, Lady Evans..." Millicent rolled her eyes. "She's fretting and says she has lost her appetite because everything is her fault. If she hadn't fallen in love with Henry Evans who turned out to be Lord Evans, she wouldn't be in this woeful predicament, forcing you to wear black ostrich feathers and now it's all too late and there's no backing out so she's..." Millicent stopped and gulped in a breath. "I've lost my train of thought."

"That's fine, Millicent. Although... Apart from missing out on luncheon, do you think Caro is going to recover from this guilt? We have a soiree to attend this evening."

"It's really difficult to say, milady. Would you like me to talk some sense into her? I do have my ways."

Evie had no doubt of that. "Just to be clear, are you referring to your impressive ability to wear your opponent down?"

Millicent grinned. "I can be quite persuasive."

Evie gave her a tentative smile. "Do your very best, Millicent."

Excusing herself, Millicent left, a joyful bounce to her steps.

Turning her attention back to Lotte, she realized she hadn't asked about the black ostrich feathers. However, she decided they still had some time to sort it all out.

"I guess it's just the two of us." Evie stood up and led Lotte to the dining room, her thoughts jumbled with that morning's events.

They sat down just as the footmen were bringing in the food.

Looking up, Evie saw Lotte studying her.

"I suppose you found all that rather odd."

"Odd?"

"Millicent has a way about her... Some people find it rather odd."

Lotte smiled. "In truth, I can't claim to have understood any of it and it might be better if I continue on my merry blissful way."

Evie couldn't agree more. Sometimes, ignorance could be bliss.

"Although, you might need to clarify a few things but only on a need to know basis."

"In other words, the less said the better?"

Grinning, Lotte nodded.

Lifting her eyebrows, Evie sighed. "I could not agree with you more."

CHAPTER 9

Later that afternoon

According to Millicent, after eating alone, Henrietta had decided to remain in her room. Millicent had also reported her failure with Caro who had insisted on spending some time alone to compose a thoughtful apology for the trouble she had caused by marrying Lord Evans.

Meanwhile, Sara and Toodles, refreshed from their rest, had gone in search of a meal to see them through the rest of the day before returning to Woodridge House to change and head off to enjoy the evening's entertainment at the theater.

Evie assumed their plans would not include Henrietta who would most likely remain cloistered with her thoughts.

Evie spent a moment puzzling over the sudden change

in her day. If she had to give an account of everything that had happened, where would she begin? With breakfast?

"I wouldn't be surprised if Tom is, right this minute, boarding a vessel to take him far away from all this madness," Evie mused.

"Is it in my best interest to ask for an explanation?" Lotte asked.

Evie gave it some thought. "No, I think it might be best to remain oblivious. Also, now that I think about it, you might be wise to heed my advice and avoid repeating words."

"Repeating words?"

"Precisely. I found myself doing it out of sheer disbelief and, wouldn't you know it, others began to do it. I fear it might be contagious."

Lotte smiled. "Contagious? Yes, I see what you mean. Actually, I am sorely tempted to ask about Tom but, as you say, it might be best to remain in blissful ignorance."

Evie had tried not to worry about his absence and wouldn't be surprised if he suddenly appeared with a new motor car. But what if he'd taken Henrietta's words to heart? What would he do? Evie drew a blank.

Standing in front of the hall mirror, Evie adjusted her hat. "I'm ready and quite eager to meet Miss Parsody Jane Buchanan. There's a lot riding on this meeting. I'm hoping it will completely absorb my attention and I'm actually quite curious about her."

Setting off, they were met by a lovely sunny afternoon, which went a long way toward helping Evie forget that morning's havoc.

They walked the short distance to the corner and turned into Grosvenor Square where the palatial houses were found, comprising several levels, including base-ments and attics, all with views of the 2.5 hectares of gardens—the countryside in the city.

These buildings had always been occupied by the most affluent who, in better days, could not only afford the exclusive address but could also afford to tear down a dwelling and erect something to surpass its predecessor. Now, some of those magnificent buildings had been broken up into separate dwellings.

Lately, the *Bentley Boys*, some of the people taking up residency in one of the buildings, had managed to raise more than a few eyebrows with their love for car racing, wild parties and their green sports cars parked *ad hoc* outside their building.

"*The Bentley Boys* must be recovering from one of their parties," Lotte said as she gestured toward several sports cars parked in the street.

"I thought only the local people knew about them."

"Everyone knows about them," Lotte said. "Ask any taxicab driver to bring you to Grosvenor Square and they will mention them."

"They must have attended a party somewhere else," Evie replied. "The only party in this area last night was the one further along in Upper Brook Street."

They found the address and rang the bell. As they waited, Evie wondered if she should install an electric doorbell at Woodridge House. Smiling, she pictured Millicent yelping every time the doorbell rang.

A couple walking by looked at them. Not a mere glance, Evie thought. Their steps actually slowed down, suggesting they might want to see who was about to gain admission into the house.

Had Parsody or her guardian, Mr. Jameson, introduced themselves to the neighbors? Or did they, as
suggested by Henrietta's remark, remain reclusive?

The passersby, Evie decided, might actually be curious
to see who had taken up residence in the grand house and
had slowed down to see if they could catch sight of the
person opening the door.

Evie stepped back and looked up. The house looked
almost too grand for two people. Then again, if the dowagers and Toodles had chosen to stay behind at Halton
House, there would only be two people residing at
Woodridge House; she and Tom.

The door opened to reveal a tall man with a mop of
white hair. Evie assumed Mr. Jameson had hired a butler
for the duration of their stay in London. It would have
been slim pickings, since there had been a steady decline
in the availability of people in service as many had chosen
different paths in life.

"Lady Woodridge and Lotte Mannering to see Mr.
Jameson and Miss Buchanan," Lotte said.

The butler did not look surprised by their presence,
suggesting he had been told of their imminent arrival.

They stepped inside a magnificent hall with marble
floors, columns, fine pieces of furniture, and a dozen
ancestral paintings.

With so many people struggling to hold onto their
properties, it wouldn't surprise Evie if the owners had
foregone a stay in town in order to rent out the dwelling.

The butler showed them through to the drawing
room, his formal demeanor never faltering. The well-
appointed room displayed fine pieces of furniture and
more ancestral portraits. Evie imagined them keeping

vigil over the house that had been taken over by complete strangers.

Entering the drawing room, they saw a young woman sitting on a chair by the fireplace. Seeing them, she shifted to the edge of her seat but did not rise to her feet. As she studied them, she reached for her hair and fiddled with a lock before curling her fingers around the armrest. Then, almost as an afterthought, she gave them a tentative smile.

Lotte introduced them.

Evie noticed a hint of uncertainty in the young woman, which became more apparent as Parsody looked toward the door, perhaps in anticipation of seeing her guardian coming to her rescue.

When she didn't invite them to sit, they took the initiative and settled on a sofa opposite her.

Evie gave her an encouraging smile and was about to say something when Lotte jumped in and said, "We've been looking forward to meeting you."

Parsody looked surprised. Once again, she fiddled with her hair and then, pressing her hand to her throat, she said, "Oh, me too."

Before they could be engulfed by an awkward silence, Evie asked, "Have you been enjoying your stay in town?"

To her surprise, Parsody stilled and her cheeks paled. If she blinked, Evie didn't notice.

Lotte leaned in and whispered, "She's interested in plants."

Of course...

Belatedly, Evie remembered she preferred solitary pursuits. "You should visit the Royal Botanic Gardens. They are magnificent."

Parsody's attention shifted away from Evie and shot toward the door.

Evie and Lotte turned and saw a man standing there.

He cleared his throat and stepped forward as he introduced himself.

Mr. Jameson was in his late fifties, perhaps early sixties, with a hint of gray on his temples giving him an air of distinction. He had a thin face with close set blue eyes and a small mouth with the lips curved up at one edge.

He went to stand beside Parsody's chair. "Parsody, have you offered our guests refreshments?"

"It didn't occur to me. I'm... I'm not used to... I mean..."

Mr. Jameson gave a lighthearted laugh. "Never mind. Gibbons is already on his way with a tray." Tapping a finger on the headrest, he continued, "Parsody and I have been looking forward to this afternoon."

If, as she suspected, they hadn't met their neighbors or received invitations to parties, what on earth had they been doing and for how long? "Have you been in town long?"

Mr. Jameson didn't answer straightaway. Giving it some thought, he finally said, "No, not really and we haven't ventured out. After traveling for so long, we felt in need of some rest."

In town? To Evie, that seemed like a strange choice. Most people found rest in the countryside.

"I was just saying Parsody might be interested in visiting the gardens." Evie looked at the young woman. "I understand you have a keen interest in plants."

"Yes," Mr. Jameson answered in her place. "Although,

now that Parsody is to be presented, we feel it is time to find other interests."

As he'd left the remark open to interpretation, Evie proceeded to assume he meant Parsody would now look to mingle in society, joining the type of social circles that would bring her into contact with people of her own class. In other words, she would be hunting for a suitable husband.

Evie couldn't help cringing. In this day and age, she could easily fall prey to an uncouth character in need of her money to recover property lost due to mismanagement. Or, worse. Parsody might find someone who merely wished to spend her fortune, as gambling and the high life had driven many men into marriages of convenience.

Evie smiled at Parsody and pushed herself to take a good look at the young woman. Ordinarily, Evie only noticed the way people looked when she had a reason to do so. Only recently, she had noticed Lotte Mannering had slimmed down and the only reason she'd noticed that was because Lotte was always appearing in one disguise or another. So, Evie was more or less forced to notice her appearance.

The harder she looked at Parsody, the more difficult she found it to describe her. Assuming she wanted to present herself in the best possible light, Evie tried to look for her best features.

She wore her light brown hair cropped in a fashionable bob highlighted with elegant waves. It suited her, but the way she fussed with it suggested the style was something adopted only recently.

Evie knew such shingling could only be achieved in

the best salons. Then again, Parsody had been living in Paris. Leading a solitary life, she might not have bothered with her appearance. Until now, that is.

She wore a dress in a fashionable geometric print and no jewelry. Bright hazel eyes stared back at Evie, but they didn't tell her anything about Parsody. Evie didn't sense any curiosity or even interest in the way she was looking at her.

"I didn't realize you were going to be presented." Not all debutantes made their curtsy to the monarchs.

Mr. Jameson cleared his throat. "We hope she will be. As it is, we are in desperate need of a sponsor. I'm afraid I have performed quite poorly as a guardian. Parsody has always enjoyed her private pursuits so she has missed out on nurturing relationships."

Meaning she didn't know anyone who could sponsor her.

"I'm afraid I have gone about this guardianship business all wrong and Parsody is now paying the price for it. Here we are, living in the heart of society and yet no one knows she even exists."

Evie knew that wasn't entirely true. In fact, she recalled Henrietta saying everyone had been talking about *the Buchanan girl.*

He lowered his gaze, cleared his throat and then said, "I wonder if you might help us, Lady Woodridge."

Straightaway, Evie knew what he wanted but she didn't wish to fall into the trap of assuming so she remained silent. Although, she had a ready response, just in case. She would, of course, have to decline, as she was already committed to sponsoring Caro and wished to devote all her time to her. It seemed only fair, especially as she and Caro had such a long history.

However, Mr. Jameson felt compelled to explain his situation in greater detail and put forth his proposal in such a way that almost made it impossible for Evie to refuse.

But refuse she must.

~

Upon their return to Woodridge House...

Evie and Lotte walked the short distance to Woodridge House in silence. Even when faced with the absence of a footman to open the door, Evie remained lost in her thoughts.

They let themselves in, their footsteps echoing in the empty hall as they made their way to the drawing room

Lotte settled down on a chair with a huff. "Since you haven't said anything, I assume you are regretting saying yes to Mr. Jameson's request."

Tipping her head back, Evie stared at the ceiling and groaned. "What was I thinking? I'm already sponsoring Caro." Now she would have to divide her time between two debutantes. Had she felt cornered by Mr. Jameson's blunt request? "You were there. How on earth did he do it?"

"Ah, my dear, the powers of persuasion work in mysterious ways."

"In other words, you are just as puzzled as I am."

"Not quite. I wasn't privy to your thoughts. I had no

idea you didn't want to say yes." Lotte shrugged. "If I'd known you wanted to turn him down, I would have jumped to your rescue. Couldn't you ask someone else to do it?"

Evie laughed. "Did I happen to mention Henrietta is not currently talking to me? Yes, I believe I have."

"What about Lady Sara?"

"Yes, of course. That would be a simple solution, but there's nothing simple about my relatives."

Evie closed her eyes and groaned. She'd have to lodge an application on Parsody's behalf. What if it was too late? Would she have to pull strings for a complete stranger?

The sound of someone rushing down the stairs and along the hall was followed by the sound of someone running back across the hall and up the stairs. Most likely the same person.

Moments later, Holmes appeared at the door and, seeing Evie, he rushed toward her.

"Have you been making people run around the house looking for you?" Evie asked as she picked him up and settled him on her lap.

Holmes lowered his little head and gave Evie a woeful look.

"I know you didn't. You're such a good boy."

That seemed to cheer him up. Wagging his tail, he made himself comfortable on her lap and cast her an adoring look to melt her heart.

Giving him a scratch under his chin, Evie said, "I suppose I should try to stir the house into action."

"Let me help you with that." Lotte jumped to her feet and walked to the fireplace to pull the bell cord.

"Thank you. I didn't want to disturb Holmes."

A confusion of footsteps echoed throughout the house followed by a yelp.

"What did you think of Parsody?" Evie asked, her tone impervious to the chaos around her.

"Not much. If Mr. Jameson intends to relieve himself of his charge, he'll need all the luck in the world. She struck me as an insipid waif."

"A waif? That's rather harsh."

Lotte waved her finger. "That's it. She didn't impress me and I didn't think much of it, but now that you ask..." She brushed her finger along her chin. "She looked uncomfortable in her own skin. Not at all the behavior of someone who's reputed to be the grandest heiress in England, if not the whole of Britain."

Evie hummed under her breath. "Yes, there was something rather awkward about her. Then again, it shouldn't surprise us. Being deprived of society can't be easy for her. She definitely lacks polish."

"Does that make sense to you?" Lotte asked.

"What do you mean?"

"She's spent the last few years traveling around Europe and she hasn't met anyone."

"You're right and she's recently been in Paris. I'm sure they stayed in the most glamorous parts of the city and you can't stay there without visiting at least one museum and being seen by the entire world." Evie frowned. "How could she possibly have managed to spend all that time traveling without making new acquaintances?"

Sitting back, Evie remembered her first trip to London with her mother. "You know what? It is actually quite possible to travel around and not meet the right people. My mother went to great lengths to have me invited by anyone and everyone of influence and consequence. If not for her efforts, I might have returned home to marry some local charmer with a penchant for yachts and fast cars."

As she pondered the mystery of Parsody's anonymity, Evie heard the sound of rushed footsteps approaching. They appeared to increase in speed. Someone was running toward the drawing room and that someone came to a skidding halt.

Chaos was about to be restored, Evie thought.

"Milady! We weren't expecting you back so soon."

Lotte laughed. "It turns out, it doesn't take much to cut an afternoon tea short. You only need to coerce the Countess of Woodridge into doing something she doesn't wish to do." Lotte sat up. "I suspect Mr. Jameson has fobbed Parsody on to you and washed his hands of the matter."

"Yes, and I don't know whether to laugh or cry." Evie turned to Millicent. "Just the person I wanted to see. I will be sponsoring one other person and we must write to the Lord Chamberlain and apply on Parsody Jane Buchanan's behalf."

Millicent looked over her shoulder and stepped inside the drawing room.

While the black ostrich feathers were the least of her concerns at that moment, she couldn't help asking Millicent if she'd spoken with the milliner.

"I'm sorry, milady... I... I've been rather occupied and haven't been able to set foot outside the house."

"Henrietta will need to release you from your duties, Millicent." When she saw Millicent bite the edge of her lip with obvious uncertainty, Evie asked, "How is Caro?"

Millicent visibly gulped, while at the same time, a moan wafted down from one of the rooms upstairs, followed by a burst of hysterical laughter.

Snapping out of her insouciance, Evie frowned. "What on earth was that?"

"I'm afraid that's Lady Evans, milady."

"But that doesn't sound anything like her."

"Well... She's not exactly herself," Millicent explained.

"Millicent. What do you mean? What has been happening? We only stepped out for a short while."

Millicent looked up at the ceiling and mouthed several words.

"Millicent?" Evie prompted.

"Sozzled. That's what she is, milady. I'm sorry, but I can't think of any other way to say it. I know there's another word, but it just refuses to come to me."

"Sozzled?" Evie repeated.

Millicent gave a stiff nod.

"How did that happen?"

"It started with a tiny tipple when... I don't like to say, milady."

"But you must, Millicent."

"She's been confused, milady and... the others thought it would help to have a word with her and offer their encouragement."

"The others?"

Evie realized Millicent had found a way to avoid naming names. She knew her granny always carried a small flask but she couldn't imagine Sara or Henrietta being liberal or encouraging with alcohol. In any case, Toodles and Sara were still out.

"You see, they didn't all go in to see her together. First,

one went in and then the other… and Lady Evans didn't wish to seem ungrateful or rude. After all, they meant well. So, when they suggested a drink to calm down, she accepted. All three times. We've been giving her cups of coffee because, you see, Lord Evans is due to arrive at any moment and that has sent her into a panic because then she'll have to explain why she's in such a state."

"Caro is drunk?"

"Yes, milady. Quite sozzled. And… I should own up to having provided her with a bottle of your finest brandy. I actually suggested she dab some on her temple. To be perfectly honest, I'm not sure if she drank from the bottle I gave her first or if she succumbed to temptation when one of the others offered her a drink."

"I take it Toodles and Sara have returned."

Millicent nodded.

Evie closed her eyes. "Millicent, you should go up and take care of Caro and, if you happen to see Lady Henrietta, try to find out if she knows anything about the Buchanan family." She might be in the midst of another chaotic episode in her house but the only way to survive it was to push ahead.

Nodding, Millicent rushed out of the drawing room.

"I hadn't thought of that," Lotte said.

"What?"

"Delving into the Buchanan family."

Evie rubbed her temple. Despite everything happening around her, Evie had managed to engage her curiosity. "People are bound to ask about Parsody and, since she will be part of our group, I'll have to provide some answers."

"Is that the only reason you're curious?"

113

"Truth be known, I'm feeling uneasy about all this. She was obviously quite young when she lost her parents. I can't understand why Mr. Jameson was put in charge. So I suppose we should also try to find out something about him. After all, his position is one of trust. He must have been a very close friend of the family. It might help to know where they lived. The estate must still be in Parsody's possession. If that's the case, then there must be servants still employed at the house or living nearby."

Lotte frowned. "This no longer sounds like mere curiosity. It actually borders on suspicion."

A confusion of hurried footsteps drew Evie's attention.

"Heavens. Now what?"

Lotte leaned back to try to get a better view of the door. "You're going to love this."

A footman entered and announced, "Lord Evans."

Holmes barked, jumped off Evie's lap and rushed past the footman, in the process, nearly colliding with Henry Evans.

"I have no idea what's come over Holmes." Evie smiled and greeted Caro's husband.

"Lady Woodridge." He inclined his head and, noticing Lotte, greeted her.

"Do sit down, Lord Evans," Evie invited. "I'm afraid Tom is not here right this minute, but he's bound to return soon. Meanwhile, we are ravenous for an entertaining story." Something to keep Lord Evans busy, Evie thought.

Lord Evans settled down opposite Evie. "Well, my mother sends her regards."

"How is Lady Louisa? Are her chickens behaving?" For

the briefest moment the house appeared to fall silent again, the mayhem that had been unleashed in her household settling like dust motes. Yes, peace had been restored.

However, she was soon dissuaded of the illusion when a burst of hysterical laughter was followed by a sailor's ditty she had once heard one of her uncles sing...

Lord Evans looked up. "Is that singing?"

"Singing?" Evie echoed.

CHAPTER 10

"*S*inging?" Evie echoed again even as she realized she should have changed the subject. *Straightaway.*

"Yes, singing," Lord Evans said. "I'm sure I heard singing."

Evie saw him blink and somehow knew Henry, Lord Evans, Caro's husband... had just transformed himself from a titled gentleman to Detective Inspector Evans. If there was some sort of shenanigans going on, he would sniff it out.

The detective held Evie's gaze for a moment. His expression revealed nothing now, further confirming the fact he suspected something was going on and his entire focus was fixed on getting to the bottom of it all.

Silence settled around them.

Lotte Mannering's gaze bounced between Evie and Henry Evans, her eyes bright with amusement.

Without taking his eyes off Evie, he asked, "Lotte, did

you, by any chance, happen to hear someone singing just now?"

Lotte's eyes crinkled at the edges. "Singing?"

He nodded. "It was a sound that approximated something resembling singing."

"So, it might not have been singing?" Lotte asked.

"It is debatable," Lord Evans agreed. "Yes, it might be open to debate and there are some people who might describe the sound as a disturbing cacophony. However, I'm inclined to think of it as a musical sound. Shall we call it that?"

Evie cut in by asking, "Have you been in town long?"

The question appeared to catch him by surprise. His eyes widened slightly, his lips parted but he did not speak.

Evie imagined him trying to remember the story he had concocted with Caro since she was to go ahead and come to Woodridge House first to test the waters.

"I... We arrived this morning and... I had some business to attend to," he explained.

Lord Evans was momentarily relieved from having to offer further explanations when Edgar entered the drawing room and set a tray on the table.

"Ah, tea." Evie stood up and, as she poured herself a cup, asked, "Lord Evans, have you heard about the incident in Upper Brook Street?"

Joining her, he said, "I heard something or other about it."

Lotte joined them and helped herself to tea and cake. "Evie and Tom were witnesses."

"Really? How so? Did you actually see it happen?" Lord Evans asked.

"No, we heard a scream and that made us curious,"

Evie clarified. "It seems the police think there was foul play involved," she remarked rather testily because Detective Inspector Rawlinson had alluded to no such thing.

"Interesting." He took a sip of tea and seemed to find comfort in the beverage, either because he was revitalized by it or because it gave him a temporary respite from talking.

Evie lowered her cup. She considered sitting down but Lotte and Lord Evans remained standing. "There's something odd about that death. You see, there's only one person who recognized the victim and she'd only met him recently and briefly." Evie hoped she'd written down the young woman's name because, if her curiosity continued to grow, she would have to begin making enquiries. "Also, apart from the young man's name, the police know next to nothing about him."

"How was he dressed?" Lord Evans asked.

Lotte snorted. "It seems clothes remain a key indicator to a person's standing in society."

"Does that surprise you?" he asked.

"No, not really. After all, I rely on disguises and, if I do say so myself, I excel at convincing people I am someone other than myself merely by changing my clothes."

"Are you suggesting the young man was pretending to be someone else?" He took a pensive sip of his drink and murmured, "Interesting."

"It's certainly an interesting topic," Evie mused. "We've determined that he might have been trying to pass himself off as someone affluent without really knowing what is required. You see, he wore the wrong suit."

He nodded. "Ah, that explains your curiosity."

"However," Evie continued, "he wore very good shoes."

"Perhaps he subscribed to the belief that a good pair of shoes would open doors for him." He helped himself to more tea. "If, as you suggest, there might be foul play, what do you think the motive was?"

"That's a very good question. We have been fixated on the young man's identity. Did I mention he hailed from Boston?"

"I see. He might not have been acquainted with local customs, which would explain him wearing the wrong suit."

"Would it?" Evie looked at the cake on offer. "The police haven't had any luck contacting his relatives. I wonder... is it possible he had no relatives?" And what did that say about him? Evie wondered.

"He might have been a confidence trickster," Lotte suggested. "Or someone out to better his lot in life. He might have fallen on hard times and set out to find himself a wealthy bride."

"All very good points," Evie offered. "What if the explanation is simpler than that?"

Lotte and Lord Evans looked at her with interest.

"He had been traveling around Europe. It's possible he might have been a young man simply exploring."

"And how do you think he ended up in an exclusive London soiree?" Lotte asked.

How and why, Evie thought.

She set her teacup down and walked around the drawing room.

Motive.

"Why would someone intentionally push him to his death?"

"Blackmail," Lotte suggested. "If we entertain the idea

of a young man of limited means traveling around, he might have seen something."

Evie's eyebrows curved up. "You think he might have witnessed something and by revealing this he put his life at risk."

Lord Evans smiled and shook his head. "I've often heard Detective Inspector O'Neill talking about your ability to weave stories and then extract a theory. And, of course, I have my own experience of seeing you in action."

Evie laughed. "Tom and I do that because we usually have little to no information to go on with. How is Detective Inspector O'Neill? We haven't crossed paths in quite some time."

Lord Evans laughed. "Don't take this the wrong way, but I suspect he might be relieved about that."

She didn't blame him…

Evie glanced toward the door.

Where was Tom?

Earlier she had joked about him catching a boat and fleeing. What if he had decided—

Evie shook her head. She could not bring herself to entertain the thought of Tom abandoning her.

She heard voices approaching from the hall and identified them as Toodles and Sara. Had they been here all along or had they just arrived?

The house had fallen silent again so she should have heard the front door opening, but she hadn't. Probably because her mind was whirling with too many thoughts.

Shaking her head, Evie remembered they had already been in the house, busy making Caro drunk.

"Birdie and Lotte," Toodles exclaimed as she and Sara entered the drawing room. "And Lord Evans. *And* we're just in time for tea. Do you know, I've never been a tea drinker and look at me now, craving a cup." As Toodles helped herself to some tea, she said, "We had the most marvelous lunch at the Automobile Club. It's members only but Sara knew someone who gained us entry." She took a sip of her tea. "We saw the most exciting group of people there. So lively. I coerced Sara into sitting at the bar for a bit and we had cocktails." She looked around. "Where is everyone?"

Trying to steer the subject away from everyone else's whereabouts, Evie said, "We've been discussing the incident. You both caught a glimpse of the victim. What did you think of him?"

Sara cringed. "My dear, I try not to think of him. I'm surprised I managed to get any sleep afterward."

"We heard some people talking about it," Toodles said.

"Did we?" Sara shrugged. "Yes... we did. It was that young girl, what was her name? The screamer."

"Lauren Gladstone," Evie offered.

"Yes, that's the one. I'm having second thoughts about her being one of my debutantes. She doesn't look as if she needs help. She was at the Automobile Club surrounded by young admirers. We heard her say the police had been asking more questions about her relationship with the young man."

"James Clementine," Evie guessed.

Sara looked surprised. "How do you know his name."

"The detective in charge of the case called on us this morning," Evie admitted.

"Really? And he spoke with you and not us?"

Evie searched her mind. "I believe you were still out on your walk."

"Yes, we might have been but, from the sounds of it, he didn't even ask to speak with us." Sara turned to Toodles. "Are you offended by that? I am."

"I suppose I should be. At my age, one doesn't wish to feel redundant."

Sara smiled. "I'll keep that in mind... for when I get to your age."

As Sara and Toodles bantered, Evie leaned back and tuned in to the sounds coming from the rest of the house. Thankfully, Lord Evans had been distracted. However, another rendition of the sailor's sea shanty might revive his curiosity.

Sara set her cup down with a clang. "I just remembered something I noticed. I believe Lauren Gladstone recognized us. I saw her looking our way and she paled." Sara turned to Toodles. "Did you notice it too?"

"I can't say that I noticed the same thing. I thought she might have been looking right past us and, yes, she paled. Almost as if she'd just seen something she didn't wish to see."

Sara yelped and looked at Toodles. "Do you remember why we hurried back?"

"That's right. We wanted to tell Henrietta." Toodles nodded. "We overheard Lauren Gladstone mention the Buchanan girl. We thought Henrietta would want to know."

"In what context?" Evie asked.

Sara and Toodles looked at her without blinking. After a moment, Toodles spoke up, "I suspect Henrietta wants to recruit her before Sara snatches her for herself."

"That's not what I meant," Evie explained. "What did you hear Lauren say about Parsody?"

"Who's that, dear?" Sara asked.

"That's the Buchanan girl," Evie clarified. "Her Christian name is Parsody."

"What sort of name is that?" Sara asked. "Then again, what sort of name is Toodles?"

Evie sighed and wondered if Woodridge House needed airing. She hoped the fireplaces weren't releasing toxic fumes. Although, that would cast some light on the odd behavior she'd been witnessing lately.

Evie tried to get them back on track. "Can you remember what Lauren Gladstone said?"

Sara looked at Evie, her gaze expressing surprise. "That's right, I said we overheard her. Someone mentioned the Buchanan girl and Lauren claimed to have seen her at the dressmakers and she claimed there was no real mystery about her. She was quite plain looking."

Evie thought only someone in competition for a husband would say that. "Did Lauren engage Parsody in conversation?"

"My dear, we were eavesdropping on a conversation. We didn't exactly have the right to question her."

Toodles set her tea down and looked around her. "Why are we all standing about?"

"No reason, Grans."

Toodles looked at one of the chairs. "I suppose it would look odd if I'm the only one sitting down."

Sara burst out laughing.

Toodles frowned. "It wasn't that funny."

"Actually, yes, it was. I just remembered the incident with you and another chair. Remember? The one you became stuck in and we had to pull you out?"

Instead of being cross with Sara for mentioning the incident, Toodles appeared to be amused.

Lost in thought, Evie sat down. Lotte and Lord Evans joined her.

Sara whispered, "I've only just realized we might have walked in on something."

Evie closed her eyes for a moment. They had been in town for several days and had attended lunches, afternoon teas, dinners, and parties. During the day, they had visited their favorite milliners and dressmakers…

If she had encountered Parsody in the street, she would not have put a name to the face because she hadn't met her yet.

Evie's lips parted and her eyes widened slightly.

Toodles smiled. "Birdie is entertaining a theory."

"Not quite," Evie said. "How did Lauren Gladstone recognize Parsody? Has she met her before?"

Everyone fell silent as they pondered the question.

"I suppose it's possible Lauren Gladstone might have overheard someone at the dressmakers using Parsody's name. Or, Lauren might have asked someone to identify her."

Lotte cleared her throat. "That is the most likely scenario. However, Lauren might have seen her at a function. While Mr. Jameson suggested they hadn't been out and about, can we really take him at his word?"

Sara's eyes brightened with enthusiasm. "Lauren attended the party so Parsody might have been present."

"Which party?" Evie asked.

"The one we attended."

"The one where the young man fell to his death?"

"Yes."

Evie thought that would be highly unlikely, although not entirely impossible. What if Mr. Jameson had refrained from mentioning anything about attending a party? After all, he had been trying to coerce her into taking pity on them.

She turned to Lord Evans. "The police took down names." And, she thought, she and Lotte had been discussing Parsody's background. This might be a way to obtain some information. "Lord Evans, do you think it might be possible to find out what the police know about her?"

"Know what about whom?" Lord Evans asked, almost as if to suggest he hadn't been following the conversation.

Good heavens.

If Evie mentioned her conversation with Lotte, Lord Evans would know she fully intended poking around and finding out what she could about Parsody.

And, she thought, he would most likely disapprove.

"Never mind. If Parsody Jane Buchanan had attended the party, she would have mentioned it when we had afternoon tea with her today."

Hearing a sharp intake of breath, Evie swung toward the door and saw Henrietta standing there.

It took her a full minute to realize she had just exposed her secret. She wasn't supposed to know anything about *the Buchanan girl.*

"I see," Henrietta said as she lifted her chin. "Someone, who shall remain nameless, has withheld information from us."

Evie clasped her hands and stilled. This was a perfect moment to pretend to be invisible.

"Henrietta?" Sara exclaimed. "What are you talking about?"

"Sara, you seem to forget we were curious about the Buchanan girl and, all along, there has been someone in this house who knew about her, someone who has visited her."

"Someone?" Sara could not have looked more puzzled.

Henrietta swung toward Evie and thrust an accusatory finger straight at Evie. "J'accuse. *J'accuse.*"

"Henrietta, have you lost your mind? Why are you accusing Evie?" Sara swung toward Evie. "I've just realized, Henrietta is right. You just alluded to having met the Buchanan girl. In fact, you said you had tea with her. And you didn't tell me. How could you?"

If ever there was a need for an interruption...

Evie sent up a silent prayer and it was answered, almost too soon, when an out of tune bellowing reached them.

"*What shall we do with a drunken sailor... What shall we do with a drunken sailor...*"

CHAPTER 11

Keep your friends close; keep your enemies closer

*L*ord Evans' foot swung to the rhythm of Caro's drunken singing, only stopping when it was interrupted by the dinner gong.

Standing up, he drew in a breath and said in a calm, resigned tone edged with sarcasm, "The footman took my luggage up. I assume I can find my room by following the sound of my wife's singing."

With everyone offering tentative smiles, he excused himself and made his way out of the drawing room.

Sara and Toodles held a whispered conversation. Appearing to come to some sort of decision, they both stood up and followed Lord Evans out, with Toodles saying, "We have decided to forego tonight's planned theatrical entertainment for the diversions offered here.

We will let Edgar know there will be two more for dinner."

Lotte stood up and set her teacup down. "I suppose I should…"

"Lotte, do join us for dinner," Evie said, her voice heavy with pleading as she hoped to find safety in numbers.

Thanking her, Lotte said, "I'm afraid I have a prior engagement." As she took a step, she signaled to the door.

Evie interpreted that as a cue to join her. She avoided making eye contact with Henrietta and walked Lotte out.

When they were out of earshot, Lotte said, "Mr. Jameson seems to think you will be taking full charge of Parsody's social activities. Am I correct in thinking that?"

"Yes, I think you are." Evie would have to accept responsibility for introducing the Buchanan girl, but she knew nothing about her character or background, and that worried her.

When they'd trekked over from Halton House to town, they had found a pile of invitations waiting for replies and, during the last few weeks, there had been a steady flow of more invitations. She had no issues with including the debutante, however, now more than ever, Evie felt she needed to know more about Parsody Jane Buchanan.

Frowning, Evie added, "Strange. When you first told me about them, I assumed Parsody had already been attending social functions."

Lotte nodded. "That was also my impression."

"Do you suppose they are now waiting to hear from us?" Of course, it was too late to organize anything for that day. She and Tom had planned on attending a party that night, but Tom still hadn't returned…

"I'll call on them tomorrow morning," Lotte suggested.

As she nodded, Evie tried not to think too much about the next day because she still needed to get through this one. "I'll see you tomorrow." Evie hesitated.

"What is it?" Lotte prompted.

"Earlier, Sara suggested something that I found intriguing. I would like to know if Mr. Jameson and Parsody attended last night's party in Upper Brook Street. If they did, then it would make sense for Lauren Gladstone to have recognized Parsody at the dressmakers."

"Don't you think that's something they would have mentioned?"

"That's just it, I'm not sure."

A footman appeared carrying Lotte's coat, hat, and handbag.

As Lotte fixed the hat in place, she said, "I'll try to find out."

After Lotte left, Evie stood in the empty hall for a full minute. It had been a long day and it wasn't over yet.

Turning, she headed for the stairs. Caro was clearly not deterred by her husband's presence, as her singing continued to reverberate throughout the house. Evie also heard people still rushing about.

Changing her mind, she turned and headed back to the drawing room where she thought she might find a moment to herself. However, when she walked in, she found Henrietta. She had taken a seat and had clearly been waiting for her to return.

Henrietta looked up just as Evie stopped at the door.

Neither one looked away.

This was either going to be a moment of truth, Evie thought, or the continuation of their awkward stalemate. Briefly, she considered backing away and exiting the drawing room to give Henrietta the opportunity to save face.

Changing her mind, she wrenched herself out of the indecisive moment and stepped forward.

Just then, Henrietta shot to her feet, proving Sara right. Henrietta could, indeed, shoot to her feet.

Lifting her chin, she looked away. Evie realized she was trying to find a way around her.

A moment of indecision followed. Evie stepped to one side to let her through at the same time as Henrietta stepped to the same side. They both reacted by stepping to the other side.

"Henrietta—"

To Evie's surprise, Henrietta put her hand up and stopped her.

"Evangeline, I feel it's time I should forgive you."

Forgive her?

"After all," Henrietta continued, "you weren't to know the harm you'd be causing to my dear friend, Lady Montague. Of course, I should also apologize for holding it all against you. Before you say it, I'm not being magnanimous."

It would never have occurred to her to say that.

Henrietta's eyes glinted and she smiled. "In fact, I should express my gratitude. Lady Montague is better off in an out of the way place." Henrietta shrugged. "I know what you must be thinking. Yes, she is my friend but the relationship has always been rather complicated. Suffice

130

to say, it's sometimes wise to keep your friends close and your enemies closer."

She'd been forgiven and thanked in the same breath?

Evie searched for a hidden meaning only to give up and, as she did, understanding dawned and Evie suddenly realized Henrietta's propensity to express her opinions far outweighed her need to establish a moral high ground.

It simply didn't suit her to remain silent.

She must have been bursting at the seams with the need to speak her mind.

Of course! Henrietta was always going to cave in first.

Evie smiled. "Friends?"

Henrietta surprised her by saying, "Not quite yet. There is still the other matter to resolve."

Evie inhaled a shaky breath. Something told her this would be a long night, but at least they were headed in the right direction.

Henrietta sat down and patted the space next to her. Smiling, she said, "Make yourself comfortable, Evangeline."

"On one condition, Henrietta." That caught Henrietta by surprise. Now Evie had to come up with a condition.

"And what would that be, *dear*?"

The sarcasm in Henrietta's voice did not go unnoticed.

"Lotte and I are struggling with a case," it occurred to say and, as expected, her revelation had the desired effect.

Henrietta showed immediate interest.

"How can I be of assistance?"

"Parsody Jane Buchanan—"

"I see, we are going to be killing two birds with one stone. The subject of the Buchanan girl is, of course, the remaining source of friction between us. You kept all knowledge of her from me. How could you?"

"That wasn't my intention, Henrietta. What with everything happening all at once, I merely lost track of what I had said to you and what I still had to say to you." Of course, that wasn't the entire truth. If memory served, she had, at first, decided to tell everyone about Parsody. Then, she had changed her mind, only to change it again... and again.

It took a moment for Henrietta to unravel the admission.

"How could you possibly have forgotten to tell me? You seem to forget you were not speaking to me," Henrietta reminded her.

"Actually..." Evie looked heavenward and knew she would never win this argument.

"Very well. Let's put the issue aside, for now. We can always come back to it later." Henrietta shifted in her seat. "How can I help?"

Evie blinked. Henrietta had subjected her to the silent treatment for weeks. Was it really over?

Before Henrietta could change her mind, Evie said, "Lotte and I are somewhat puzzled by Parsody. More specifically, we are curious about her past." Evie told her the little they knew about her.

Henrietta took her time responding. "Interesting. All this time I've been hearing people murmur about the Buchanan girl, I assumed someone knew her family."

"Are you saying you don't know anything about the family?"

"No. I mean, yes, that's what I'm saying. Isn't it odd? I always seem to know something about everyone."

That only justified Evie's need to know more about Parsody.

Henrietta mused, "When you say she's been abroad, I can't help thinking she's been in exile."

That made sense. Every year, she met more and more people and Evie was sure there were many people who knew of her or had met her briefly. The connections existed and everyone's name had a way of surfacing.

The Woodridges from Berkshire. The Palmers from Essex. The McGraws from Lincolnshire and so on and so forth.

Was there anyone who knew something... *anything* about the Buchanan family?

"Is there a reason why you haven't asked them directly?" Henrietta asked.

Evie floundered. "Well, it really only came up after we met them." She tapped her finger on her chin. "This is rather strange but, after meeting Mr. Jameson, I feel he would find a way to avoid answering the question directly."

"You can only know that for sure if you ask," Henrietta suggested.

A simple solution, Evie thought and she hoped Lotte met with success. Yet, why did she feel Mr. Jameson would avoid answering a direct question? It was only an intuitive suspicion and she knew she couldn't really substantiate it with a reasonable explanation. They'd only met him the one time and he might have been overly concerned about righting a wrong. After all, he had already confessed to having performed quite poorly as a guardian.

Henrietta smiled. "I'm sure you will get to the bottom

of it all, my dear, but I will do what I can." Henrietta stood up. "You mentioned her parents perished with the Titanic. I think we might still have some newspapers from that time. That might be a good place to start. There might be some mention of her parents."

"That's a very good idea, Henrietta. I don't know why it didn't occur to me."

Henrietta chortled. "It didn't occur to you because you've only now become suspicious of them."

Was she really suspicious?

When she'd listened to Lotte's scant information, she hadn't been bothered by it. Although, she had reacted to finding out Parsody had no other family or even friends.

Henrietta walked to the door and turned to ask, "Are you coming up?"

"Yes... in a minute."

Nodding, Henrietta held her gaze for a moment. Appearing to come to some sort of decision, she smiled and left.

Evie looked at the clock and grimaced. Tom still hadn't returned. If she had to search for him, she wouldn't know where to start looking.

He had been gone for hours. His behavior was so uncharacteristic, Evie felt she had reason to worry.

What if something had happened to him?

Should she alert the authorities?

Surging to her feet, she walked out of the drawing room and saw Edgar coming down the stairs.

"Just the person I wanted to see. Edgar, where will I find Edmonds at this time of day?"

"Edmonds, my lady?"

Evie nodded.

Glancing at the clock on the mantle, he said, "He is most likely in the kitchen."

"Thank you." When Evie turned toward the hidden door leading down to the kitchen, Edgar hurried after her.

"My lady? Is there something I can help with?"

"Not really, Edgar. I merely wish to speak with Edmonds."

"Perhaps it might be easier if I ask him to come up, my lady."

"Yes, of course." Belatedly, Evie realized she'd been about to intrude on the servants' space. "I'll... I'll be in the drawing room."

A short while later, Edmonds found Evie in the drawing room.

He wore his chauffeur's uniform. His tie sat slightly askew so Evie imagined he had indeed been relaxing.

"I hope I didn't interrupt your leisure time, Edmonds. I actually need a favor."

"Certainly, my lady."

"It's Mr. Winchester. He went out today and he hasn't returned. Would you have any idea where he might go if he needed to... let's say..." How could she put it? "Well, let's say he needed to get away."

"Get away, my lady?"

"It's a long story, Edmonds." Most gentlemen, Evie knew, would head off to one of their clubs but Tom didn't have a club. At least, not that she knew of. "Do you happen to know if he has a fondness for a particular place?" Could he be nurturing his grievances in a pub?

Heavens. They already had one inebriated guest...

When Edmonds didn't answer, Evie decided he might

need some sort of assurance. "Edmonds, you don't really need to tell me. I only wish to know if you happen to know where to look for Mr. Winchester."

Edmonds gave a reluctant nod.

Evie brightened. "Wonderful. Is it very far?"

Edmonds gave it some thought.

Evie noticed him looking up, not at the ceiling, as she usually did, but toward the corner. Evie knew that if she followed his gaze and stepped out of the drawing room, she would be looking straight at the staircase.

"Good heavens." Her exclamation startled Edmonds. "Are you about to say Mr. Winchester is here?"

"I'm not sure if he wishes it to be known, my lady. This is awkward…"

Yes, it was awkward. Evie understood Edmonds' loyalty to Tom but, of course, he worked for her.

Evie thanked him and made her way upstairs, murmuring to herself, "When I became the Countess of Woodridge, I had no idea I would have to acquire mind reading skills and tread such turbulent waters."

She stopped outside Tom's room and pressed her ear against the door.

What if he didn't wish to be disturbed?

What if he had no intention of ever coming out of his room? He was always so calm and composed, not letting anything affect him. Of course, everyone had a breaking point. Had Henrietta's remark been too much for Tom?

As the questions piled up in her mind, Evie sensed someone standing behind her.

Good heavens, caught in the act, again.

Straightening, Evie turned and saw Edgar.

She gave him a tight smile. "I've just been informed

Mr. Winchester has returned and…" And, Evie thought, she really didn't need to explain herself. Lowering her gaze slightly, she noticed Edgar carried a pair of trousers folded over his arm. "I think I might be standing in your way." She hurried along the hallway and dashed inside her room.

Millicent swung toward her. "Milady! I was about to go looking for you."

"Millicent. How is Caro?"

"Still in fine spirits, milady. If anything, the drink did her a world of good, putting her in a better mood."

As if to confirm it, a burst of laughter echoed around the house.

"Wonderful. Now we know what to do if Caro gets cold feet again."

Millicent's eyes widened. "Milady. Surely you don't mean to make Lady Evans drunk on purpose."

"Did I say that? I'm sure I didn't." Evie laughed, her thoughts straying to Tom. When had he returned and why hadn't he sought her out? She couldn't wait to find out.

The process of dressing for dinner, always seen as a leisure activity not to be hurried, wore Evie out.

"I wonder if there is…" Evie shook her head.

"What, milady?"

Evie fished around for an excuse to send Millicent out of the room but, apart from starting a sentence, she couldn't come up with something credible. "Never mind."

As Millicent adjusted the straps on her dress, Evie studied her reflection. "It's almost a shame to wear this dress."

"Why?"

"Because I don't get to look at it." The elaborate

geometric design in various shades of gray with black edges, was accentuated with clusters of glass beads and spangles. As usual, the back was designed to draw the most attention.

"Which earrings, milady?" Millicent held two different pairs.

"Drop, I think. Unless you prefer the clustered ones."

Millicent nodded and handed her the jet clusters.

"I do hope I don't clash with anyone. I don't suppose you know what the others are wearing?"

"I'm sorry, milady, I didn't have time to poke around."

"Well, it's just as well. It's not as if I'd actually change my mind about wearing this dress."

"But you'd like me to have a look... just in case."

Evie sat down to fix her earrings. "Would you? You're such an angel, Millicent. Thank you."

When Millicent rushed out of the room, Evie counted to three and then tiptoed to the door. Opening it a fraction, she looked down the hallway and saw Millicent turning a corner.

Hurrying out, she walked toward Tom's room and knocked on the door.

When there was no answer, she knocked again.

Surely, he hadn't already gone down.

All too soon, Millicent returned. Evie ran back to her room, sat down and tried to catch her breath.

The door opened and Millicent walked in. "Lady Henrietta is wearing blue. Lady Sara is wearing brown and gold. Toodles is still undecided. She is considering a dark green gown but is also tempted by a burgundy one. And Lady Evans is struggling into her light blue dress."

"Struggling?"

Millicent lifted a finger as if to draw attention to the silence. Two seconds later, Caro burst into song again. "It's the singing, milady. Whenever she bursts into song, Lady Evans thrusts her arms out, making it rather difficult for the maid to fix the dress into place."

"Well, then I suppose this gown will be perfectly fine."

They spent half an hour chatting and going through the finer details for Caro's presentation ball.

Finally, Evie stood up. "Millicent, I hope you'll take the rest of the evening off. You've spent the day running around. I don't want you wearing yourself out."

She made her way down to the drawing room. As she approached, she took comfort at the sound of murmured conversations.

She walked in, her steps confident, her smile in place.

She saw Toodles, Sara and Henrietta, all chatting amiably.

Another step provided a full view of the drawing room and Lord Evans and Caro. While Henry smiled and responded to something Sara said, Caro sat next to him sipping from a cup. A cup of coffee, Evie assumed.

"Ah, here's Evangeline."

Yes, but where was Tom?

hen she entered the drawing room, Evie thought she must have looked distraught at not finding Tom there. Fortunately for her, Henrietta interpreted her look of concern and said, "Tom is in the library. I had Edgar hunt down those newspapers I told you about and Tom went there directly."

"I hope this doesn't mean dinner will be delayed," Toodles said. "Or that you will both shut yourselves away in the library and leave us all out of whatever it is you're looking for."

Evie swung on her feet, saying, "The library. Yes, I should have thought of that."

She hurried across the hall. Reaching the door, she stopped and gave a determined nod.

Evie opened the door and walked in. "Tom." Her eyes darted around the library, searching for him and she found him standing over a table with a pile of newspapers in front of him.

"Countess, come and look at this."

Curious, Evie walked toward him. At the very least, she had expected some sort of vague explanation for his absence. She didn't expect an apology, even if she had felt abandoned.

"What is it?"

"Henrietta said you were searching for information about the Buchanan family. Although, she didn't explain why you were interested. I think I've found something." He tapped his finger on a page. "It's dated a couple of weeks after the ship went down. It's a photograph of the couple. The article mentions a plan to erect a plaque in the village near the family home in Lancashire."

"Does it mention the name of the village?"

"No."

At least they had a general location. "I do hope Lotte manages to get some straight answers from Mr. Jameson. Did Henrietta tell you about my concerns?"

Tom nodded. "She started to say something but then Henry drew her attention to another subject."

"How strange."

Tom smiled. "I believe Lord Evans wanted to steer the conversation away from something that sounded like police business."

"But our interest in the Buchanan girl has nothing to do with police business."

Tom shrugged. "Perhaps he merely wished to avoid any notice of the elephant in the museum."

"The what?"

"It's from a story I recently read. *The Inquisitive Man.* It's a story about a man who goes to a museum and notices all sorts of tiny things, but fails to notice an elephant." Tom laughed. "Caro being the elephant."

"I see. You noticed..."

"I heard her singing when I returned. I assume it had something to do with drinking?"

Evie told him about Caro's guilt and how the others had tried to soothe her concerns with a medicinal glass of brandy, or two or... three.

Suddenly, she realized that was her opportunity to ask him about his exodus. "It happened soon after you left. And that reminds me, you were gone for quite some time. I was beginning to worry you might never come back."

"Not come back? Where would I go?"

"Somewhere else where you wouldn't have accusations thrown in your face."

Tom smiled. "Countess, it would take a lot more than a jab from Henrietta to drive me away."

"A lot more? And what might that be?" What was his breaking point?

"I have no idea."

Evie tried her best to keep her frustration at bay when she asked, "What kept you away so long?"

Tom grinned. Digging inside his pocket, he retrieved a piece of paper.

"What's that?"

"A special license."

"A what?"

Annoyingly, he answered with a question.

"Do you have any idea how difficult it is to find an Archbishop?"

"No, I've never had reason to look for one. Why would you need one?"

"To marry in haste."

"What?"

"It was my kneejerk reaction to Henrietta's remark."

"Tom, you can't possibly be serious."

"Are you turning me down?"

"No, I'm… I'm turning down a rushed wedding."

"After all the trouble I went to… Wait, do I need to get down on one knee again?"

Evie's chin lifted a notch. "Again? I don't remember you ever getting down on one knee."

"Yes, I did and I gave you a ring. Do I have to procure another ring?"

"I thought that was a display for the benefit of the others."

"I see." Tom drew in a long breath and pushed it out. "I am going to have to do it all over again."

"I can't believe you spent all day hunting down a special license."

"Actually, I didn't. Something else sidetracked me. Once I'd sorted out the business with the Archbishop, I hailed a taxicab and headed back to Woodridge House. We were just coming up to Berkeley Square when I saw Stuart White. As he was on foot, I climbed out of the taxicab. By the time I paid the fare, Stuart White had put some distance between us so I just followed him."

Evie didn't want to admit she'd almost forgotten about Stuart White. As Tom spoke, she recalled the young man standing on the street struggling to light his cigarette on the evening they had responded to the scream.

Tom continued, "I followed him along Piccadilly. Instead of trying to catch up to him, I decided to keep my distance and see where he was headed. I almost lost him when he turned into St. James's Street. He stopped to look at a store window so I had to stop. Unfortunately, the store proprietor recognized me. He came out and engaged me in conversation. When I saw Stuart White walking away, I had to cut the conversation short so I could follow him but, by then, he'd put even more distance between us."

"Tom, please tell me you finally caught up with him."

Tom nodded. "Just as I turned a corner into Pall Mall, I saw him go inside the Automobile Club."

"And?"

"I had to make up the distance. By the time I went in, he was nowhere to be seen. Then, would you believe it, someone cornered me."

"Who?"

"Brigadier Peterson-Monkwell. Remember him? He wanted to know more about my campaign to protest against knee breeches. Apparently, he'd been giving it some serious thought." Tom grinned. "I believe I have an ally. Anyhow, he's a difficult fellow to shake off. When I succeeded in extricating myself from his company, I made the rounds of the restaurants, lounges and bars and didn't find Stuart White."

"It's possible he might be staying there."

Tom shook his head. "I asked. Anyhow, I think I might have missed him coming out again. I spent an hour wandering about the area but didn't spot him again. He covered quite a distance on foot so I assume he is staying somewhere in the vicinity."

"I'm sure he'll eventually surface again." Evie's eyes dropped to his coat pocket and she found herself thinking about the special license he had procured. He really had taken Henrietta's remark to heart. She was actually surprised he hadn't dragged the Archbishop back with him to perform the marriage ceremony right here and now. "The police are bound to catch up with him. That is, if they are still intent on investigating the matter."

Nodding, he asked, "And how was the rest of your day?"

Evie stopped blinking. "I doubt I can piece any of it together. It's all become rather a blur."

Tom surprised her by slipping the edge of the special license out of his coat pocket. "We could always make use of this and escape."

"Hold on to it. Who knows, it might come in handy."

He tucked it back in. "I suppose we should return to the drawing room."

"Yes, I'm sure they're about to send Edgar to fetch us. Toodles warned me she's hungry. I almost forgot. Henrietta and I have made our peace, more or less. Would you believe it? She made the first move."

Tom laughed. "She could only stay silent for so long."

They entered the drawing room just as the others were rising to their feet.

"I guess I was wrong. They weren't going to send for us."

"And yet they are stepping aside so you can lead them in. It seems traditions and good manners never go out of fashion."

Evie waited for everyone to take their seats before saying, "Tom came back with the most wonderful news. Show them, Tom."

Tom produced the piece of paper and waved it.

"He procured a special license. Would you believe it?"

"What? You wouldn't dare." Henrietta spoke up first,

and her sentiments were echoed by everyone else, including Caro who was struggling to sit up straight.

"Birdie. Tell me you don't mean to run off and get married without us."

"You wouldn't dare deprive us," Sara stated. "Everyone expects the nuptials to take place at the local village church. To do anything different would cause such disappointment, no one would speak to you ever again."

"I'm glad to know how everyone feels," Evie said.

Despite Caro's nudge, Lord Evans was the only one who didn't express an opinion.

Evie looked at Tom who sat across the table. "Tom, it seems everyone wishes to be present for our nuptials. However, do hold on to that special license. You never know, we might need it."

Evie couldn't be sure, but she thought she heard Henrietta murmur, "Devious."

After all that hubbub, dinner was a subdued affair. It hadn't been Evie's intention to silence everyone. She had never seen her relatives bereft of speech or, at least, as close to is as they had ever come. Evie guessed they were all mulling over her revelation and were being cautious, at least until they decided where Evie drew the line and what would actually prompt her to make use of the special license, thereby depriving them of a wedding.

Of course, she would never do that to them, but she saw no harm in keeping them guessing.

Not only was dinner a quiet affair, it was also brief. Everyone retired to the drawing room with Lord Evans and Caro the first to bid everyone a good night. The others followed soon after, saying their day had been eventful and they needed some rest. Tom and Evie were left gaping at each other.

Patting his coat pocket, he said, "We seem to have emptied the room."

"It's still rather early." Given the opportunity, Evie always enjoyed retiring to the library to spend a few hours reading. The fact she and Tom could do that together had forged their relationship. Of course, they had invitations to several parties taking place that night. Indeed, they had already decided to attend one of them, but then Tom had disappeared. Now it seemed too late in the evening to make such an effort.

She was about to suggest they take a walk when Tom stood up.

"Let's see if we can hail a taxicab."

"And go where?"

"The Criterion?" he suggested. "I don't really feel like exploring new places."

"Very well. Yes, I do need a distraction." Standing up, she headed for the door. "I need to get my coat."

In her room, she looked for a coat to match her dress and settled for a velvet cape with fur trim. A further search yielded a silk purse with a chain handle. Sturdy enough to hold her small pistol. Just in case, she thought.

Tom was waiting for her by the front door. "I hailed a taxicab." Looking up at the staircase, he added, "Quiet has been restored."

For now, Evie thought as they stepped out of the house. "I wouldn't be surprised if they are all waiting for us to leave so that they can venture out and follow us."

Instead of driving along the main roads, the driver

147

turned into side streets and, almost as if the powers that be wished to poke fun at Tom, he drove along Mill Street.

"This looks familiar," Evie murmured. "It's Saville Road. This is where your tailor is."

Tom did not take the bait. "That was a stroke of genius, Countess."

"What was?"

"Revealing the existence of a special license. Correct me if I'm wrong, but you actually delivered a veiled threat meant to hang over their head and keep them in line. At least, until one of them forgets and steps out of order."

Evie gave him an impish smile. "Who knew I had it in me? But you're right, they will forget. And, of course, once we're married, I'll have to come up with something more creative."

"To keep them in line?"

Evie smiled. "To maintain some sort of order in the house."

"Pity," he mused. "They can be quite entertaining."

"Are you suggesting you actually enjoyed Henrietta pointing the finger of accusation at you?"

"Not really. Although, I must admit it was rather amusing. Back to your threat, which I found surprising. You must have found Henrietta's silent treatment frustrating but what did the others do?"

Evie snorted. "I'm sure I told you what they did to Caro."

"Surely you don't believe they did it on purpose."

"Are you defending them?" Evie shook her head. "I suspect they knew precisely what they were doing. I wouldn't be surprised if they came up with the plan to tackle Caro one at a time so Caro wouldn't suspect them of trying to get her drunk."

"And why would they do that?"

Evie rolled her eyes. "They were probably at the end of their tether. From the very start, Caro insisted she wasn't good enough to be a lady and they couldn't understand her reasoning."

Tom laughed. "Because no one in their right mind would refuse to be a titled lady?"

"Caro will be back to normal just as soon as we get this presentation out of the way."

Tom patted his coat pocket. "I should have put the special license in a safe place. We might need it again."

"Not to worry, Lord Evans is here now. I'm sure everyone will be on their best behavior."

The driver stopped behind a long line of taxicabs, all waiting for people to hop out.

"Shall we get off here?" Evie asked.

As Tom handed the money for the fare, the driver murmured, "Most people want to make an entrance."

Evie smiled. "We prefer to be discreet." Walking the short distance to the entrance, Evie took in the sights and sounds of town. Conversations flowed around them, mingling with laughter.

They'd had invitations for several parties that night but Evie wanted to avoid spending an entire evening coming up with polite and witty conversation. This would be a good place to find some enjoyment and forget about the last couple of days. Best of all, they wouldn't have to talk to anyone.

They walked in, checked their coats at the cloakroom,

and went down the stairs, following the sounds of a lively tune.

Rather than secure a table, they went straight to the dancefloor were Tom swept Evie into blissful oblivion.

"That little purse of yours is rather heavy," Tom murmured.

Evie smiled. "Yes, it's quite handy and dangles perfectly on my wrist."

While she danced, she didn't have a care in the world and it seemed neither did Tom.

And then it happened...

Right in the middle of a Foxtrot, Evie winced.

Not missing a beat, Tom asked, "What?"

Evie tried to dismiss the stray thought. She shook her head. "Nothing."

"Nothing? I'm sure it's something."

Growling, Evie gave a stiff nod.

Tom slowed down. Looking around, he spotted an empty table. "Let's sit down." He pulled out a chair for Evie and then sat next to her.

A waiter approached and they placed an order for drinks.

"Well?" Tom prompted.

"I'm sure it's nothing." She told him about Sara and Toodles going to the Automobile Club.

"I didn't see them," Tom said.

"I only now thought about it. When you went there, you were focused on looking for a young man, Stuart White. Anyhow, they sat at the bar. Lauren Gladstone was sitting nearby."

"The screamer?"

Evie nodded. "They eavesdropped on her conversation. Anyhow, at one point, Lauren looked up. Sara thought she'd recognized them from the party but Toodles was convinced Lauren looked straight past them."

"And?"

"And what if Sara and Toodles weren't entirely wrong? Except, instead of recognizing them, Lauren Gladstone recognized Stuart White?"

Tom sat back. "What do you think it means?"

"I'm not entirely sure and I'll have to wait until tomorrow to ask them for details, but it's possible they might have said Lauren paled."

"She saw someone she wasn't expecting to see," Tom suggested.

"Yes, and what if that person was Stuart White? You said you lost him. He might have wandered in when you were looking for him elsewhere." Evie closed her eyes and laughed. "I do believe that is my craziest theory to date."

"I'm surprised at you, Countess. You're usually the first to mention Detective Inspector O'Neill is not overly fond of coincidences."

Evie shrugged. "He's not. This might or might not be a coincidence. What if I'm right?"

"If you're right, then you've made a connection. A significant one at that. Lauren and Stuart were both at the party."

Evie waited for him to finish the thought. When he didn't, she filled in the gaps as best she could.

What if Lauren had done more than find the body?

The more she thought about it the more convinced she felt people were withholding information.

Tom took a sip of his drink. Setting his glass down, he

looked at Evie and smiled. A second later, his gaze shifted slightly and he frowned.

"What?"

"Don't turn. Remain calm. Rawlinson has just sat at the next table."

Detective Inspector Rawlinson?

"Is he alone?"

"No, he's with a woman."

"I suppose he's entitled to a night of dancing." Leaning in, she asked, "Has he seen us?"

"If he has, he is doing a very good job of not showing it."

She hadn't noticed him on the dancefloor. Then again, she hadn't really been looking as her focus had been on pure enjoyment of the moment.

"Are we going to pretend we haven't seen him?"

"Too late, he's seen us and he just gave me a small nod of acknowledgment."

"Can I look now? It would look odd if I don't. After all, he just acknowledged you. It would be entirely normal for you to then tell me you'd seen him." Evie glanced over her shoulder and smiled at the detective.

Out of curiosity, she looked at the young woman with him. Her feet were tapping away under the table and she looked at the couples dancing with the eagerness of someone who could think of nothing better than to join them on the dancefloor.

The young woman elbowed the detective and appeared to be urging him to get up and dance. In response, the detective looked toward their table.

"Did you just see that?" Evie asked.

Tom nodded. "He's getting up."

Evie glanced back and saw the detective taking the young woman by the hand and guiding her toward their table.

"Are they coming to join us?" Evie asked.

Nodding, Tom said, "I believe the detective has just invited himself over and I'm sure we have just been recruited to help him out of a bind."

"What sort of bind?"

"I don't quite know. It's just a guess."

"Lady Woodridge and Mr. Winchester."

"Do join us, detective," Evie invited.

With a nod, the detective and his companion settled at their table.

"My dear brother has no manners. How do you do? I'm Althea Rawlinson."

The detective's sister?

She didn't see a wedding ring. That made the young woman an available candidate. A quick glance around the room was enough for Evie to identify several interested parties casting glances her way...

The young woman's green eyes sparkled. "You look surprised to see my brother out and about with his sister. You shouldn't be." She lowered her voice. "We're on a case."

"Althea," the detective warned.

"What? I thought you told me they knew all about it?"

Had the detective come here to follow a lead?

"There he is," both Tom and the detective exclaimed.

They were both looking toward the bar. Evie followed their gazes and immediately recognized Stuart White.

CHAPTER 13

*D*etective Inspector Rawlinson shot to his feet and headed straight for the bar. Tom followed, while Evie and Althea remained behind watching with keen interest.

"This is delicious. Theodore now owes me a new gown."

Evie's eyebrows hitched up.

"He's had constables scurrying about all over the place looking for that man and I told him he only needed to go to the liveliest place in town and wait for him to turn up, and here he is."

"Marvelous, but how did he recognize him? Tom and I encountered him ever so briefly. While Tom spoke with him, I only saw him from a distance and it was nighttime."

Althea smiled. "That was another one of my bright ideas. I think he'll need to spring for shoes too. I told Theodore to ask the barman if he knew Stuart White and, as he did, I suggested he engage the barman's services and have him point him out. For an agreed fee, of course."

Althea giggled. "That made Theodore grumble. He'll do a lot more grumbling when he sees the cost of the dress I have in mind."

Evie saw the detective tap Stuart White on the shoulder. The young man turned and nearly dropped his drink.

That brought to mind the first time they'd seen him when he'd struggled to light his cigarette. She decided that he either had a nervous disposition or he was startled by the detective's presence because he was the last man he'd expected to see.

Since the detective had yet to say whether or not he was investigating a crime, Evie assumed he was merely crossing another name off his list and being thorough by speaking with everyone who had attended the Upper Brook Street party.

He struck her as being the rather cautious type, in itself an admirable trait as she was sure he wouldn't let anything escape his notice.

Without tearing her attention away from the scene, she reached for her glass and took a sip. Somehow, she managed to retain her hold on the glass even as she registered surprise when Stuart White erupted to his feet and tried to make a run for it.

"Dear me. That was rather foolish," she murmured and took another sip.

Stuart White's attempt to flee was thwarted by Tom, who'd been standing out of his line of vision.

"This is definitely very interesting," Althea Rawlinson declared. "An innocent man does not try to make a run for it."

"Are you interested in police investigations?" Evie

asked as she watched Tom and the detective have a brief word with Stuart White.

"Not particularly. I simply enjoy reading people. There's so much to be discerned from merely observing how people behave."

"Stuart White might not be guilty of anything really serious. We think he has a nervous disposition." Evie explained about the young man's experience during the war.

Althea Rawlinson listened to her. When Evie finished, Althea lifted an eyebrow.

"You don't agree?" Evie sat back and answered her own question. "Now that I think about it, from what I have observed, it takes quite a lot to trigger those horrible memories. Those who harbor dreadful experiences seem to try their best to keep them under control."

Althea nodded. "We have a few men in our village who were scarred by their experiences. It's almost as if something inside them was ruptured or they left something behind in the battle fields and have never been the same. Generally, they keep to themselves." Althea Rawlinson studied her for a moment. "Did you say you first saw him at the scene of the crime, which happened to be a party in Upper Brook Street?"

Evie nodded. "And my companion, Tom Winchester, saw him earlier today at the Automobile Club. And here he is tonight, at the Criterion." She'd be inclined to say not everyone displayed their inner wounds in the same fashion. This young man was certainly not keeping to himself. However, she couldn't ignore Stuart White's reaction outside the Upper Brook Street house. It had suggested he was vulnerable to shocking scenes.

"They're leaving." Evie wasted no time in standing up. "Coming?"

Althea was already on her feet.

Evie didn't think the detective and Tom would escort Stuart White to the police station. Otherwise, Tom would have said something.

"I suspect they might be headed for someone's office."

They both hurried their steps, weaving their way around the tables and avoiding people coming in.

"Which way did they go?" When they reached the lobby, Evie whirled around and tried to find Tom among the throng of people making their way down the stairs. Had they gone up?

Althea tugged her sleeve. "I think I saw them disappear along that corridor."

"Perhaps we should wait here. They're bound to appear again," Evie reasoned. "We don't want to get lost in the bowels of this place."

Althea stomped her foot and huffed out a breath. Realizing Evie had seen the display, she smiled. "How can you remain so calm?"

"They're bound to have found somewhere quiet, somewhere behind a closed door," Evie reasoned.

"And you don't feel excluded?"

Evie smiled. "Sometimes, I feel it's best to choose my battles."

"Theo tries to hide behind his closed doors, but I always find a way in."

"Do you live with him?"

"No, but I do live nearby and I feel dutybound to make sure his rooms are maintained in good order." Shrugging, she added, "That's my excuse."

"I thought you lived in the country." Evie couldn't think why had that impression. Perhaps the detective had mentioned something about it.

Althea gave her a small smile. "Yes, in fact, not far from Halton House, but I spend most of my time in town."

"We've only just met. How did you know that's where we live?"

Althea's eyebrow hitched up.

"I see." The detective had researched her and he'd been discussing her.

Evie had no trouble imagining the scene where the detective grumbled about the nosy Countess of Woodridge being in town instead of happily ensconced in her country house.

Althea's attention swung toward the stairs so suddenly, Evie clutched her purse, just in case.

Looking up, Evie saw two constables making their way down the stairs.

"Their appearance can't possibly be a coincidence," Evie murmured. Glancing around her, she saw Tom appear.

He headed straight for her. "Countess, it might be time to go home." He cupped her elbow.

Surprised by the sudden turn of events, she exclaimed, "What? Why? What has happened?"

He leaned in and whispered, "I'll tell you on the way back."

"But what about Althea? We can't just abandon her. And…" She looked toward the constables. "Are they here for a reason?"

Tom nodded. "They'll be escorting Stuart White home."

"Escorting? Is that another way of saying he is under arrest?" Their talk with Stuart White hadn't taken that long. How much could he have told the detective?

Tom shook his head. "Very well, we'll wait for Theodore."

"Theodore? Since when are you on first name terms with the detective?"

"Since he called me Tom. It's only fair."

"So what should I call him?"

Tom grinned. "You might need to continue being formal."

Evie decided she wouldn't feel offended. "Yes, it might be wiser."

Laughing, Tom whispered, "Because you'll have greater influence as the Countess of Woodridge?"

"Indeed, and you can nurture your relationship as his friend."

The detective emerged from the corridor with Stuart White walking beside him. After a brief word with the constables, the detective left Stuart White in their charge, and then walked toward them.

"Theo," Althea smiled. "I do believe you owe me an apology, as well as a trip to the dressmakers."

Tom offered to share a taxicab and Evie took the opportunity to invite them in for a nightcap.

While keen to discuss the developments, Evie felt relief when the detective thanked them but declined the offer, saying he'd had a long night and he needed to escort his sister back home. *To her own home.*

Evie was about to insist but decided against it. She'd really had all the excitement she could handle for one day and one night and needed to refresh herself with a good night's sleep. Besides, Tom would surely share everything that had been discussed.

However, during the drive back home, he remained silent. When they reached Woodridge House, he explained, "I didn't want to discuss the matter in front of the driver."

Before entering Woodridge House, they both stopped to look up and down the street.

"Not a creature is stirring," Tom murmured and guided her up the steps.

Inside, the lights had been left on in the hall. Tom took her coat and they made their way to the library.

"One drink and then I'm turning in for the night," Evie declared.

Tom poured the drinks and settled beside her, opposite the fireplace.

Drawing in a deep breath, he said, "Stuart White is afraid."

"Afraid?" Evie shook her head. "I really do need to stop doing that."

"He said there was someone following him."

"Is that how he explained his reaction?"

Tom nodded. "He looked terrified and babbled on about having to constantly look over his shoulder."

"Does he know who is following him?"

"No, he didn't say."

"Either he's imagining it or it's all part of his nervous disposition."

Tom gave it some thought. "Something about your tone suggests you're entertaining a few doubts about his disposition."

"I might be. It just doesn't make sense. If he is suffering

from his experiences during the war, I find it strange for him to be constantly out and about." She told him about Althea's observations. "You must admit, most people we've encountered who suffer from some sort of mental disturbance brought about by their experiences in the war do tend to keep to themselves."

"And some, I'm sure, feel they need to push on and overcome everything holding them back," Tom murmured.

Frowning, Evie asked, "What did he have to say about his presence at the Upper Brook Street party?"

"He insists he didn't know James Clementine."

"What about Lauren Gladstone? Does he know her? Remember, you followed him to the Automobile Club and that's where Sara and Toodles were and..." Evie tried to recall the sequence of events. "They saw Lauren Gladstone pale and we think she might have been surprised by someone's presence."

Tom nodded. "He said he went in there to look for a friend but then realized the meeting was for the next day."

"A likely excuse."

Evie's remark surprised Tom. "You doubt him?"

"Yes. I've decided I'm not going to believe anything he says because it simply doesn't make sense. It all sounds like a convenient excuse."

Tom stood up and walked to the desk. Leaning over it, he wrote something down.

Returning to his seat, he said, "He has rooms in Charles Street. I thought I should write it down before I forget."

Taking the piece of paper, Evie placed the address.

"That's nearby. How did you find out?" Evie nodded. "Of course, the detective asked him."

Tom laughed. "Is that a new trait? You answer your own questions?"

Evie agreed, "Sometimes, I speak too soon."

Tom picked up his drink and studied it. "Since you're going to doubt him, I assume that means you think he did know James Clementine."

"Yes. Now we have to try to imagine where he knew him from." Evie set her glass down and walked over to the desk where she found a notebook and a pen. Sitting down, she said, "Let's make a list and let's start with travel. We know James Clementine carried his passport. Did the detective say where he had been traveling? No, I don't think he did, and if he did, I simply can't recall. What if Stuart White had also been traveling recently? Could they have met?"

"Yes, that's possible, but how do we find out?"

Grinning, Evie said, "You could ask your new friend, Theodore. I'm sure there are a lot of questions he didn't think to ask Stuart White."

Tom gestured toward the piece of paper Evie held. "Or, we could visit Stuart White."

"Heavens, what an intrepid idea. Do you think the constables will remain at the house guarding him? What if they deny us entry? I know. We could take him a basket with some lovely scones or some teacake."

"You're doing it again. Providing your own answer to your own questions."

Evie hummed. "Tomorrow promises to be yet another busy day. Lotte is visiting Parsody and Mr. Jameson and you have your appointment in the afternoon."

"Appointment?"

Evie laughed. "Mr. Strutford, the tailor, is expecting you tomorrow afternoon for a final fitting." Evie closed her eyes and thought about the day after that…

She would have to be creative and quite deliberately underhanded…

"Do you think Caro will be back to her old self again tomorrow?" Tom asked.

"I do hope so. In fact, I'm sure she will be. Lord Evans is here now and she's bound to want to do her best. Remember, she doesn't want to put a foot wrong and embarrass him." Evie looked down at her notes. "We haven't talked about Lauren Gladstone."

"That's because we've been focused on finding Stuart White guilty of lying to us."

He hadn't been entirely honest with them. Evie would bet her house on it. Although… the house wasn't actually hers to gamble with.

She looked around the library and searched for something that might belong to her.

"That's strange."

Tom looked at her and shook his head. "No, I've tried but I'm afraid I can't end the sentence. Perhaps we're not well matched, after all."

"Don't be silly. I wouldn't want you to finish my sentences. I much prefer to remain an enigma. Anyhow, I just realized there is nothing in this room that belongs to me. Except you, of course, and vice versa."

"Would you like me to purchase a house to call our own? We'll eventually need somewhere else to live."

"Heavens. Another abode? No, that won't be necessary. When Seth grows up and marries, it will be our job to…"

"Make a nuisance of ourselves?" Tom suggested.

"I was going to say it will be our job to make his life interesting. Do you think we'll still be dabbling in investigations?"

"I should think so, yes. Unless, of course, you find something else to occupy our time. You might wish to become an explorer."

"That sounds rather dangerous. People risk perishing in faraway lands." Stopping for a moment, she smiled. "How odd. When I was younger, I was taken all over the country to explore the wilderness and wild west. Then, when my mother brought me to England, she feared I wouldn't like it because it was all too sedate. Look at me now, turning down the opportunity to become an explorer."

"There's a time for adventure and a time for home and hearth," Tom murmured.

Evie yawned and stretched. "I might need to start taking notes along the way because I don't remember half of today. I'd like to say tomorrow promises to be better but I'd only be lying to myself."

Tom shrugged. "Considering what I have to go through tomorrow, I'm afraid I have little sympathy for you, my dear."

"Now that you are on first name terms with the detective, do you think he was satisfied with Stuart White's responses?"

Shaking his head, Tom gave it some thought. "Being on a more familiar footing with the detective hasn't given me a better understanding of how his mind works."

"Perhaps he's employing some sort of underhanded tactic. Organizing the police escort might make Stuart

White think the detective cares about his wellbeing." Evie winked at him. "By this time tomorrow they might be on first name terms and then he'll ask the tough questions."

"I noticed you're on first name terms with his sister."

"Yes, and she rather impressed me. She's a keen observer. I'll have to introduce her to Lotte." Evie's eyes widened. "I've just had a fabulous idea. We could send Millicent to see Stuart White. She could take a basket of food and use her skills to find out what she can about him."

"And what will that free us up to do?"

Evie shrugged. "I'll think of something. Or, perhaps, we should make ourselves available for the unexpected."

"You mean, the inevitable. Something is bound to happen."

CHAPTER 14

The next morning

A spy?

Evie wasn't sure but she thought that's what Millicent had mouthed. Had she shocked her with the request? The night before, she had discussed the idea with Tom and he'd agreed Millicent would have a better chance of gaining entry to Stuart White's abode.

"Well? What do you think? I don't wish to force you. Tom and I think you would do a wonderful job collecting information."

Millicent sat down only to spring back up.

"Do sit down, Millicent."

Nodding, Millicent lowered herself onto a chair. "You want me to take a basket…"

"Yes."

"And what if the constables stop me at the door?"

"You could offer them some cake," Evie suggested. "Or you might just say the Countess of Woodridge is very concerned about Stuart White and wishes to offer him some comfort food. Of course, you might have your own idea of how best to tackle the matter. You know Caro has been my cousin thrice removed. Perhaps you'd like to play a new role."

Millicent's eyes brightened. "That would be lovely and so much fun. However, I think I might stand a better chance being myself."

"Yourself? Are you thinking of wearing down the constables by subjecting them to your persuasive ways?"

Millicent grinned. "My particular talent of wearing people down is quite effective. I should go see what's available in the kitchen. By the way, everyone has made their way down to breakfast."

Everyone?

"Lady Sara and Toodles?"

Millicent nodded.

"And Lady Henrietta?"

"She led them down. I believe they are waiting for you and Mr. Winchester."

"I suppose that means they know Tom and I went out last night."

Millicent smiled. "I was helping Lady Sara last night and she kept looking out the window. When she saw you and Mr. Winchester setting off, she raced to tell Lady Henrietta and Toodles. They had some hot chocolate brought up to Lady Henrietta's room, where I believe they kept vigil."

"Did anyone get any sleep last night?"

"I believe they waited up for as long as they could."

Evie imagined they had wanted to discuss her threat of eloping. "I just remembered I might have said something to upset them. Actually, I did upset them." When Evie told Millicent about Tom's special license, Millicent paled.

"Milady, surely you wouldn't deprive us. We are so looking forward to seeing you in a wedding gown."

"Remind me to visit a dressmaker while we're in town."

Millicent's eyes widened. "Milady! You'd think that would be a priority. I mean... My apologies, milady. I should not have said that."

Laughing, Evie set her at ease. "I'm not about to bite your head off just because you spoke the truth. If you must know, I'm rather annoyed at Henrietta for putting Tom on the spot. We'll marry when we feel the time is right and not a moment sooner."

"Well, that's a relief." Millicent gasped. "Begging your pardon, milady. I did it again."

"Millicent, you're allowed to say what's on your mind. Well, up to a point. I really don't wish to put Mr. Winchester on the spot again. Sometimes, I feel his tolerance of my family is running thin. He says he finds them all amusing but everyone has their breaking point." Evie looked around her dressing table and tried to remember where she'd left her notebook.

"Is this what you're looking for?"

"Yes, thank you. What was I saying?" She looked up for a moment. "I must admit, there was a moment when I thought he might have fled."

Millicent laughed. "Milady, if Mr. Winchester ever decides to flee, I'm sure he will take you with him."

Agreeing with her, Evie stood up. "I'm ready to face them." She looked inside the notebook and found the piece of paper Tom had given her the night before and handed it to Millicent. "That's Stuart White's address. Ask Edmonds to drive you there, please. I'm sure Stuart White is harmless, but I would prefer to err on the side of caution."

Millicent nodded. "I should go down and see what sort of tempting treats I can pack for Mr. White."

"That's the spirit." Evie made her way out of the room. When she reached the stairs, she found Tom leaning against the banister, his arms folded, his feet crossed at the ankles. He was either waiting for her or he was running through their theory. If he fell, would he land with his feet facing the door or away from it?

Sensing her, he looked up and smiled. "I heard everyone decided to have breakfast downstairs today."

Evie smiled. "What if I had decided to have breakfast in bed?"

Tom scowled at her. "You've never done that. Why would you do it now?" He stared at her, his eyes filled with disbelief. "I see. I suppose you think it would be amusing if I had to face them alone. Well, for your information, I have my newspapers to hide behind."

"Heavens, I do hope they haven't messed up your newspapers. You know, Toodles likes to browse through them and she tends to pull pages apart and she always puts them back in the wrong order. Of course, if she finds something of interest, she's likely to ask for a pair of scissors."

Taking Evie's hand, Tom led her down the stairs. "Keep up, Countess."

They slowed down only when they reached the dining room.

"Tom, calm down, take a deep breath, and count to three. It's what I usually do to prepare myself."

"And does it work?"

Evie hummed under her breath. "Well, not always..."

"Countess, this is a matter of urgency." Releasing her hand, he rushed in and searched the table for his newspaper.

Edgar cleared his throat. Stepping forward, he handed Tom the morning newspapers. "Your newspapers, Mr. Winchester."

Toodles growled, "I thought you said they hadn't arrived yet."

"My apologies, Toodles. I only now saw them on the sideboard." Edgar bowed his head and stepped back.

Tom tucked them under his arm and proceeded to help himself to breakfast.

"Good morning, everyone." Evie went to stand beside him and nudged him.

"Good morning," Tom threw over his shoulder. "My apologies, we had a late night."

Evie rolled her eyes. He had just provided everyone with a conversation starter.

"Evangeline, do tell us. We heard you go out last night. Did anything of interest happen?" Henrietta asked.

Sitting down, Evie noticed two people missing. "Have Caro and Lord Evans not come down?"

Sara smiled. "They went out for a morning constitutional and will have breakfast when they return. Lord Evans said something about needing some fresh air.

Although, I have no idea where he hopes to find that in town."

Evie closed her eyes and took a sip of her coffee. Henry's presence would settle everyone, she was sure of it. Yes, for as long as he was here, everyone would be on their best behavior.

"Birdie. You were going to tell us about last night."

Tom settled in his place and hid behind his newspaper while Evie gave them a brief summary of their night.

"So Stuart White has been found." Henrietta was impressed. "And now you've sent Millicent on a scouting mission. That's very adventurous of you. What can we do?"

"Let me think…"

A footman entered and delivered a message to Edgar who cleared his throat and announced Lotte Mannering.

The lady detective waltzed in. "I hope I'm not inter-rupting. I know this is rather early for a social call."

Henrietta laughed. "There are times when I think we're all sitting on a theater stage, with actors making their grand entrance and bringing some delightful news."

"Lotte? Has something happened?" Evie asked as she gestured to a place across the table from her.

Lotte settled down and shrugged. "I thought I'd come and tell you in person I took the liberty of asking Parsody to afternoon tea here. I know I should have consulted with you first but, last night, it suddenly occurred that we hadn't had much success with getting information out of them. Not that we thought we had to at the time. Anyhow…" Lotte looked around the table. "I thought we would have better luck with a larger group."

"Did they agree to come?"

Lotte nodded. "I received a note this morning. They're quite eager."

Catching Edgar's attention, Evie nudged her head toward Lotte and signaled to the serving dishes on the sideboard. Edgar, bless him, interpreted her meaning and prepared a plate for Lotte.

When Edgar set the plate down in front of Lotte, she smiled. "Thank you. I don't mind if I do. I left home in rather a hurry. Although, some might say my empty pantry chased me away."

"Perhaps we should all make an effort to be here this afternoon," Evie suggested.

"Is this something we can help with?" Henrietta asked.

"Yes, absolutely." Now they needed to formulate a few key questions. Evie remembered the newspaper article Tom had found. "Tom, what was the name of the village?"

"I'll have to have another look at the article. I'm afraid I don't remember. Wait a minute, it's just come me. The village wasn't actually mentioned."

Evie explained how the village locals had planned to erect some sort of plaque in memory of Parsody's parents. "As I'm going to be taking charge of introducing her around, I would like to know as much as I can about her family. I wouldn't want to promote someone whose family might bring the name of Woodridge into disrepute by association." Looking up, she asked, "Tom, is there anything interesting in the newspaper this morning?"

"Not yet." He sat up. "Wait... Here's something. The police have actually requested anyone with information about James Clementine to contact them."

That had to mean they were treating the death as suspicious.

"I wonder if they have managed to find any relatives."

Henrietta looked around the table. "Forgive my lack of alertness. I realize you are discussing another matter, but I'm puzzling over something you said. Why would the local villagers erect a plaque? Isn't that something the family would take care of?"

"I hadn't thought of that. Perhaps Mr. Jameson took care of building some sort of memorial and the villagers wished to commemorate the couple's lives in their own way. I hope that's the case because it would then mean they were well regarded in the community."

"That's certainly something we can delve into," Henrietta declared. Of course, Miss Buchanan would have been too young so she would not remember. Do you know if she stays in the family home?"

"Lotte and I only know she has been traveling extensively."

"Why?" Henrietta asked.

"It might not have been her decision. This is something her guardian might have decided and, he might have a very good reason for it."

"And what do you think that might be, Evangeline?"

"If I had to guess, I'd say Mr. Jameson has business interests that took him abroad. Or maybe they were just personal interests. Also, some people believe travel broadens the mind and can be quite educational."

"From what you've told me, Parsody doesn't strike me as having benefited from a broad education," Tom murmured from behind his newspaper.

Henrietta shook her head. "You said she's an heiress. I'm sure he must be a man of means. Otherwise, he would not have been chosen as her guardian." Looking at

Toodles and Sara, Henrietta nodded. "We have our work cut out for us."

Thinking back to the conversation she'd had with Tom the previous evening, Evie wondered if, in years to come, she would be her own version of Henrietta.

She'd need to nurture a full colored personality. Then again, Tom might be right in thinking they might have moved on to some other interest. She couldn't help smiling at the image of Seth's relief.

"You should tell Lotte about last night," Henrietta said. Laughing, she added, "Perhaps you should publish a daily broadsheet. The Woodridge News. Never mind, I'll tell her and if I leave anything out you can fill in the details."

Evie listened as Henrietta summarized everything she had said earlier. Of course, she made the retelling of the information that much more exciting, gesturing with her hands like a seasoned thespian and using her voice by fluctuating her tone, hitching with excitement and lowering with amazement.

When she finished, Henrietta looked at Evie. "Did I leave anything out?"

"No, you were very thorough."

Tom set his newspaper down and turned his attention to his breakfast. He looked up and found Evie's gaze bouncing between Henrietta, Sara, and Toodles.

Meeting Tom's gaze, Evie frowned. Their exchanged glances suggested they were up to something.

Tom and Evie followed the silent exchange and when their glances met again, they both shrugged.

"We might need a referee," Toodles murmured.

Henrietta cleared her throat. "That won't be necessary. We are all mature adults."

"I beg to differ," Toodles declared. Looking at Evie, she said, "These two," she signaled to Sara and Henrietta, "will be vying for Parsody's attention. They both want her as their debutante. There, it's out in the open."

"Perhaps we should let Miss Buchanan decide for herself," Sara suggested.

"You say that with confidence because you believe she will favor a younger person such as yourself," Henrietta complained.

Sara began to speak only to stop when Caro and Lord Evans walked in.

"I told Henry we should hurry back because if we didn't, you would all be out and about and getting on with your day and I would have missed my opportunity to..." Caro stopped and inhaled a sharp breath. "I need to apologize for my behavior last night. It was inexcusable and I promise it will never happen again."

"My goodness," Henrietta exclaimed. "That would be a pity. You were quite entertaining, my dear."

Lord Evans pinched the bridge of his nose. "Lady Woodridge, please don't encourage my wife."

Henrietta smiled. "Which Lady Woodridge are you chastising, Lord Evans?"

When Lord Evans didn't respond, Caro cut in, "Don't mind Henry. He obviously got up on the wrong side of the bed."

Lord Evans, who had been helping himself to breakfast, turned and said, "That's because, in the middle of the night, I found myself pushed off my side of the bed and I had to make do with the other side and I nearly fell off again when you decided to roll back."

"The room was spinning and rocking," Caro

complained. "I was merely trying to keep up with the motion. Drinking clearly does not agree with me. It makes me restless and I already apologized for that."

Evie looked heavenward.

She had been relying on Lord Evans to introduce a sense of sanity.

Henrietta leaned in and murmured, "This is better than going to the theater." Looking toward the door, she added, "I wonder who will come in next?"

One by one, they all turned to look at the door and, right on cue, Holmes poked his head in and whined.

Taking a sip of her coffee, Evie asked, "Has Holmes been taken out?"

Edgar stepped forward. "I will see to it straightaway, my lady. Yes, Master Holmes clearly wishes to be taken for his morning constitutional."

Nodding, Evie was about to turn back to her breakfast when she noticed Edgar signaling to a footman who followed him out. They must have stood just outside the door because she was sure she heard Edgar ask the footman to keep him abreast of any new developments...

CHAPTER 15

Later that morning...

Millicent set her basket down and settled in the front seat of the Duesenberg beside Edmonds. Arranging her skirt, she spread her hands out on her lap, looked ahead and lifted her chin.

The edge of Edmonds' mouth hitched up as he asked, "Is milady all set?"

"Don't you be cheeky. Did I ask to sit in the back? No, I didn't. So don't you go suggesting I have airs."

"That's giving me an earful," Edmonds murmured as he set them on their way.

Millicent grinned. "It was more of a tongue lashing."

"Are you practicing for when you get married?"

Millicent swung toward Edmonds. "What do you know about that? Have you heard something? Who's talking about me?"

Edmonds lowered his head. "It was just a remark. I mean, you will eventually marry Edgar. At least, that's what everyone expects."

Millicent turned to look ahead again. "Yes, eventually. We obviously can't marry before Lady Woodridge and Mr. Winchester because that would make things awkward, what with us going away on honeymoon." Glancing at Edmonds, Millicent realized she'd said more than she should have. "Sorry. I suppose when someone asks how you are they don't really expect you to tell them."

"What?"

"Never mind. Drive on."

Edmonds tapped his hat and focused on his driving.

"Look! There's Edgar with Holmes." Sitting forward, Millicent waved and called out, "*Edgar! Edgar!*"

Across the street, Edgar had been telling Master Holmes about his bad timing in wanting to go for a walk right when things were becoming interesting, when he suddenly heard his name called out. Seeing the Duesenberg, he squinted and noticed Millicent.

"I suppose she won't stop waving until I wave back." Edgar looked around him before giving Millicent a discreet wave.

Back in the Duesenberg, Millicent snorted. "Sometimes, I forget Edgar's proper manner is not an act." Pointing ahead, she yelped, "Watch out for that woman."

Edmonds' grip tightened around the steering wheel. "Why?"

"She might cross the street. Do you want to be responsible for cutting her life short?"

"If she had any intention of crossing the street, she'd

be edging toward the curb, but she's nowhere near the curb."

"But you never know. She might suddenly decide to cross the street on an impulse." Millicent closed her eyes and tried to remember everything Lady Woodridge had told her about Stuart White. She had no reason to worry or feel jittery. She had a task to accomplish and her only concern was in returning to Woodridge House empty-handed. How would she explain that?

Edmonds hunched his shoulders and focused on his driving. He brought the Duesenberg to a stop outside the address Millicent had given him, and turned to look at her.

"Are you sure this is the address?" Millicent asked. "I wouldn't want to go knocking on the wrong door."

Edmonds read out the number and Millicent checked it against the piece of paper Lady Woodridge had given her. "Yes, I suppose it's the right one, but there's no harm in wanting to be sure."

"He must do well for himself," Edmonds remarked. "Rooms in these houses don't come cheap."

When he made a move to hop out, Millicent stopped him. "What are you doing?"

"I'm accompanying you."

"You don't need to. I'm the maid. How would it look if I show up at his doorstep with a chauffeur?"

"In other words, you want me to wait out here. What if he turns violent?"

"He's not dangerous." At least, she didn't think he was. "Do you see any coppers about? Lady Woodridge said there were going to be two constables."

"No, I don't see any, but they might be in disguise or

sitting in one of the motor cars. If I see them approaching you, I could tell them to spare themselves the headache."

Millicent scowled at him. "I think you meant to say trouble."

"No, I'm sure I meant to say headache."

Millicent hid her smile by lifting her chin. "I won't be long." She crossed the street. Walking up the steps to the front door, she thought she saw a curtain shift on the second floor.

To her surprise, a butler opened the door. "I'm the Countess of Woodridge's maid, here to see Stuart White."

He nudged his head toward the stairs. "First door on your left."

Millicent climbed the stairs, her steps cautious. Glancing over her shoulder, she saw the butler looking up at her. She hurried her step and reached the door. Taking a moment to compose herself, she repeated his name several times, just to make sure she didn't forget it. Finally, she was ready, but she had to knock three times before the door opened a crack. "Stuart White?"

"Who wants to know?"

Despite opening the door only a fraction, Millicent could see he wore a fancy smoking jacket, although it was longer than the ones she'd seen. It was definitely silk or maybe satin... with bold stripes in red and buff. Shaking her head, she decided it looked more like a robe.

Millicent introduced herself. "Lady Woodridge thought you needed some pampering." She lifted the cloth covering the cakes and allowed the aroma to work its charm.

"Come in."

The library, Woodridge House

"I wonder how Millicent is getting on. She's been gone a long while." Evie paced around the library, her notebook in hand. "Yes, yes. I know. I'll wear out the carpet."

Tom chortled. "If you'd like, I could drive down to Charles Street."

"No, no, no. You need to stay right here where I can keep an eye on you. No excuses, Tom. You will keep your appointment."

"Worth a try," he murmured and hid behind the newspaper again. "Although, I still don't understand the need for a fitting. The tailor took the measurements. What can possibly go wrong? It's not as if the knee breeches could be any shorter."

"Yes, they could," Evie murmured.

"Forget I said that."

Lotte stepped back from the table and held up a fashion magazine. Tapping one of the pages, she asked, "Do you recognize any of these young women? This is a photograph from a fashion show."

Evie studied the grainy photograph. "No."

Lotte nodded. "Where there's one photograph, there's bound to be more. It's only a month old."

Evie looked at the cover. "It's a French magazine."

"Does it matter? I've been thinking about the police asking for information related to James Clementine. Some of the debutantes might have traveled to Paris."

Evie followed Lotte's train of thought. "The detective

mentioned he'd traveled extensively. Are you thinking he spent time in Paris?"

Lotte nodded.

The fact no one had admitted to knowing James Clementine still puzzled Evie. Lauren Gladstone had said she'd met him briefly. But there had to be someone, somewhere who could tell them more about him.

Evie hummed and decided they might actually be getting carried away and straying from an obvious trail. "There must be some older magazines somewhere. Sara enjoys reading them. I'd ask her about them but she and the others went out an hour ago saying they wouldn't return until the afternoon."

The doors to the library opened and Edgar walked in.

Evie gave Tom a slanted look and smiled. "Edgar, are you free this afternoon? Mr. Winchester wonders if you might be able to accompany him to the tailor for his fitting."

"This afternoon, my lady?"

"Yes." Evie noticed Edgar's shoulders lowering. He looked both disappointed and resigned.

"Yes, of course. I'd be only too delighted to accompany Mr. Winchester." Edgar turned to leave only to swing back. "My apologies, I almost forgot... Millicent has just returned and wishes to speak with you."

"At last. Thank you, Edgar."

As Millicent brushed past Edgar, she frowned at him. Evie actually suspected she might have poked her tongue out at him.

Tom set his newspaper down and stood up. "Millicent, we were about to send a search party for you."

"I'm ever so sorry I took so long, milady. I sat down to

a cup of tea with Stuart White and then one thing led to another... He's quite chatty."

"Really? Why did I have the impression he didn't enjoy talking?"

"He rambles," Tom said.

Millicent gave a vigorous nod. "He did quite a bit of rambling."

"What did you talk about?" Lotte asked.

"I asked him about his robe." Millicent described it. "He seemed to be surprised to be wearing it. Almost as if he hadn't noticed. Then, he looked at it as if he'd never seen it before."

Evie tried to determine what the robe had to do with... anything. Then she remembered this was Millicent and all would be revealed in good time. From experience, she knew asking any questions would derail Millicent's thoughts and getting her back on track would take some doing.

"Did he look out of sorts?" Lotte asked.

Millicent gave it some thought. "I hadn't met him before so I have nothing to compare with. In my opinion, he didn't look the way a young man should look. His skin looked pasty and he could do with a hearty meal and some fresh air."

Lotte snorted. "Most men his age look that way in the morning."

"Anyhow, I suspected he might have had a long night." Millicent turned to Evie. "I know you told me he was escorted back by the constables but he might have stayed up. That's when I looked around the room and I noticed the mess. There were newspapers and books strewn about the room and cups of tea or maybe coffee and quite a few empty glasses. Oh, and a cabinet stocked with alcoholic beverages."

That, in itself, Evie thought, wasn't unusual.

Millicent looked up at the ceiling and murmured something to herself. "What was I saying? Oh, yes, the robe. I asked him where he'd had the robe made. Instead of telling me what I wanted to know, he started rambling. It took me a moment to realize he'd changed the subject."

Good grief. Evie rolled her eyes. Why couldn't people answer a simple question? Stuart White made her think of Mr. Jameson and his tendency to avoid answering direct questions. It was almost as if they were hiding something or trying to avoid revealing something they didn't want known.

"That's when I started taking mental notes of everything in his room and noticed the mess. I'm not sure I could call it a drawing room. Everything looked out of place and more like a library than a drawing room. Maybe that's what gentlemen's rooms look like. I wouldn't know because this was my first time visiting a bachelor's abode but I've read plenty of stories describing them, so I shouldn't be surprised by the general untidiness." Millicent nibbled the edge of her lip. "The chairs were leather. You know, like the type you find in libraries. Anyhow, I looked around and tried to memorize everything. Just in case what I was seeing meant anything because, obviously, the robe must mean something. Only, he didn't want to tell me." Millicent's expression turned woeful. "I really tried to get the information out of him, milady. I asked him several times but he was immune to my persistence."

Lotte frowned. "Why?"

Evie anticipated Millicent's response and expected her

secretary to take the dialogue in a different direction. She knew Lotte had merely expressed her thoughts aloud. Why hadn't he simply told her. Why would he wish to avoid answering such a simple question?

"Because he wouldn't tell me where he got it and he should have. It's an innocent enough question. At least, I think it is. And if he didn't know where it came from, well... then, he should have told me he didn't know... but he didn't."

Edgar cleared his throat as if to draw Millicent's attention to her babbling.

She swung toward him and scowled. "I'm only saying what I think and what I saw. That's why her ladyship sent me there."

"What else did you notice, Millicent?" Evie asked. Although, in reality, she needed a few minutes for the information Millicent had provided them with to stop floating around her mind and settle.

"I told myself to remember and now I've forgotten. Just as well I wrote it down." She searched inside her handbag and produced a scrap of paper. "There was a bottle which looked interesting. *La fée verte.* One of the words had one of those little strokes above it."

Evie tried to decipher what she'd said. Millicent had made the words sound like Bertie's fee. "*La fée verte?*" Evie repeated in her rusty French.

"Is that what it's supposed to sound like?" Millicent shrugged. "I wrote it down because the bottle looked pretty and it was sitting out so he must have been drinking from it. What struck me as odd was the pretty drawing of a fairy. I've never seen a bottle with a fairy on it. I've seen fairies. I mean, not in real life because everyone knows fairies don't exist, at least, we think they don't, but they might." Millicent's cheeks colored. "What I mean to say is that I saw the fairies in an illustration in a magazine. I think it was a Christmas issue. Now that I think about it, I think the story was written by that Sherlock Holmes fellow. Anyhow, it was a green beverage. Maybe it was that Crème de Menthe drink I don't like."

"Absinthe," Lotte murmured.

"Isn't that drink illegal?" Evie asked.

"Yes. Too many people suffered from absinthe madness so it's been made illegal," Lotte explained.

Evie walked over to the desk. Digging around a drawer, she brought out some paper. "This might be something or it might be nothing." How many times had she said that? Whenever she and Tom discussed a problem, she fixated on a tidbit of information which, invariably, turned out to be quite useful. In her experience, nothing should be dismissed as insignificant.

She took a chair over to the table and settled down to write in bold letters, "Absinthe drinker."

Millicent's eyes widened. "Does the drink make you see fairies, milady?"

"I don't know, Millicent, but it's been known to have quite strong effects on people. It could be the reason why he thinks someone is following him."

"Where do you think he got the absinthe from?" Tom asked. "A recent trip to Paris? There might be a black market for it."

Evie set the page she'd been writing on aside and picked up another piece of paper. "Paris. We know James Clementine traveled extensively."

"Everyone who travels goes to Paris," Lotte said.

"Yes, so it's possible he was there recently. Could this be the connection we're looking for or am I grasping at straws?"

Tom frowned. "If they were both in Paris at the same time and Stuart White met James Clementine, why didn't he tell the detective?" Tom put his hand up. "Now I'm grasping at straws."

"Not necessarily," Evie murmured. "Let's not dismiss any ideas yet, and certainly not the obvious one staring us in the face."

"Are you about to suggest Stuart White is the killer?" As he asked the question, Tom's gaze lowered. After a brief moment, he looked up. "That would mean I helped him make his escape in the taxicab."

They were silent for several minutes. Then, Millicent said, "It could reveal something. I mean, the connection to James Clementine could…"

"Actually, Millicent, I think you are on the right track. Tom and I have considered the possibility of James Clementine's death not being an accident and in order to prove that, we feel we must find a connection." Evie turned to the table and the two pieces of paper she had written on. Then she looked at the magazine. Turning, she said, "We have some obvious facts. James Clementine and Stuart White attended the same party."

Everyone nodded.

"James Clementine died. How? We don't know if he fell or if he was pushed. We now suspect he'd been to Paris. Thanks to Millicent's observation, we now think Stuart White had recently been in Paris." Evie smiled. "That is a huge assumption. It's possible someone gave him the bottle of Absinthe as a gift. For the sake of argument, let's assume he purchased it himself in Paris. Also, Millicent has established another fact. Stuart White is evasive to the point of not answering a simple question."

Lotte nodded and Tom said, "You're on the trail, Countess."

"Diminishing trust in people. I think I might have mentioned that to Lotte. I'm almost convinced Stuart White is not telling the truth. There's a reason why he was so shaken by the sight of James Clementine's body."

Tom nodded. "He knew James Clementine."

"Yes, and now we're wondering if they met in Paris." She looked at the photograph Lotte had pointed out in the magazine. "Lauren Gladstone said she'd met James Clementine only recently at a soiree."

Tom nodded. "An afternoon tea and I'm having difficulty picturing him there."

Evie thought this was as far as they could go before their theory was derailed by a lack of facts. "The detective needs to find out if Stuart White has recently been to Paris. There is something suspicious about James Clementine's death. The police have asked the public for information so I believe this is more than an assumption. If the police can't manage to trace his activities prior to coming to England, I doubt they will be able to solve the case."

It didn't make sense. Why would people deny knowing the victim? Did they fear the connection would lead the police to something bigger?

Evie looked at Millicent, who said, "I'm not sure my mind was actually going all the way there, milady. However, if what I said helped you, then my job is done."

Evie nodded. Closing her eyes, she tried to recapture her train of thought.

"Countess, you'd just placed the two young men in Paris."

"Thank you." Evie pointed at the fashion magazine. "The detective is trying to find someone who knew James Clementine and, so far, no one has come forth. I find that hard to believe. James Clementine went to a party attended by people who might have been in Paris recently." She wrote on another piece of paper. Swinging around to face them, she held up the piece of paper. "Paris. I wonder if we can assume James Clementine also made the rounds of social gatherings there? What if he met someone or saw something?" She stopped for a moment.

Would she be putting so much emphasis on Paris if Millicent hadn't mentioned the Absinthe?

Evie's gaze shifted from Millicent to Tom to Lotte. "You probably think I'm off with the fairies." Smiling, she saw Edgar standing by the door.

He wasn't alone.

Everyone turned toward the door and saw Detective Inspector Rawlinson.

Lotte sidled up to Evie and murmured, "This should be interesting. You must have made quite an impression on the detective for him to be seeking you out."

"We don't know if that's the reason for his visit," Evie whispered and lowered the piece of paper she'd been holding up. Just how much had he heard?

The detective stepped forward. "Lady Woodridge, my apologies. A footman opened the front door and I couldn't help being drawn in here."

"That's perfectly fine, detective. Do come in." All her

thoughts had scattered and she couldn't quite remember what they'd been discussing.

The room fell silent and remained so until it was interrupted by the clock striking the hour.

Edgar cleared his throat and excused himself saying, "I should see to luncheon."

"My apologies, my lady. I did not notice the time."

"Edgar," Evie called out. "There will be one more for luncheon. Detective, please say you'll join us."

He inclined his head. "If you insist."

She smiled. "I do." Evie gestured to the door. This would be her chance to get some straight answers out of the detective. "Perhaps we could all go to the drawing room."

Even as she spoke, the detective moved to the table and stood with his hands on his hips, looking down at the notes she'd made.

"You have been busy, Lady Woodridge."

Evie guessed she would have to provide an explanation.

The door to the library opened again. Evie immediately thought of Henrietta's remark about being on a theater stage. Had the others returned?

A footman entered and announced, "Miss Althea Rawlinson."

"Althea?" the detective exclaimed.

Evie sidled up to the footman and asked him to tell Edgar there would be another guest for luncheon.

"What are you doing here?" the detective demanded. "Did you follow me?"

"Follow you?" Althea lifted her chin. "I happened to be

in the vicinity and saw you and… Never mind all that."
She smiled at Evie.

"It's lovely to see you." Evie turned to Lotte. "I actually wanted to introduce you to my dear friend, Lotte Mannering. Lotte, Althea has the most intriguing ideas and she's wonderfully observant. I think she would be a perfect addition to the agency."

The detective gaped at Evie. "Agency?"

"Althea, do join us for lunch."

CHAPTER 16

"The day isn't even half over, Countess," Tom murmured as they all made their way to the drawing room.

"Lady Woodridge," the detective, who'd been walking a step ahead of them, stopped and turned. "Do you think I could have a word with you and Tom. It won't take too long."

Evie looked at Tom and then at the detective. "Yes, of course." She mentally rushed through the last few minutes and tried to determine what might have triggered his need for a private word. Something must have caught his attention, enough for him to decide to act without further delay.

Drawing a blank, Evie prepared herself to be surprised.

They returned to the library. Evie gestured to a chair but the detective insisted it wouldn't take too long.

He cleared his throat and, holding her gaze for a moment, he appeared to hesitate.

Evie imagined he was trying to formulate what he would say to her. Or, perhaps, how he would phrase his question. It didn't seem to be an easy task.

"Did we overstep a boundary, detective?"

"What? No. Not really."

"Well, that's a relief. At least, I hope it is."

"I do, however, have some questions. My constables…"

Aha!

This had to be about Millicent's visit to Stuart White.

He cleared his throat again. "My constables contacted me to say your maid called on Stuart White."

"Yes, I thought he might like some cake."

"Cake?"

Evie nodded. "Actually, how did your constables know she works for me?" Millicent hadn't mentioned anything about the constables speaking with her. Had they spoken with Edmonds?

When the detective didn't answer, Evie said, "I hope her presence didn't interfere with your investigation."

"No, not exactly. However, something is puzzling me. When the constables saw her approaching the building, they decided to question her. However, they were intercepted by your chauffeur who gave them, to quote him, a piece of friendly advice."

"Indeed." Evie couldn't begin to imagine what Edmonds had said to them.

"Your chauffeur told my constables they would be tackling your maid at their own risk. He then told them they should spare themselves the headache."

Headache? "You mean trouble."

"No, I'm sure they said headache."

Evie tried not to smile. "And did they heed his advice?"

"They did, but only after your chauffeur assured them the maid was only carrying some food. Can you confirm she was not carrying a weapon?"

"Why would my maid carry a weapon?"

"It's the way your chauffeur expressed himself. You see, we are taking Stuart White's fears seriously and your chauffeur seemed to suggest she is rather dangerous."

Tom chuckled.

"Detective, you have no need to worry. Millicent is quite harmless," Evie assured him.

He nodded. "She was in there for a long time."

"Would you like to have a word with her? I'm sure she'll be only too happy to tell you about her visit."

Smiling, Tom shook his head.

Unfortunately, the detective witnessed this. "You don't seem to agree, Tom."

"I agree about Millicent being quite harmless. I just don't think it's a good idea for you to question her."

"Why?"

"Because, as Edmonds said, you might wish to spare yourself the headache."

He took a couple of minutes to consider Tom's response. "Very well. I'll trust you can vouch for her." The detective looked at Tom and then at Evie.

Evie could tell he didn't look convinced. However, if he had any more questions, he didn't appear to want to ask them right at that moment.

Evie led them through to the drawing room. When she entered, she saw Lotte and Althea, but there was no sign of Millicent.

Seeing her, Lotte said, "You were right about Althea. Best of all, she would have the perfect cover."

That intrigued Evie. "What might that be?"

"She's a society portraitist. That means, she has a way to gain easy access."

Althea smiled. "True, so long as a suspect is interested in having their portrait painted."

Evie thought she heard the detective groan under his breath and she was sure he would have a great deal more to say to his sister… later on.

One of the side doors opened and Edgar stepped in to announce, "Luncheon is ready, my lady."

"Thank you, Edgar. Please ask Millicent to join us." Turning, she saw Tom's lifted eyebrow so she felt compelled to explain, "Millicent is my secretary and she might need to record something."

They walked through to the dining room, with Evie inviting everyone to sit wherever they pleased, "We're quite informal here."

Evie noticed Althea chose the chair diagonally opposite the detective, no doubt as an attempt to avoid his direct censure.

The detective, Evie noticed, kept his eye on the door. She guessed he was anticipating Millicent's arrival.

When she finally appeared, she took a couple of tentative steps inside and stopped.

Evie looked around the table. The only available place was directly opposite the detective and next to Althea. "Do sit down." Evie introduced her to the detective. "And, this is Althea Rawlinson, the detective's sister."

Tipping her chin up, Millicent hurried to take her place.

Evie glanced at the detective. He'd accepted her invitation to lunch and she knew he could just as easily have found an excuse to leave. But he hadn't.

Did he have another reason for extending his stay?

Evie heard Millicent whisper, "Am I in trouble?"

Smiling at her, Tom shook his head.

A fish course was brought in. The wine was poured. Evie noticed the detective did not object. Lotte remarked on the weather and everyone took turns to express their opinion.

Evie knew Lord Evans and Caro wouldn't arrive unexpectedly because they were enjoying an outing together. And, while Toodles, Sara, and Henrietta had said they would be busy until the afternoon, Evie knew that could always change.

She didn't think the detective would answer questions about the case but, at some point, Evie thought she should find out if there had been any new developments. Of course, the most strategic moment would be right in the middle of luncheon, but if she missed her opportunity, she would definitely ask him before he left.

Clearing his throat, the detective said, "I believe I interrupted a rather interesting conversation."

Remembering the jumble of thoughts she had entertained earlier, Evie tried to laugh it off. "We were tossing about some ideas. Mostly wild ones, I might add."

"I've heard say those are usually the ones which yield results for you, my lady."

"On occasion, yes."

"I'm sure you employ some sort of deductive thinking," Althea observed.

"I like to think so."

The detective glanced around the table before saying,

"I'd be interested to know why you think someone would deny knowing James Clementine."

Before answering, Evie gave it some thought. "They might wish to avoid becoming involved. To some, this is the most important time in the social calendar. Indeed, in their lives."

"You're referring to the debutantes."

Evie nodded. "Straight after the war, there were private balls held for the debutantes. Court presentations finally resumed last year. It might sound antiquated, but most people still worry about making the wrong impression and being in any way connected to scandals."

"I'm fully aware of that," the detective admitted. "However, I'm more concerned with the lack of civic duty."

"You could run another article in the newspaper assuring people of their anonymity," Evie suggested.

"That's certainly something I could offer but there is always the possibility of word getting out and the person's identity being exposed."

Lotte closed her eyes to savor the wine and then asked, "Why do you think James Clementine was killed?" She took another sip and added, "I'm sure the police have yet to decide if a crime has been committed. Of course, my question is only hypothetical."

"I'll admit his death looks like an accident," the detective revealed. "There were no actual witnesses to his fall. That's something we find highly suspicious. Especially given the nature of the gathering. There were quite a number of guests and I assume they were moving from room to room. Working on the assumption, and I should point out this is a huge assumption, that someone killed him, then the killer chose his moment with precision."

Choosing the moment when no one would witness the incident, Evie thought, only to realize the detective hadn't quite answered Lotte's question. Was he being evasive?

He gave everyone a moment longer to digest the news.

Had she noticed anyone looking suspicious? Had the killer lingered in the house, standing in the crowd, hiding in plain sight?

"Detective," Evie said, "On the night we met, when we explained we'd been drawn to the house after hearing the scream, you asked us if we'd seen anyone leaving the house."

The detective nodded.

"Do you think the killer fled the scene?"

"Yes, it is something we need to consider."

It had been a quiet night. They'd seen a motor car driving by but it had come from the top end of North Audley Street, heading toward Upper Brook Street. Then, when they'd reached the corner, they'd had a clear view of the street and she couldn't remember having seen anyone walking away from the house. In fact, she clearly recalled noticing the way the guests were lingering, not quite willing to leave.

The detective studied his glass of wine. "As for the reason for his death. Your guess is as good as ours. While we know where James Clementine had traveled to before coming to London and the two social events he attended, we don't know whom he socialized with and have no knowledge of his activities in-between those two events."

Evie took a sip of her drink. Setting the glass down, she stared at the contents. "I wonder what brought James Clementine to London. Detective, how long had he been in town?"

"He arrived three days before his death."

And they knew he'd attended an afternoon soiree and the party at Upper Brook Street. "I wonder..." It took her a moment to realize everyone was waiting for her to finish her thought. "I wonder if he came to London looking for someone."

"Someone he met in Paris?" Tom asked.

"Yes."

The detective smiled. "From what I managed to over-hear, I believe Lady Woodridge is better equipped to deliver a sound theory." He looked at Evie. "You mentioned Paris but I didn't quite follow the thread of your idea."

Evie shrugged. "I assume when the police investigate a crime, they question witnesses and try to place possible suspects near the scene of the crime. It looks like no suspects have been identified. So, we've been taking our attention further afield, to the time before the incident." Since no one contradicted her, Evie assumed that's what they had been doing. In reality, they had merely been tossing around ideas to see where it all took them. "The theory hasn't quite taken shape in my mind, but I believe I was entertaining the possibility of placing several people in Paris, perhaps at the same event." She shrugged. "That's assuming James Clementine had traveled to Paris."

To her annoyance, the detective did not confirm it or deny it.

"At a place where they might have met James Clemen-tine," he said.

"Yes. Although, now that I think about it, it is highly unlikely someone like James Clementine or Stuart White would have attended a fashion show. I mention that

specific setting because Lotte brought it to our attention."
When she saw the detective frowning, she added, "The
theory, such as it is, relies on people who attended the
Upper Brook Street party also being in Paris. Perhaps as a
lead up to the season. Young ladies would have traveled
there to purchase new gowns and some would have
attended the sort of fashion shows put on by the most
prestigious fashion houses. That's where my idea dwin-
dles because I can't actually picture someone like James
Clementine attending one of those shows. In fact, I doubt
we're even on the right track about Stuart White knowing
him."

"Why not?"

Everyone's attention shifted to Millicent.

Millicent mouthed an apology and lowered her gaze.

"Millicent?" Evie encouraged her with a nod.

"Well, I couldn't help noticing… Today, when I visited
Stuart White, I mentioned his room was rather disorga-
nized. Actually, it was messy, in a chaotic sort of way. As
we chatted, I couldn't help myself. I do like to keep busy,
some would say it's a nervous trait, but I think it's just a
habit from always being busy, doing things day in, day
out. So as we chatted, I picked things up and put them in
their place. Stuart followed me around the room and then
we moved to the next room. There were clothes strewn all
over, on chairs and sofas and even on the floor. I picked
them up and straightened them and asked where they
could be put away and, suddenly, there I was in his
bedroom—"

The sound of a serving spoon clanging against a
serving platter startled everyone.

Edgar cleared his throat and, glancing at Evie, mouthed an apology.

Millicent's voice hitched, "As I was saying, I found myself in his bedroom." Millicent shot Edgar a warning look. "*Putting his clothes away* in the wardrobe and that's when I saw the contents of his wardrobe. He is very fashionable."

Evie glanced at the detective. After a full minute, he blinked.

Tom gestured to a footman. "I think the detective needs more wine."

The detective did not refuse.

Just as he picked up his glass, Millicent said, "Oh, I remembered the point I was trying to make." Millicent shot Edgar another warning glance.

Lowering his wine glass, the detective asked, "And what might that be?"

"Lady Woodridge mentioned James Clementine had worn a dinner jacket instead of the customary tailcoats. Stuart White had quite a collection of suits. Some were actually outlandish. The sort of clothes one sees the bright young things wear. Like those wide legged trousers with short cropped coats, usually striped. The fabrics don't even match but I think that's the whole idea. Well, he also had a dinner jacket."

"Is that unusual?" he asked.

Millicent gave it some thought. "No, not really."

Nodding, he picked up his glass.

"Except for one thing," Millicent said.

The detective's hand lowered and he set his glass down again.

"Well, as I said, there I was, putting his clothes away.

Mind you, he didn't complain. Anyone else would, but I think he's used to having someone pick up after him." Millicent glanced at Evie. "I'm sure that suggests he comes from a well-to-do family, but we probably already knew that because of where he lives."

Evie knew Millicent had meandered away from the main topic, so she prompted Millicent, "The dinner jacket."

"What about it, milady?"

"You noticed something about it."

"Yes... Yes, I did. The detective didn't think it was unusual to have a dinner jacket in his wardrobe. What I found unusual was the fact he had a dinner jacket with matching trousers and, right next to it, a pair of trousers but no dinner jacket."

"Ah, I see." Evie nodded.

"Countess?"

Evie looked across the table at Tom. "Millicent is suggesting there is a missing dinner jacket." She turned to Millicent. "Did you ask him about it?"

Millicent grinned. "I did."

"And what did he say?" Evie asked, just in case Millicent was sidetracked again.

"He thought about it for a moment and then he said he'd found a stain on it and he'd sent it away to be fixed. I found that strange because I was let in the house by a butler and I assume he takes care of those sorts of things."

"I don't follow," the detective admitted.

"The dinner jacket, detective. From the start," Evie said, "I wondered about the dinner jacket James Clementine wore. We also wondered where he'd been staying."

"Are you suggesting James Clementine had been wearing Stuart White's jacket and staying with him?"

Evie smiled. "When Tom and I theorize, we take quite a few liberties and allow ourselves a great deal of creativity. It could be something or it could be nothing."

Tom picked up his wine glass and raised it. "Indeed. Lady Woodridge believes Stuart White has been lying. This might be absolute proof he knew James Clementine."

"And why do you think he hasn't owned up to it?" the detective asked, his tone cautious.

"The green fairy might have something to do with it," Millicent suggested.

The detective pushed the words out, "The green fairy?"

"I'd forgotten about *la fée verte.*" Evie leaned back slightly to allow the footman to remove her plate. "We haven't quite worked out the details of this theory but this is where it might all become quite interesting. On the one hand, we think Stuart White is experiencing some of the effects connected with this beverage."

"*La fée verte?*"

"Do keep up, Theo." Althea turned to Millicent. "I assume you found a bottle of Absinthe in Stuart White's room."

Millicent nodded.

"Tom said Stuart White believes he's being followed." Evie shrugged. "This might be the product of his imagination inspired by the beverage."

"But it's illegal," the detective said.

Althea rolled her eyes. "There are so many things that are illegal and yet some people have no trouble getting their hands on them." She looked at Evie. "You have prohibition in your country and yet, I'm sure, people are still enjoying their alcoholic beverages."

"Then again," Evie tapped her wine glass. "Someone might really be following him. How do you know Stuart White didn't witness the incident? He appeared to be well and truly shaken up."

The detective sighed. "So, you think Stuart White knew James Clementine and he quite possibly met him in Paris…"

Althea interrupted by saying, "Where he went to buy his illegal Absinthe."

"You don't need to travel all the way to Paris to obtain an illegal drink. I'm sure of it, after all, you only just suggested it." The detective took out his notebook.

"Yes, but the story Lady Woodridge is creating relies on Stuart White traveling to Paris," Althea explained.

"What about the dinner jacket?" Millicent asked. "You shouldn't forget the dinner jacket because that could be important. It might actually confirm Lady Woodridge's suspicions about Stuart White knowing James Clementine." Millicent nodded. "Detective, you should write that down because, if you're anything like me, you're bound to forget or be sidetracked."

The detective brushed a finger along his temple. "The dinner jacket." He pushed out a breath and made a note of it. "We haven't been able to identify the place where he was staying and, from memory, Lady Woodridge suggested James Clementine might have stayed with someone as a guest," he murmured, almost as if to clarify the point.

"Yes, detective. We are suggesting he stayed with Stuart White and he also borrowed the dinner jacket."

Evie watched him make a few more notes. "Have you tracked down the maker of the shoes?" Evie asked.

"Not yet."

"No one has mentioned motive," Lotte said.

"Lady Woodridge has an interesting theory about that," Tom remarked.

The detective looked at Evie. "Does it, by any chance, have anything to do with Paris?"

Evie couldn't tell if the detective was poking fun at her or being serious. "The theory was actually inspired by you, detective. I'm sure you told us James Clementine had been in Paris and had then traveled to England. Or, perhaps you didn't." She waited a moment for him to confirm or deny it. When he didn't, she continued, "We decided that might be a vital piece of information. In fact, as Althea pointed out, we have based our entire theory on that."

The detective frowned.

Realizing she'd forgotten to make her point, Evie added, "We think something happened in Paris."

"Something?"

Evie shrugged. "He might have seen something or someone."

"I assume your theory relies heavily on the killer also traveling from Paris to England."

"Well, yes. As a matter of fact..." Evie smiled. "We do get carried away. You must think we've been enjoying *la fée verte*."

"The thought didn't even cross my mind." He turned his attention to his food.

Evie suspected he was deep in thought, possibly tossing around everything they'd talked about.

As they neared the end of the meal, he looked up. "Lady Woodridge, do you remember asking me about the young man who'd been fished out of the Thames?"

"Benjamin Hammonds." She looked at Tom. "I take it you haven't found anything else in the newspapers."

"No, I haven't."

"Well, that's strange. If I remember the article correctly, the police were treating his death as suspicious."

"Indeed," the detective agreed. "I have spoken with the detective in charge."

He had her full attention, but she couldn't help interrupting and asking, "Why exactly are they treating the death as suspicious?" She remembered him saying it was probably nothing but a suicide.

He looked around the table, and she imagined him trying to determine the suitability of the subject. He obviously knew his sister very well. Lotte was a seasoned lady detective. Millicent's eyes were wide with interest and Evie had already shown she could bear to hear otherwise unpalatable details.

"There were bruises on his neck."

Signs of a struggle, Evie thought.

"Have the police identified any suspects?"

"No. However…" The detective looked down and appeared to come to some sort of decision. "I mention this now because Benjamin Hammonds had visited Paris." The detective shrugged. "It could be something or it could be nothing."

CHAPTER 17

I *t could be something or it could be nothing?*

Before Evie could determine whether or not the detective was being serious, he checked his watch.

"Is that the time?" And before anyone could confirm the time, he thanked Evie for lunch and stood up.

"Do please stay for some coffee, detective." He couldn't possibly leave now when she had so many questions begging to be answered.

"Perhaps another time, my lady."

Evie's voice hitched. "When did Benjamin Hammonds travel to Paris?" He still needed to confirm or deny this. Evie thought the question would kill two birds with one stone.

The edge of his lip lifted. He regarded Evie with interest. "That's a pertinent question."

"Detective." Evie pushed out a breath. "We've been discussing vague ideas. Being precise would spare us a lot of running around in circles." As she spoke, she wondered if he was going to reveal the information.

"He traveled there six months ago."

Six months ago?

"And James Clementine?" She knew his visit had been more recent but she needed him to confirm it.

His answer was disappointing.

He had been there only a week ago. The times didn't coincide so they couldn't make a connection. However, after a full minute, the detective decided to provide more information.

"Over the past few months, James Clementine traveled there twice. The first time was six months ago."

Evie's lips parted but she didn't speak. She glanced at Tom and knew he had put the two young men in the same place and at the same time.

"Is it possible their deaths are connected?" she finally asked. One young man had drowned and the other one had fallen to his death.

He gave a distracted nod. "We're looking into it." The detective turned to his sister and gave her a pointed look.

Evie imagined he wanted Althea to join him. She watched what could only be described as a private and silent conversation between the siblings.

It all ended with Althea saying, "Lady Woodridge, Millicent has been telling me about your interest in having a portrait painted. We could discuss it over coffee."

"That would be lovely." The idea of wanting to have a portrait painted was news to Evie but she went along with it. Either Althea had no desire to toe the line and comply with her brother's prompt to leave or she actually wanted to remain and discuss the portrait or Lotte's suggestion about becoming a lady detective.

The silent exchange between the siblings resumed and ended when Althea smiled and lifted her chin.

Taking his leave of everyone at the table, the detective sighed and left.

"Just once in my life, I'd like to know what is happening," Millicent murmured.

Evie stood up. "Shall we retire to the drawing room for coffee?"

"Don't you actually mean the library?" Tom asked. "That's where your notes are and we have much to discuss."

"Heavens, yes." Evie's eyes brightened. "I'm keen to hear your thoughts before you leave for your appointment with the tailor."

"Worth a try," Tom whispered.

As they crossed the hall, Millicent sidled up to Evie. "Milady, are you really going to have your portrait painted?"

"I hadn't actually given it any thought."

"I think you should. I hope I didn't speak out of turn earlier. For a moment there I thought the detective was struggling to understand what I was saying."

"You did very well, Millicent. In fact, I believe you encouraged the detective to share the information he had about the young man who was fished out of the Thames."

"Benjamin Hammonds."

Evie nodded. "And that's something else you should be commended for. You did very well to notice it and to bring it to my attention. Thank you, Millicent."

Millicent's cheeks colored. "I'd like to say I'm not used to such praise, but you're always quite generous with it."

"Credit where credit is due, Millicent. Now, do you

have your notebook with you? It would be good if you took some notes."

Millicent dug inside her pocket and produced her small notebook and a fountain pen.

Lotte walked in and sat down, her glass of wine in hand. "Too good to go to waste," she remarked.

Evie stood in the middle of the room, her gaze pensive. "I can't quite decide why the detective revealed that information about Benjamin Hammonds. I only mentioned him briefly and, at the time, he hadn't had any information." She glanced at Althea. "Am I wrong in thinking he had a reason?"

"Theo can be sneaky. Also, he's really not keen on snoopy detectives who don't actually work for the police. He might have been trying to divert your attention. Is the information relevant?"

"Absolutely. It would be interesting to see if they can connect Benjamin Hammonds to either Stuart White or James Clementine." The more she thought about it, the more she believed they were on the right track.

If she traveled to Paris today, she would most likely stay at the Ritz where she would meet friends and acquaintances. Once she returned home, the subject would come up in conversation and, she had no doubt in her mind, there would be remarks such as someone seeing so and so who remembered meeting her.

"Two people who met in Paris dead," Tom mused. "Yes, that would be interesting. Countess, despite what Althea said, I'm sure Theo wants you to solve the case for him. He just doesn't want to make it too easy for you."

Althea snorted. "He'd never admit it but I do believe he values your input."

"Tom thinks the police have circulated a photograph of me so that everyone will recognize me and, quite possibly, stay out of my way."

"Countess! I said no such thing," Tom complained.

"I'm sure you alluded to it." Evie turned to Althea. "Tom and I understand there are boundaries. We certainly don't meddle in police business and we never intrude on their territory."

"But you have solved a few cases," Althea said.

"Accidentally. We merely happened to stumble upon enough clues, which we then tossed around and mulled over." The case would be solved with or without her.

Just then, Evie realized they could walk away from all the unanswered questions and lose themselves in the social activities they had traveled to town for and it wouldn't make a difference to the case.

She tapped the pieces of paper on the table. "Are we going to jump to conclusions and assume the young man who drowned in the Thames met Stuart White and James Clementine? Yes, I think we should. And we now have the advantage of knowing Benjamin Hammonds did not drown himself."

Tom agreed. "We should also remember that Theo believes James Clementine's death is suspicious."

Evie brushed a finger along her chin. "Because there were no witnesses in a house swarming with people." The killer had either taken advantage of an unexpected opportunity or he might have planned ahead. "I think we should focus on Stuart White. After all, he is still alive."

"Would you like me to keep an eye on him?" Tom asked. "If he leaves the house, I could follow him. Who knows? I might encounter the killer following him."

Evie raised her eyebrow. That prompted Tom to check his watch and roll his eyes.

Millicent frowned. As she scribbled away on her notebook, she whispered, "I see." A second later, she shook her head and added, "No, I don't."

Hearing this, Evie said, "Millicent, we are tossing around the idea that a killer followed both young men to London."

Lotte raised her glass. "Motive.

"I'm sorry, Lotte, I'm afraid I can't produce anything new. I still think James Clementine might have seen something." Evie swung away and walked to the window. "At this point, I think anyone could come up with a dozen reasons why these two young men were killed."

Millicent cleared her throat, "They might have witnessed a theft and blackmailed the thief into handing over the loot."

The loot?

Evie turned and smiled at Millicent. "That's very creative."

"I can't claim full ownership of the idea. I'm sure I read something along those lines in one of my penny dreadful stories."

Edgar walked in and set a tray down on the table. "My lady. The dowagers and Toodles are on their way in."

Evie was about to ask how he knew when she heard them talking and laughing.

Toodles asked a footman, "Where are they? The library? Why doesn't that surprise me."

"What did we miss?" Henrietta asked as they walked in. "We have a visitor. And who might you be?"

The detective's sister responded with a smile, "Althea Rawlinson, portrait painter."

"Marvelous. We need some new pictures. Everyone hanging on our walls looks out of date. Sometimes, I feel like a stranger in my own home. Rawlinson? That can't be a coincidence. Are you related to the detective?"

Althea nodded. "He's my brother."

"Althea is going to assist us in investigations," Lotte declared. "At least, she will once I convince her to join us."

Evie helped herself to some coffee. "How was your morning?"

"Quite eventful. I have made progress with two of my bachelors."

"Henrietta stole one of my debutantes," Sara declared. "Where am I going to find another one at such short notice?"

"How did Henrietta manage to do that?" Evie imagined a scene where Henrietta claimed to have seen the Prince of Wales and, of course, Sara would have been distracted...

"I didn't hear the conversation." Sara huffed out a breath. "One moment the bachelor and the debutante looked desperate to escape her and, before I knew what had happened, they were talking as if they'd known each other since birth."

"I will not stand here and defend myself," Henrietta declared. "We have guests arriving soon and I would like to change." Smiling, Henrietta waltzed out of the library, with Toodles and Sara following on her heels.

Evie glanced at Althea. "My apologies, I don't believe you were properly introduced to everyone."

"Fear not," Tom said. "They'll make themselves known to you."

There were times, Evie thought, when she couldn't quite decipher Tom's intentions. His eyes brimmed with amusement so she assumed he found the situation entertaining. However, she couldn't help wondering if he felt trapped by it all. In a sense, he found himself in an impossible situation. His relationship with her meant he had to accept everything and everyone connected to her.

Edgar cleared his throat, without making the slightest effort at subtlety.

"Tom, I believe Edgar is reminding you of your appointment. You don't want to be late."

Tom muttered something under his breath Evie couldn't quite make out and followed Edgar out of the library.

The police had categorized Benjamin Hammonds' death as suspicious because of the bruises found on him. She imagined there had been a struggle, perhaps preceded by an argument.

His death might have been the result of a malicious act, with no rhyme or reason. Benjamin Hammond could have been lured there by the killer or he might have arranged to meet someone, who'd turned out to be a killer. If Benjamin had agreed to a meeting, what had been the reasons behind it, what had been his intention?

Lotte drained the last of her wine. Setting the empty glass down, she said, "Motive."

Yes, indeed.

Motive.

The detective was not in charge of this particular case but what if it was connected to his investigation?

She turned her thoughts to James Clementine. Thanks to Millicent's observations, they had now decided to give serious thought to the possibility he had known Stuart White.

They needed to speak with him.

Frustrated, Evie exclaimed, "Why does anyone kill? For gain. For revenge? Fear? Jealousy?"

Sitting forward, Lotte hummed. "Fear. I like that."

Evie walked in a small, tight circle. "Yes, it rather fits in nicely with the idea of the victim witnessing something. The killer might be afraid of discovery." She stopped. "Tom said Stuart White is afraid and he believes he is being followed. Do his fears have something to do with the case? Are they real or are they a product of his drinking? Or is he afraid because he too had witnessed something?"

Evie and Lotte turned to look at Althea. Noticing this, Althea sat up. "What?"

"Can you think of anything to add?" Evie asked.

"I'm afraid not. I've been listening and thinking Theo should employ some of your tactics."

"Which ones?" Evie asked.

"There's the creative aspect of your theories. You appear to rely on probabilities." She shrugged. "Imagined scenarios."

"Yes, and we are well aware of the fact the police carry out their investigations based on facts and evidence they collect along the way. Unfortunately, we don't have access to that information."

Millicent set the newspapers aside and shot to her feet. "We need some French newspapers." She swung on her feet and marched out of the library.

"I believe Millicent is on a mission to find French newspapers," Lotte said.

That made sense. Millicent had found the article about Benjamin Hammonds in a local newspaper and they were trying to link everything to a meeting in Paris. What if there were other deaths related to this and they took place in Paris?

"Does your entire household become involved in your investigations?" Althea asked.

Evie exchanged a smile with Lotte before saying, "On occasion." Looking at the clock, she shook her head. "We need to turn our thoughts to Parsody's visit. Remember, we wish to find out all we can about her background. Althea, you're welcome to join us. Miss Buchanan is an heiress and might wish to have her portrait painted."

Althea laughed. "I believe I have just been recruited by your agency. What fun."

CHAPTER 18

*W*ith a couple of hours to wait until the guests arrived for afternoon tea, Lotte Mannering retired to one of the rooms to close her eyes and think, Althea set off on a walk, and Evie found herself alone in the library.

Evie expected Millicent to return at any moment, either crestfallen because she hadn't been able to find any French newspapers or, triumphant and carrying a stack of them.

Left alone in the library, Evie spent some time studying the notes she had made and moving the pieces of paper around to see if they could trigger a new idea.

At one point, she decided to close her eyes and empty her mind, and she must have dozed off because when she opened her eyes again, there were three pairs of eyes looking at her.

She shot upright and straightened her skirt. "Good grief. What time is it?"

Toodles teased her, "Did you know you talk in your

217

sleep?"

"I do not. Do I?" Evie looked at the clock and scrambled to her feet. "Heavens, I'm going upstairs to straighten myself. They'll be here at any minute. And… I don't talk in my sleep. What did I say?"

Toodles laughed. "She's not awake yet."

Grumbling, Evie hurried out and rushed up the stairs. She met Lotte, who was coming down the stairs and they both grumbled and continued on their separate ways.

When she made her way back down, Evie headed straight for the drawing room, stopping in the middle of the hall when she saw Tom coming in, with Edgar following him. They both carried a handful of parcels.

Tom's eyebrows were drawn down into a dark scowl and Edgar was looking up at the ceiling. Evie imagined him thanking the heavens for delivering him back to safety.

"Tom. You're back."

"Why do you sound surprised?" He hitched his head toward Edgar. "I had him joined at the hip. If I took off, I would have had to cart him along with me. Can you picture a long voyage with Edgar in tow?"

"I think he would make a terrific traveling companion."

Tom glanced over his shoulder. "Sorry, old chap. Didn't mean to hurt your feelings."

Employing his most dignified tone, Edgar replied, "That's perfectly fine, Mr. Winchester. I understand all too well."

Evie knew she needed to handle the situation with the utmost delicacy. "I see you've returned with parcels. Does that mean your court dress is all ready?"

"Countess," Tom snapped. "Please don't make it worse by referring to these garments as a dress."

"You know what I mean, Tom."

"Yes, and I know you too well. That wasn't just a slip of the tongue. You meant to say *dress*." Tom turned and unloaded his parcels onto Edgar's outstretched arms. "Do with them what you will."

Relieved of his burden, Tom rubbed his hands together. "What did I miss?"

Sounding incredulous, Evie admitted, "I fell asleep."

"You fell asleep? Here I was thinking you would have solved the case by the time I returned." He looked toward the drawing room and then the library. "Where is everyone?"

"I left them in the library but I'm guessing they're now in the drawing room. I was just on my way there." Evie took a step and hesitated.

"What?"

"Nothing but a stray thought, which emerged after my nap. Only, I rushed upstairs so I haven't thought about it too much. I remember entertaining a similar concern a couple of nights ago when we returned from the Upper Brook Street incident."

"Concern? Which one?"

"When we went to the Criterion, the killer could have been there. He could have witnessed you and the detective approaching Stuart White."

"Why do you think that?"

"Because the killer might have followed Stuart White and he might have been waiting for an opportunity. We can't dismiss Stuart White's fears. He must have a reason to feel the way he does."

"I thought you were satisfied to think he was suffering from the effects of Absinthe consumption."

"No, Tom. We can't dismiss his suspicions," Evie insisted.

He appeared to nibble the inside of his lip. "If, as you suggest, the killer was there, he'll know we are somehow involved."

"Tom, I hope you're not about to suggest we walk away."

"No, I wouldn't dream of it, but we should take more care." He frowned. "I didn't see anyone looking suspicious."

"Nor did I. Then again, I don't expect a killer to go around advertising his intentions."

Tom held her gaze for a moment. "You thought he might have been at the Upper Brook Street party."

"Yes."

"In plain sight."

Evie shrugged. "Lauren Gladstone found the body."

"Surely you don't suspect her?"

"We haven't really talked about her. Why should we assume she's innocent?" Evie's shoulders rose and fell. "It's just a thought. Remember, these days, everywhere I look I see suspicious people."

"I didn't see Lauren Gladstone at the Criterion. Then again, I wasn't looking for her."

The clock chimed the hour. Evie signaled toward the drawing room, saying, "We shouldn't keep them waiting. Although, it seems strange to spend the afternoon entertaining a debutante when we should be looking into this matter."

"Perhaps this is precisely what we need."

They headed to the drawing room and found Toodles and the dowagers regaling Caro and Lord Evans with an amusing story about their matchmaking game.

"Evangeline, you have just missed the most amusing tale. Toodles did a wonderful impersonation of Sara."

Taking a seat, Evie greeted Caro and Lord Evans, and asked about their lunch.

"Surprisingly uneventful," Lord Evans said.

"He couldn't stop looking over his shoulder." Caro's eyes lifted heavenward. "It's almost as if he wanted something to happen."

"I thought I'd explained it all to you," Lord Evans complained. "It's the hazards of my profession."

Caro rolled her eyes again. "In the end, I told him we should return to Woodridge House because something was bound to be happening here. I almost changed my mind when I remembered Millicent had said you were entertaining a debutante. I decided not to tell him about it because Henry had spent the morning complaining about seeing nothing but young women running around giggling, and talking over each other. I hope you don't mind us being here."

"Of course, not. The more the merrier." Evie looked toward the door. "Where's Lotte? I saw her coming down…"

"She's with Althea in the library." Henrietta did something Evie had never seen her do. She stretched her arms out and then pressed her hands against her cheeks, in some sort of expression of dismay. "I don't know why it didn't occur to me sooner. I suppose we've all been too preoccupied with debutantes and bachelors."

Evie had no idea what she was referring to.

"Henrietta, you haven't told Evie. Very well, I'll tell her." Sara shifted on her seat and looked at Evie.

"But it's not your tale to tell," Henrietta argued. "If you tell her, you'll make me sound unhinged."

Ignoring Henrietta, Sara said, "They're looking up the name Buchanan in the Who's Who. Henrietta has a copy of Debrett's and the Who's Who by her bedside, and I swear she reads them every night and yet, it didn't occur to mention the obvious. If the Buchanans were anyone of note, they'll be in one of the books."

Evie glanced at Henrietta and saw her having a silent conversation with herself.

She then appeared to come to some sort of agreement with herself and exclaimed, "No, I can't for the life of me remember why I didn't think of suggesting it. I'm sure Sara distracted me. She can be rather a handful." Henrietta turned to the door. "Here they come. No, wait… false alarm."

Standing up, Evie excused herself. "I'll go see what's keeping them."

She crossed the hall, her thoughts on Lauren Gladstone.

"Motive," Evie murmured.

What reason would she have for killing James Clementine? And, if she'd killed James Clementine, had she also killed Benjamin Hammonds?

Try as she did, she couldn't come up with a single stray thought that might cast some light on the problem.

When she entered the library, she found Lotte, Althea, and Millicent standing by the table, poring through a pile of magazines.

Seeing her, Millicent apologized for taking so long in

returning. "I tried six of the neighboring houses before I found one with a subscription to French magazines, but no newspapers."

"You did very well, Millicent."

"We're glad Millicent met with some success. Unfortunately, we can't say the same for our efforts." Lotte tapped a large tome. "We looked for the Buchanan family of Lancashire but didn't find anything in the Who's Who."

"That's odd. That book is supposed to list everyone of note, but it explains why Henrietta has never heard of the family."

A footman appeared at the door and alerted Evie to the arrival of Parsody Jane Buchanan and Mr. Jameson.

Evie looked at the stack of magazines. As Millicent continued to go through them, she wished their guests would have a change of heart and leave. Right that moment, she wanted to remain in the library and recruit Toodles and the dowagers to help her comb through magazines.

She wouldn't be surprised to discover some of the people who had come to town for the social season had recently visited Paris and might have come across either of the victims or even Stuart White.

"Milady." Millicent drew Evie's attention to one of the magazines.

Thinking she had found something relevant to the investigation, Evie leaned in. "What is it, Millicent?"

"This gown. It's beautiful."

Evie agreed. "However, Millicent, do please remember—"

"And look at this young woman sitting in the front row of this fashion parade."

Evie studied the photograph. "I don't recognize her."

"You don't have to. The article identifies her and the other young ladies watching the fashion parade. It's Lauren Gladstone."

Evie turned to the front cover page and looked for the date. "This is from six months ago."

~

Moments later...

Evie left Millicent to continue searching through the magazines and made her way to the drawing room. She found everyone chatting, but it didn't take her long to sense the tension in the room. Awkward tension, she thought.

"Here's Evangeline." Henrietta gave a tentative smile.

"I do apologize for my tardiness." She sensed Lotte and Althea behind her. Stepping aside, she made the introductions, saying, "Of course, you know Lotte Mannering and this is Althea Rawlinson. She's a portrait painter."

Mr. Jameson stood beside Parsody Jane Buchanan who sat opposite Toodles and the dowagers, while Caro and Lord Evans sat on another sofa.

"Parsody was just telling us how excited she is to be presented and since she doesn't know anyone here, I've been telling her about the people she should meet."

Evie noticed Henrietta sounded almost smug. Had she managed to win Parsody over to her side?

"And I was about to ask about the Buchanan family." Henrietta shifted her attention to Mr. Jameson. "I knew an Orson Buchanan, but that was many years ago. I don't know what has become of him." Henrietta chuckled. "Yes, Orson Buchanan. That was his name. Was he related?"

Evie couldn't remember Henrietta ever mentioning Orson Buchanan. Had she just made him up?

"Parsody was far too young then," Mr. Jameson explained. "Her recollections are vague and, considering her loss, she sometimes prefers not to remember."

Evie and everyone else turned their attention to Parsody as if by looking at her they could all somehow perceive some of her hidden memories.

It took a moment for Evie to realize he hadn't actually answered the question.

Henrietta sighed. "So sad. Losing your parents at such a tender age."

Parsody had as yet to say anything. Looking morose, she seemed to be quite content to let Mr. Jameson do all the talking for her. The moment the footman set a tray of cakes on the table she instantly brightened and didn't wait for an invitation to help herself.

Despite knowing Parsody hailed from Lancashire, Evie wanted to try to establish a more precise location. Getting up to join Parsody, Evie asked, "Which part of the country did you say you were from?"

The young woman's cheeks colored. To Evie's relief, she provided an answer, albeit a vague one.

"North." Parsody bit into a piece of cake.

"Will you be settling there again?"

Studying her cake, she shrugged, "W-we haven't decided yet."

They were joined by Henrietta, who asked, "Have you practiced your curtsy?"

"Mr. Jameson has taken care of all that. He hired an instructor."

"Has he also organized your presentation gown and ostrich feathers?" Henrietta asked.

"Yes. I had the gown made in Paris. I had to have some minor alterations, but now it's perfect."

When Parsody took a quick bite of her cake, Evie wondered if she felt she had said too much.

Lotte joined them and asked, "Where in the north did you live?"

Having finished her cake, she eyed the serving platter and, reaching for another piece of cake, she murmured, "Lancashire."

That confirmed the information Tom had found in the newspaper article but it didn't tell them anything new.

Lotte gave a firm nod, which Evie interpreted as determination to get more out of Parsody.

Looking around the drawing room, Evie saw Lord Evans and Tom chatting with Mr. Jameson who kept glancing at Parsody.

She gravitated toward them and found them talking about Paris. At the first opportunity, Evie asked him why he had chosen to travel with Parsody instead of remaining in England where he could provide her with a stable home.

"Business interests took me abroad. It seemed more practical to travel together. For a while there, of course, I thought it safer to live in Switzerland."

"Did you spend much time in Paris?" Tom asked.

"Several months." Mr. Jameson nodded. "We took a house. It seemed easier that way."

Easier than what?

Evie puzzled over his responses. He seemed to provide information without saying very much.

"Parsody was saying you hadn't decided if you'll be staying on. Is the house in Lancashire still open?"

"I organized tenants to move in. They're quite fond of the place and have been living there for a number of years."

Evie smiled. "I must say, you have Lady Henrietta intrigued. She prides herself on knowing everyone. And yet, for the life of her, she can't place the Buchanans."

Mr. Jameson looked down at his cup of tea. "Shortly before their death, Parsody's mother inherited the house and estates from a distant relative. I'm sure Lady Woodridge has heard of Sir Matthew Devlin. If not, she must surely have heard of the Devlin coal mine."

Coal! That explained Parsody's great wealth, and she now knew why they hadn't been able to find the Buchanan name.

As Tom and Lord Evans turned their attention to the coal mining industry, Evie wandered off and switched her thoughts over to her latest suspect.

Lauren Gladstone.

She couldn't be more than twenty years old.

Would someone so young be capable of cold-blooded murder? And what possible reason would she have?

She had been in Paris six months ago and they now knew both victims had been there at the same time.

Right in the midst of that thought, Henrietta sidled up to her and whispered, "I might let Sara have the girl. Never mind her wealth, I believe Holmes has more personality in his little paw."

Evie tried to remember Lotte's first impression of

Parsody. It hadn't been kind. "She definitely lacks exposure to society. At least we know more about her background."

Evie told Henrietta about Sir Matthew Devlin and the Devlin coal mine.

Henrietta glanced over her shoulder. "Yes, but what do we know about Mr. Jameson?"

Heavens. "I'm just going to have to take my chances. Although, I have no idea how I'll explain Parsody's lack of polish." Evie had organized a ball for Caro at Woodridge House. Now, she would have to include Parsody.

Evie looked over her shoulder and saw Caro chatting with the young debutante. Caro seemed to be doing all the talking. Lotte and Althea stood to one side studying Parsody while Tom and Lord Evans continued their conversation with Mr. Jameson.

Evie tilted her head in thought.

"I know that look," Henrietta murmured. "What are you thinking? Let me guess..." Henrietta turned slightly and followed Evie's gaze. "Have we asked if Miss Buchanan and Mr. Jameson encountered James Clementine in Paris?"

Evie gaped at Henrietta.

"Is that what you were thinking? Did I guess right?"

"No, but it's a splendid idea."

Henrietta looked overjoyed. "I always knew I had it in me. May I be the one to ask?"

"By all means, please do."

Without any need for further encouragement, Henrietta wove her way around the drawing room. For some strange reason, she headed toward Parsody the long way around, along the way stopping to admire a vase and a painting. Evie imagined Henrietta wanting to be discreet and employ the tactic of deception.

As she watched Henrietta's meandering journey toward Parsody, Lotte and Althea joined her.

"I'm afraid my perception of Parsody has not wavered," Lotte declared. "She is a monument to wallflowers." Lotte shook her head. "Did I actually suspect Parsody of being a sheep in wolf's clothing? I can't imagine why."

"But you did! At least we know there are no skeletons in her closet," Evie mused. "No one that dull could possibly be hiding anything."

Lotte glanced at Mr. Jameson. "Have you learned anything new about her guardian?"

What if *he* was hiding something?

"I'd like to think he was named guardian because Parsody's parents had absolute trust in him." She looked toward the door.

"Are we expecting someone else?" Lotte asked.

Laughing, Evie said, "No, but I've become accustomed to expecting interruptions."

She bit the edge of her lip. Her list of unanswered questions and concerns had not diminished. She hoped Millicent had been keeping track of them by writing them down.

Thinking about Millicent, she remembered her discovery of the missing dinner jacket. An idea sprung to mind. "The label. Why didn't we think of it before?"

In response to Althea's look of puzzlement, Lotte murmured, "She'll explain it all as soon as it becomes clear in her mind."

"Dear me. It's so simple. There is one foolproof way to

find out if the jacket worn by James Clementine belonged to Stuart White. If the label matches the trousers, then…"

Lotte finished the thought for her, "Then we will have proof Stuart White knew him."

"Yes." Evie saw Henrietta move away from Parsody and head toward Mr. Jameson.

Sounding excited, Althea asked, "Are you going to tell Theo or would you like me to do it?"

"Althea, that's a wonderful idea. I'm sure it will be more expedient if you do it. He has access to the jacket and, of course, he can gain access to the trousers. There's a telephone in the library."

Evie considered joining Henrietta but she was already headed toward them. Even before she reached them, Evie could tell she looked disappointed.

Reaching them, Henrietta said, "I'm afraid I got no response from them."

"Nothing?"

"The name James Clementine drew a complete blank from Parsody. I'm not sure how that girl hopes to find a husband. I phrased the question in such a way as to entice her interest, but she didn't ask a single question about him."

"That is odd. His name has been in the newspapers." Then again, Evie thought, not everyone read the daily news so she couldn't really expect it to be common knowledge. "What about Mr. Jameson?"

"He gave it some thought and admitted the name sounded familiar but not because he might have met him, he made that perfectly clear. He then explained he and Parsody had not mingled in society whilst in Paris. Then, he remembered reading about him, which explains why the name sounded familiar." Henrietta lowered her voice to a whisper. "Lord Evans looks highly suspicious."

"Of what?"

"I'm certain he thinks you're involved in some sort of clandestine investigation."

Evie looked at Lord Evans and caught him looking at her. Not long after their marriage, he had asked Caro to avoid becoming involved in investigations. Evie knew she had been labeled a bad influence. While Caro had taken a stand, Evie didn't wish to cause any trouble for her.

"I should alert Edgar," Henrietta murmured, "he'll want to know there are two more guests for dinner."

Evie turned to her. "What? Who else is coming?"

"Mr. Jameson and Parsody. I took the liberty of inviting them. The girl has to start somewhere and it will give me an opportunity to observe her table manners. I hope you don't mind." Henrietta must have noticed Evie's dismay. "Oh, dear. You do mind."

Evie set Henrietta at ease. Although, she would have preferred to have dinner among friends and family so they could discuss the developments of the case.

Shortly after Henrietta delivered the news, Mr. Jameson and Parsody thanked them for afternoon tea, and took their leave, presumably to return home to rest and change for dinner.

Edgar took care of showing them out and Evie took the opportunity to sink into a chair and close her eyes.

"Countess?"

"I think we'll need to cancel our engagements tonight. We have guests for dinner."

CHAPTER 19

*A*lthea walked in just as Tom was handing Evie a glass of brandy.

Caro went to sit beside her. "If it's all too much, Henry and I could entertain ourselves tonight elsewhere."

"Heavens, no. I'll need all the support I can get. Do please have dinner with us."

Caro bobbed her head from side to side.

"Oh, dear. You actually wanted to escape the awkward situation."

"Did I say that? I'm sure I didn't." Caro looked down at her hands and smiled. "I must admit, Miss Buchanan requires a lot of patience and effort, but you can rely on us."

"Thank you."

Tom chortled. "They might actually become more interesting in the evening."

"One can only hope." Evie looked up. "Althea. What did your brother think of the information you gave him?"

"He welcomed it." Althea looked around the room.

Everyone except Caro had sat down with a glass of brandy. "Have I missed something?"

Henrietta put her hand up. "I suppose I should own up to the blunder."

"Henrietta, you meant well. In fact, you were quite gracious. I can't exactly say the same for myself. I couldn't wait to get rid of them," Evie admitted and explained the rest to Althea. She watched the young woman's expression change from puzzled to amused. At some point, Evie thought, she would have to become accustomed to people having that reaction about her family.

"If it's any consolation, Theo actually promised... Well, I made him promise to keep us informed."

That sounded promising. Evie looked at the clock and hoped he chose to share his findings well before Mr. Jameson and Parsody returned for dinner because she would want to discuss the development with the others.

Henrietta shook her head and apologized again.

Taking a sip of his brandy, Tom said, "You really shouldn't feel guilty. I thought he'd actually invited himself."

Evie sat up. "What?"

"I don't recall the exact wording, but I think he suggested he and Parsody would be dining alone. Again." Tom nodded. "Yes, he emphasized that part and that's when Henrietta suggested they join us." He looked at Lord Evans. "Do you remember how he phrased it?"

"What? Oh, I'm sorry. I'm afraid I lost track of the conversation. The man has a knack for saying a great deal without actually saying anything."

"How true and frustrating. As well as puzzling." Henrietta raised a finger as if to say something else and then shook her head. "No, I don't understand the fellow."

Someone hurried toward the drawing room.

Henrietta clapped. "Goodie. Someone is coming. It just occurred to me that if we sit here long enough, the killer might actually make an entrance and reveal himself."

Everyone turned toward the door.

The steps slowed down.

Finally, Millicent appeared and whispered, "Milady."

Evie stood up and excused herself.

"Milady." Millicent sounded out of breath. "I bring you good tidings."

Evie couldn't begin to imagine what news she was about to deliver.

"I took a break from perusing the magazines, mostly because I wasn't sure what I was looking for. Anyhow, I went to confront the milliner." Millicent shook her head. "I gave that milliner a good piece of my mind. Now he will stop at nothing to make sure he makes up for the trouble he caused with his blunder. I do believe you will be receiving special treatment from now on. He made a mistake, milady."

Confused, Evie asked, "What does that mean?"

"I came back as quickly as I could to deliver the news. The ostrich feathers, milady. They're white. I mean, they were supposed to be white, after all. I told him how much trouble he caused. Of course, I didn't give him all the details. I wouldn't want Lady Evans' drinking spree or Mr. Winchester's hunt for a special license to be spread about."

Evie thanked her. She knew she ought to feel relieved,

but a part of her had accepted the fact she would be attending the presentation as Nicholas' widow.

"That's not all, milady." Millicent pointed to a table. "I found more magazines."

"Well done, Millicent."

"If you need me, I will be in the library."

Evie returned to the drawing room and shared the news.

"What do you mean it was a mistake?" Henrietta exclaimed. "Does that man not realize the trouble he caused? He threw the household into an upheaval."

Tom patted his coat pocket. "I got a special license. I'm sure it will come in handy."

"I suppose we must look on the bright side. If you hadn't dashed off, you would not have encountered Stuart White or followed him to the Automobile Club." Evie sat down. "I wonder…"

"What?" everyone chorused.

Shrugging, Evie said, "It's far too late to invite Lauren Gladstone."

"And Stuart White?" Lotte asked.

"Yes. It would be interesting to see how they react to each other's presence but, as I said, it's too late."

Henrietta and Sara held a murmured conversation. After which, they both stood up.

What were they up to? "Henrietta? Sara?"

"You'll have to excuse us, Evangeline. We have some business we need to attend to. And, don't worry, Evangeline. We will alert Edgar to the possibility of extra guests for dinner." Turning to Althea, Henrietta said, "Althea, would you care to join us?"

Looking confused, Althea hesitated for a moment. Then, she stood up and followed them out.

Tom laughed. "Like a lamb to the slaughter. I wonder if she realizes, now that she has met us, her life will never be the same." He picked up the bottle of brandy. "More brandy?"

"I think I'm almost ready to have one," Caro admitted.

Lord Evans cleared his throat.

"What?"

"Your memory seems to have faded. Only a few hours ago, you were swearing you would never again indulge."

"Then, will someone please tell me what is happening?"

"I'm not sure," Evie admitted. "I suspect Henrietta and Sara will try to coerce Lauren Gladstone into coming here this evening, and I think Althea has been given the task of luring her brother here with Stuart White in tow."

Tom agreed. "Yes, that's my guess."

Caro huffed out a breath. "At the risk of sounding rather slow... Why?"

"Lady Woodridge believes Miss Gladstone will recognize Stuart White," Lord Evans explained.

Caro scowled at her husband. "I thought you weren't paying attention."

"I'm afraid I cannot escape my vocation, my dear."

Evie crossed her arms and frowned. On the bright side, she commended Henrietta for taking the initiative. Finally, they could answer one nagging question, but where did that leave them?

If they knew each other and they had met in Paris six months before, what did that signify?

"Countess."

"Yes, Tom."

"Could you please share your thoughts?"

Agreeing, Evie asked, "What do you think Stuart White's reaction will be to seeing Lauren Gladstone?"

"We might need some coffee." Tom walked to the fireplace and pulled the bell cord. He then sat down opposite Evie. "Earlier, you'd begun to suspect Lauren Gladstone. If you are correct, then Stuart White will express surprise. Actually, we've already seen how he reacts when surprised so he might try to flee."

At which point, Evie thought, the detective would want to subject Stuart White to a series of questions. "Heavens, what if Mr. Jameson and Miss Buchanan latch onto us? We'll never be rid of them?"

Lotte's eyebrows hitched up, while the others stared at Evie without blinking.

Noticing this, Evie cringed and apologized. "Tom asked me to share my thoughts. I'm afraid that one slipped out and has nothing to do with the investigation."

Caro worried her bottom lip. "I'm afraid we can't escape their acquaintance now. Let's hope they tire of London and return to Paris. We should definitely avoid any talk of house parties, just in case they decide to invite themselves."

"How exactly did you come to meet them?" Lord Evans asked.

Evie looked at Lotte who confessed to introducing them to her.

"Mr. Jameson found us." Evie looked up in thought. "Lotte, he must have come across one of your advertisements."

Lotte agreed. "I should freshen them up and change the wording in such a way as to discourage dull people."

Lord Evans stood up. "I think a walk will do us good."

Smiling, Caro joined him. "You just want to take me away from temptation."

"Temptation?"

"Yes, the evil drink."

As they made their way out of the drawing room, Lord Evans whistled a soft tune which resembled the sailor's ditty Caro had sung the previous night.

Lotte excused herself saying she needed to return home to change clothes for the evening.

Toodles set down her glass, saying, "I think I'll take advantage of the peace and quiet."

"Speaking of quiet," Evie said, "I didn't hear you say anything about our guests."

"Birdie, sometimes, it's best to adhere to the old adage. If you don't have something nice to say, don't say anything at all."

"I hope you won't develop a migraine and bow out of tonight."

"I wouldn't dream of forgoing the entertainment."

Toodles made her way out, leaving Tom and Evie alone in the drawing room.

"And suddenly, it's just the two of us. I can't remember the last time we were alone together. Should we go see what the dowagers and Althea are up to?" Tom suggested.

"I'm not sure how to interpret that. Are you saying you don't wish to be alone with me? That's what it sounded like."

"Yes, you're right. In that case, I suggest we follow Henry's suggestion and go out for a brief walk."

"I'll fetch my hat."

"And I'll get Holmes. I'm sure he'll appreciate a walk."

Moments later, they were standing outside Woodridge House.

"Which way?" Tom asked.

"I'd like to avoid Grosvenor Square, please."

Tom laughed. "Are you trying to avoid your new friends?"

"Tom, you seem to forget what happened the last time I encountered one of my unsavory acquaintances. In case you have, I'll remind you."

"No need. I can never forget the reasons why we stumbled upon a car rally." He gestured to the right, away from Grosvenor Square.

Evie slipped her arm through his. While Tom took a step, she dug her heels in.

"What? Did you forget something?"

"No." Lifting her chin, she murmured something under her breath.

"I didn't catch that."

Evie rolled her eyes. "It's a woman's prerogative to change her mind."

"Good heavens. You want to retrace our steps."

Evie grinned. "How did you guess?"

"I didn't. I believe I have acquired the ability to read your mind and I'm quaking in my boots."

"You're not wearing boots. You're wearing lace-up shoes."

"You know perfectly well what I mean."

"Yes, I suppose I do. Anyhow, you must indulge me. Retracing our steps might freshen our minds and provide information we hadn't thought about before."

Tom chortled. "If we missed anything it's because we have been otherwise engaged with your bizarre family."

Holmes barked.

"My feelings precisely. Tom! I'm shocked."

"But not surprised, I'm sure."

Evie lifted her chin. "You've always known full well what you were getting into, so if this is your idea of backing out of our wedding... then, I'm afraid I will have to object."

"Get out of our wedding? Are you mad? After all the trouble I went to obtain a special license?" He watched her for a moment. "I see. You're teasing me. You've become quite adept at that."

"You've taught me well, Mr. Winchester. Now, let's focus. This is where we heard the scream."

Holmes sniffed the air.

"Yes, and we had to decide where it came from."

They both looked down at Holmes. He took a step in one direction, hesitated, and then led them toward Upper Brook Street.

Evie tried her best to ignore the passersby and the motor cars driving by.

"We only heard one motor car drive by. Otherwise, the streets were rather quiet. If someone had run away from the scene, I believe we would have heard them. Assuming they left the house."

When they reached the corner, they stopped for a moment before crossing the street.

"We picked Stuart White as someone standing out from the crowd."

Evie remember Tom had approached the young man. "I didn't realize you carried a lighter. You don't smoke."

"They can come in handy. Someone is always after a light." He stopped and looked back and then toward Upper Brook Street. "We suspected the killer made his escape along this way. What if he headed in the opposite direction?"

"That's possible. However..."

Tom nodded. "Yes, however, everyone was looking that way, waiting for the police to arrive. Someone would have remembered seeing him leave." He cleared his throat. "Assuming it's a man."

They continued walking in silence. Half an hour later, they headed back.

"Anything?" he asked.

Evie laughed. "You make me sound like a medium, and I have just the perfect name for myself, Madame know-it-all."

They turned the corner into North Audley Street and saw the Duesenberg and Henrietta and Sara entering the house.

"I thought they were in the library. I guess their business took them out of the house. I wonder how they fared." She hoped they'd succeeded. Although, their success needed to be matched by the detective's willingness to bring Stuart White to Woodridge House.

"You're not hurrying your step," Tom said.

"All good things come to those who wait."

"Admit it, you're afraid of what we'll learn."

Evie took a deep swallow. "I'm afraid Henrietta has shown an unpredictable side to her I hadn't known she possessed."

Tom hummed. "We should be ready for anything."

CHAPTER 20

*H*enrietta, the Dowager Countess of Woodridge, had asked for a favor.

"I'm still not sure," Evie murmured, "but I think I am now indebted to Henrietta."

"Sorry, milady. What was that?" Millicent asked as she emerged from the boudoir.

"Just talking to myself, Millicent. Is that the dress I'm wearing tonight?"

"Yes, I hope you don't mind. Since you won't be required to wear black ostrich feathers for the presentation and you seemed so accepting of it and, in fact, you were even resigned to it and said it was perfect as it would…" Millicent floundered. "Anyhow…"

Evie watched Millicent stare into space and blink. She knew Millicent had been distracted by something and had lost track of what she wanted to say, so she decided to help her out. "You thought I might want to wear something black tonight. Yes, that is a perfect suggestion. Thank you, Millicent."

"That's not to say you should wear black until Mr. Winchester decides to finally drag you... I mean..."

"Yes, I know what you mean, Millicent, and you are quite right."

Millicent inspected the beaded dress and murmured, "It might be an omen, me choosing this dress for you, milady."

"How so?"

"You and Mr. Winchester always spend several days digging around and playing with ideas and suddenly, everything begins to make sense, or you hit upon an idea which leads you to identify the guilty party. I suppose what I'm trying to say is that black is a fitting color to wear when you're about to make a grand declaration. You see, if you wore something bright and cheerful, everyone would think you are ghoulish, looking quite jolly when you point the finger of guilt at someone."

"Won't they hold the same opinion when they see me wearing black?"

"No, because you won't be wearing cheerful colors."

"That's a brilliant deduction, Millicent."

"Would you like to wear the black ostrich feathers tonight? Perhaps just one. The milliner wanted them back, I'm sure he did, but I held on to them. After all, he made the blunder and that set off a series of events, which I hold him totally responsible for."

Evie thought it might be over the top but she didn't want to disappoint Millicent.

"Very well. It might bring us luck. With so much black, we're bound to have a positive result tonight." As she spoke, she crossed her fingers.

They had set the scene and the players would be in

place. Tonight, they would have some key questions answered and they would either prove her theory correct or completely quash it.

She finished dressing and surprised herself by saying, "I've been entertaining an idea but I believe it had a lot to do with us wishing we could be rid of Mr. Jameson and Miss Buchanan."

"From what you've told me about them, they sound like an odd pair, milady."

"Yes, they are. Anyhow, the night all this happened, Mr. Winchester and I saw a taxicab drive by. We wondered if the killer had headed away from Upper Brook Street and now I'm wondering if he might have changed his mind and actually jumped in the taxicab."

"And how does Mr. Jameson fit into your theory?"

"Well, the taxicab drove by and headed toward Grosvenor Square. It then stopped. I assume a passenger got out. Then the taxicab drove back along Upper Brook Street and that's where Mr. Winchester hailed it. You see, if someone climbed out of the taxicab in Grosvenor Square, it would be quite a coincidence because Mr. Jameson is staying there."

"And he would be guilty and hauled off to prison and you wouldn't risk having him invite himself again."

Evie grinned. Lowering her voice, she admitted, "Yes, it's rather wicked of me."

Millicent's eyes lowered. "And what would happen to poor Miss Buchanan? Wouldn't you feel responsible for her? If you did, and I'm sure you would because you're that sort of person, you'd have to invite her to stay with you at Halton House and Lady Henrietta and Lady Sara would have to join forces and try to find her a husband."

Evie had no answer for that particular scenario. Millicent was right. If anything happened to Mr. Jameson, Miss Buchanan would become her responsibility.

"Yes, well... it was only wishful thinking." Driven by a desire to be rid of them, she thought. "Admittedly, I do sometimes get carried away. This might be a lesson for me." Evie nodded. "Facts. I should adopt a professional approach and do as the police do. Gather the facts and follow the trail."

She finished dressing in silence.

Millicent fixed her hair and decided against using the black ostrich feather, saying it might be too much.

"You're right, Millicent. You always have such a good eye. Thank you."

"I haven't finished going through all the fashion magazines, milady. The detective will most likely want to use the library initially so I'll wait until everyone goes in for dinner and then go down and fetch them and bring them up. If I find anything, I'll send a footman in with a note."

Thanking her, Evie made her way down and encountered Tom waiting for her at the foot of the stairs. Holmes sat beside him and when he saw Evie, he wagged his tail.

"Holmes seems to approve," Tom said. "I do too. You look splendid."

"Thank you. You look rather fetching in your tailcoat. Have the others come down?"

"Only briefly. I saw them appear at the top of the stairs but they stopped, turned around and disappeared."

"That's odd."

"I assume it had something to do with the fact they were all wearing blue. I hope they coordinated their renewed efforts, otherwise they might all emerge wearing the same color again." He gestured toward the library. "Althea is waiting in the library and the detective has just arrived. He's with her." Tom lowered his voice. "I sensed some tension between them. I believe Theo objects to her becoming involved."

"It's Theo now?"

Tom grinned. "That's what Althea calls him and Theodore sounds too formal."

"And I suppose I'm still to call him detective." She looked toward the library. "Is Stuart White with him?"

"No."

"No?"

"Stuart White is outside in a police vehicle."

"Is he under arrest?"

"It's a tactic. Theo wants to wait for Lauren Gladstone to arrive first." He tapped the side of his nose. "It's all about timing, my dear, and the element of surprise." Tom nudged his head toward the library. "Shall we?"

"What about Lotte? Has she arrived?"

Tom shook his head.

"We can proceed without her."

"I'm afraid we'll have to."

Evie tried to picture the evening unfolding and could not see beyond that precise moment. "Yes, I'm as ready as I'll ever be."

They entered the library and found the detective and Althea glaring at each other.

Tom whispered, "First task of the evening, Countess. Break the ice."

"Detective, thank you for coming at such short notice."

The detective swung toward Evie. "Lady Woodridge."

His tension melted away. "The labels matched." He could not have been more succinct.

She had to ask the obvious question. "Did Stuart White own up to knowing James Clementine?"

"He did."

"And they met in Paris?"

"I'm afraid that was as much information as I managed to get out of him. Unfortunately, I found him in a state of inebriation."

Evie couldn't help asking, "Is he really drunk or is he pretending?"

"I suppose we will soon find out." The detective checked his watch. "I take it Lauren Gladstone is about to arrive?"

"Yes, she should be here soon. Would you like a drink?"

The detective declined the offer saying he should keep a clear head.

Evie joined Althea and picked up one of the magazines piled up on a table in front of the sofa.

Althea whispered, "Theo's been glaring at me so I'm distracting myself with these."

"I guess he's not at all pleased with your new venture."

"He is livid and I can tell because he hasn't spoken a word to me. You see, he's afraid of losing his temper and shouting." She tilted her head. "Sometimes, I think he's an odd creature. He still believes his silence will make me see reason."

"I'm sure he'll soon become accustomed to the idea," Evie offered.

"My brother is rather attached to resisting change. You should have heard him when I decided I wanted to become a portrait painter. He wanted to investigate my clients before allowing me to spend any time with them. In the end, I had to work in secret." She smiled. "It was actually quite thrilling. When he seemed to become resigned to the idea of me trotting off to strangers' houses, I knew he was up to something and, sure enough, he'd been having me followed to make sure I arrived and left safely." Althea drummed her fingers on her lap. "The waiting is making me anxious."

Evie didn't want to make matters worse by admitting she felt on edge. "Has Henrietta spoken to you about having her portrait painted?"

"Yes, she's quite keen. I believe I have been invited to Halton House."

"You'll be very welcome there."

Althea straightened the hem of her dress. "You should know Lady Sara has also expressed an interest."

"And Toodles?"

Althea smiled. "Yes, I was leading up to that."

"They should sit together." Evie looked up in thought. "Then again, perhaps not."

"What do you mean?"

"You'll soon find out. I wouldn't want to spoil the surprise for you." Smiling, Evie turned the page and skimmed the contents. "Oh." Without looking up, she sensed Tom turning to look at her. Evie sat up. "It's an article and Parsody is mentioned." The article was accompanied by a photograph of a mannequin modeling a dress. "Monsieur Dubois held a private showing at her home." She continued reading. When she reached the end of the page, she realized there was more on the next page.

Evie looked up, "Monsieur Dubois must have been

keen to secure her business." She turned the page and, as she was about to read the rest of the article, she noticed another photograph had been included.

Evie stared at it. After a moment, she held the magazine up for a closer look.

Setting the magazine down, she looked up and exclaimed, "I know who the killer is."

Everyone except Althea stilled.

Leaning in, Althea looked at the photograph. "Well, that's interesting."

Tom stepped forward and looked at the photograph. He was followed by the detective.

Evie stood up and walked to the table where she found the notes she had made earlier. She arranged the separate pieces of paper in a different order and added several more notes.

Tom came to stand beside her and was joined by the detective and Althea.

"Countess? Please tell me you're about to say you found a motive."

"That photograph raises a question we hadn't considered or even imagined." She tapped the notes she'd made. "If I'm right, then we have our motive." She made another note. "Remember how I suggested someone had seen something?"

Tom nodded.

Evie scribbled on another piece of paper.

The detective's eyebrows curved up. "I think you might be right."

Yes, but how did they prove it?

Evie stepped back from the table. "We need a timeline

of events for James Clementine and we can't really establish one because he's dead."

The detective nodded. "He was there six months ago and, again, three weeks ago."

"And that's when he set off to London."

To meet his death, Evie thought.

The detective raked his fingers through his hair. "We'll have to work very quickly."

Edgar walked in. "Lady Gladstone and Miss Gladstone have arrived, my lady. I have shown them through to the drawing room where Lady Henrietta, Toodles and Lady Sara are entertaining them."

"Edgar, do you have any impressions about them?"

He seemed struck by the question but recovered promptly. "Miss Gladstone does not look pleased. However, Lady Gladstone is smiling."

Evie hadn't asked Henrietta how she'd managed to talk them into coming. She only knew Henrietta had asked for a favor. That meant she was now beholden to Lady Gladstone. That wouldn't sit well with Henrietta who was usually the one calling in favors.

Thanking Edgar, Evie turned back to the table.

The detective studied the notes. Stepping back from the table, he adjusted his tie. "We should proceed as planned. I will bring Stuart White in."

That surprised Evie. She had expected the detective to ask for a full explanation of the photograph they'd seen. The notes she had added raised a few key questions and made a strong case to support what she had been suggesting all along.

James Clementine had seen something in Paris and

that knowledge had caused his death, but they still needed proof.

Evie imagined the detective would need to contact his counterpart in Paris and they, in turn, would need to make further enquiries to establish some irrefutable facts.

"Lady Woodridge, I believe you have the situation in hand. However, as I said, we should proceed as planned."

When he stepped out of the library, Althea explained, "That means he has placed his trust in your hands. And that means he actually trusts your judgment. Well done."

"Yes, but why? I only provided a setting to prove one of my theories, although, the fact the labels match is enough for me. Of course, it would be better if Stuart White could sober up and answer some questions. I would dearly like to know if he met James Clementine in Paris recently or six months ago." She pointed to the magazine. "That photograph changes everything and I'm not entirely sure I can fill in all the gaps." Turning, she looked at the door, which stood open.

A moment later, Edgar stepped aside to allow the detective to enter. He was accompanied by Stuart White. If he was drunk, he appeared to have forgotten about it.

The detective made the introductions. When Stuart saw Tom, he tensed. A second later he appeared to recognize him either from the night of the incident or the night at the Criterion. He looked confused. Evie wondered if he was thinking about the night James Clementine had been killed or the night Tom and the detective had approached him at the Criterion.

Evie had no idea what story the detective had used to lure Stuart White here. He wasn't under arrest, but he appeared to be under police custody, at least until he answered some questions.

Evie tore her eyes away from Stuart White and looked at Althea. She remained seated and she was reading the article about Parsody Jane Buchanan.

Yes, she had discovered the killer. Lotte wasn't in the library. Regardless, Evie could hear her ask, "Motive."

What had driven the killer to target two people?

CHAPTER 21

*T*hey had already discussed the sequence of events. Althea had taken care of informing the detective and she had been rather pleased about issuing orders to her brother.

Evie gestured to one of the chairs while Tom poured him a drink. As he handed it to Stuart White, Evie wasted no time in saying, "You met James Clementine in Paris. That much we know." In actual fact, she had guessed and her entire theory depended on Stuart having met James.

He looked surprised. Taking a quick sip of his drink, he then shook his head. "What makes you say that?"

"We have a witness who placed you in Paris six months ago." Of course, they didn't, but he didn't know that.

Instead of denying it, Stuart White finished his drink and held the glass out for a refill.

Evie wanted to press him for more information about his friendship. Instead, an idea sprung to mind. Any minute now, Lauren Gladstone would walk through the door. Her reaction to seeing Stuart White would hopefully reveal something that would connect them. If that failed, Evie expected Stuart White's reaction to give them away. He was certainly primed for it.

However, after seeing that photograph of Parsody, she needed to establish a new connection. Even if she succeeded, Evie knew she would have to be creative and fill in the gaps herself.

"We know James Clementine met Parsody Jane Buchanan. He must have told you all about meeting her." He would either confirm or deny it. Or even claim no knowledge of the matter.

Stuart White held his empty glass out.

Instead of pouring him a drink, Tom held the bottle hovering above the glass. He waited for Stuart to give some sort of sign he was going to answer and, only then, he poured him another drink.

Stuart White gulped his drink down before saying, "He was smitten."

Evie lowered herself onto a chair.

She'd been right.

She'd been right?

Her wild theory had, in fact, been a clue, right there, under their noses. But why had Stuart denied knowing James?

"What happened? Did he follow her to London?"

"He was crazy. He came to me and made no sense." He held the empty glass out again but Tom shook his head. Realizing he wouldn't get another drink unless he cooperated, Stuart White said, "He went traveling and then returned to Paris but she wasn't there. That's when he came here."

"Is that when he caught up to Parsody?"

He pressed his lips together and shook his head.

"You're afraid," Evie said.

He nodded.

"You're afraid you'll meet the same fate, especially if the killer finds out you knew James Clementine."

He gave a fierce shake of his head and his voice hitched, "I never met her. I didn't know. I don't have anything to do with it."

Keeping her tone calm, she asked, "Didn't know what?"

"I need another drink."

Tom refilled his glass.

Holding the glass with both hands, Stuart White drank the contents and babbled, "Did I say I knew him? No, I didn't. I'm sure I didn't."

Tucking the bottle against his chest, Tom stepped back.

Evie leaned forward. "Stuart, we know he borrowed your dinner jacket."

Startled, he looked at her. When he spoke, his voice shook, "His luggage was lost. He... he had nothing to wear, not even shoes."

Shoes? "Did you lend him a pair of shoes?"

He nodded. "My new ones too. I don't suppose I could get them back?"

Before he could recover his composure, Evie said, "Benjamin Hammonds also met Parsody and he traveled with you and James." It was a wild stab in the dark.

His eyes nearly bulged out of their sockets. "How do you know his name?"

Right then, Evie suspected he didn't know Benjamin

Hammonds was dead. Although, it made no sense. Millicent had told her there were newspapers and books strewn about his rooms. Surely, he must have read about the young man's death.

She decided to play it safe and not mention Benjamin Hammond's death for fear he might clam up.

Out of the corner of her eye, Evie saw Tom alerting Edgar. As planned, Edgar went to ask Lauren Gladstone to join them.

The moment of truth, Evie thought, and felt her heart drum a beat all the way to her throat.

They already had enough information to make an arrest. This meeting would only confirm a further suspicion.

Tom poured him another drink and Evie was sorely tempted to ask for a glass. She curled her fingers around the armrests and kept her eyes glued to the door. The detective moved to stand by the fireplace.

When she saw Lauren Gladstone, Evie turned to look at Stuart White.

She knew the moment Lauren stepped inside the library because Stuart's eyes widened and he shifted to the edge of his seat, looking as if ready to spring to his feet and flee.

"Miss Gladstone, I believe you know Stuart White," the detective said.

Lauren Gladstone gaped at him. Shaking her head, she swung around, her intention quite clear. However, Tom stood at the door, blocking her exit.

"I had nothing to do with it. I…"

Stuart White paled. He swayed on the spot and keeled over.

The detective rushed to him. "Tom, just how many drinks did you give him?"

"One too many, by the looks of it."

"I doubt we'll get any more information out of him until he sobers up."

Evie thought she had all the confirmation she needed. The detective, however, would want to ask Lauren Gladstone more questions.

Evie looked at Tom and stood up. "Shall we go in to the drawing room? Two more guests are about to arrive."

When Lauren Gladstone took a step, the detective stopped her. "Not you, Miss Gladstone. I would like you to stay here." He motioned to a couple of constables. "They'll keep you company."

As Evie and Tom emerged from the library, they saw another two constables standing in the hall.

Evie had no idea what would happen next. As she'd been preparing for the evening, she had expected they would finally get some answers and then get on with their evening.

Now, everything had changed.

That photograph of Parsody had changed everything.

They were joined by the detective and Althea. Stopping in the middle of the hall, the detective spoke first.

"We will get all the information we need from them."

"Will it help your case?" Evie asked.

"I'm certain of it."

Evie looked toward the drawing room. The dowagers and Toodles were in there with Lauren's mother. She knew this was going to be awkward and perhaps even dangerous.

Before they could decide how to proceed, a footman answered the front door.

Tom edged closer to Evie. She expected him to suggest she stand behind him but she was ready to stand her ground.

The detective leaned in and murmured, "Lady Woodridge, this goes against all protocol and I've had to suspend my better judgment."

He appeared to want to say more but was interrupted when Lotte Mannering walked in.

"A welcoming party," she exclaimed. "For me?"

Evie had never been so happy to see the lady detective. "Lotte. You've missed everything."

"Do tell."

Tom grinned. "I got Stuart White drunk."

"Did he talk?"

"He said enough."

"And now you're in the hall... because..."

Evie looked toward the drawing room again. No one had said anything but everyone seemed to have reached the same decision. It would be safer to do it this way.

"They're here." Evie watched the footman open the door.

Their guests entered. The footman took Mr. Jameson's coat and hat and Parsody handed him her cloak.

They stepped forward and, seeing the welcoming party, they stopped.

"Lady Woodridge!" Mr. Jameson's gaze shifted to the others and then landed on the detective.

"Mr. Jameson." Evie looked at the young woman beside him. "And... I'm sorry, we haven't been properly introduced."

Mr. Jameson took a visible swallow.

The constables moved in and went to stand behind them.

It took a moment for the young woman to react. She looked at Mr. Jameson and murmured something.

Mr. Jameson's face tightened.

Evie stepped back and gestured to a group of chairs by the fireplace. "Do make yourselves comfortable. I believe you have some explaining to do." She knew she was taking liberties and half expected the detective to step forward and say he would take it from there.

Mr. Jameson did not protest. Not even when the constables searched him for weapons.

Evie glanced at the detective. She didn't want to say anything that might jeopardize his investigation but he appeared to be fine with her taking the lead.

Althea stepped forward and handed Evie the magazine. "It seems we have a case of mistaken identity or something along those lines." She studied the photograph of Parsody Jane Buchanan. After a moment, she held up the magazine. "I can't begin to imagine why this young woman has been pretending to be Miss Buchanan, but I'm sure you would like to enlighten us."

Mr. Jameson remained silent, so Evie continued, "We know James Clementine met Miss Buchanan six months ago." They knew that because Stuart White had just told them. "He returned for a visit a few weeks ago and discovered she had traveled to London. He then pursued her here."

Evie knew Stuart White would eventually tell them James Clementine had sought him out. He couldn't deny it. After all, James Clementine had borrowed his clothes and shoes.

"By then," Evie continued, "something had happened to Miss Buchanan." Why else would a young woman pretend to be Parsody? She hoped he would fill in that gap.

Despite the police presence, and the fact he had no weapons on him, Mr. Jameson acted impulsively.

Snatching the young woman, he tried to use her as a shield, issuing his threats to kill her as he backed away and toward the front door.

Of course, he did not get very far.

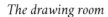

The drawing room

Toodles and the dowagers sat facing Evie, their eyes wide with curiosity and the lingering shock they had experienced when they'd all emerged from the drawing room in time to witness Mr. Jameson trying to make his escape.

Reacting to the scene, Lady Gladstone had screamed.

Her scream had alerted her daughter, Lauren, who had rushed out of the library and had also screamed.

The disturbance had been witnessed by Caro and Lord Evans, who had only then been making their way down.

Responding to the screams, Millicent had rushed down. She had sidled up to Evie in time to watch the constables taking Mr. Jameson into custody.

Leaning in, she'd whispered, "I'd been reading one of my penny dreadful stories and it took me a moment to realize no one in the story was screaming, so it must have been real... and, it was."

The detective allowed Lady Gladstone to take her daughter home on the understanding that she would make herself available for further questioning the next day. With Mr. Jameson in custody, Stuart White was also released under the same conditions.

When the dust had settled, everyone had withdrawn to the drawing room and Henrietta had sat in silence for a full ten minutes.

Finally, she murmured in a voice that conveyed her lingering shock, "Evangeline," but she was drowned out by Tom's offer, "Drinks?"

"Do we need drinks to hear what happened?" Sara asked.

Tom looked up in thought. "Perhaps not. You might want to keep a clear head."

"I'll have one, thank you," Althea stood up and joined Tom. "I can't seem to sit still."

"It's the excitement," Tom explained.

"I could barely keep up. One moment, you were all discussing these outrageous theories and, before I knew what was happening, the killer had been identified." She turned to Evie. "How? My head is still spinning."

Henrietta found her voice. "Evangeline! Please tell us what happened. I'm not getting any younger..."

"My apologies, Henrietta." Evie had already given them a brief account but it obviously hadn't been enough for Henrietta. "That photograph of the real Parsody Jane Buchanan. I wasn't expecting to find that," Evie admitted. "We were looking for anyone who might have attended the Upper Brook Street party and might also have been in

Paris at about the same time as James Clementine. Until that moment, we were only trying to get Lauren and Stuart to admit to knowing each other. The photograph changed everything."

Tom handed Althea her drink. "Yes, I assume we were relying on Lauren Gladstone and Stuart White to eventually confess to having seen the killer at the party."

Evie agreed. "Yes, I was hoping they would lead us to him. As for the photograph, well, it actually makes sense. We all found the fake Parsody odd. I think we made concessions for her because she had led a reclusive life, but the fake Parsody just didn't know how to play the role with any conviction." Evie looked at Caro. "The first time you pretended to be my cousin thrice removed, you had absolutely no trouble. Everyone believed you."

Caro smiled. "I'll take that as a compliment. Perhaps I should consider a career on the stage."

Lord Evans closed his eyes for a moment. Standing up, he walked up to Tom. "I'll take that drink now, please."

"Evangeline," Henrietta prompted her again.

"I think Henrietta needs to hear the rest," Toodles suggested.

"I'm afraid I don't have the full story. We'll have to wait, quite possibly until tomorrow. We'll know more then but only if the detective manages to get a full confession out of Mr. Jameson. I'm sure he will because Mr. Jameson is well and truly cornered."

"But you must have an idea," Toodles said.

"Countess, you thought something had happened in Paris."

"Yes, I can only assume something happened to the real Parsody, either by accident or intentionally, and that young woman was engaged to step in and play the role." She turned to Lotte, who had been sitting quietly in a corner. "From the start, you said she was an heiress. Does that mean she had come into her inheritance? For all we know, Mr. Jameson has no money and has been relying on Parsody's inheritance."

Henrietta nodded. "That makes sense. But… Why did he kill that young man?"

"Which one?" Sara asked.

"Either one, I suppose."

Evie nodded. "Because both James Clementine and Benjamin Hammonds had met the real Parsody Jane Buchanan." Evie shrugged. "I'm assuming the detective will be able to get Lauren Gladstone to admit to having seen Mr. Jameson at the party. You see, I believe James Clementine attended the party with one purpose in mind."

"To find Parsody Jane Buchanan."

Everyone turned and saw Millicent standing by the door.

Evie gestured for her to come in and sit down.

Nodding, Millicent scurried to a chair and sat on the edge.

"Yes, Millicent. I believe that's what he had hoped for."

"Instead, he met Mr. Jameson," Millicent said.

"I'm sure that's what happened." Evie sat back. "However…"

Everyone shifted on their seats.

"Benjamin Hammonds was killed several days before James Clementine met his end." Evie tapped her chin. "I won't be at all surprised if Benjamin Hammonds encountered Mr. Jameson first. I'm sure the detective will get that out of Mr. Jameson. We know Benjamin's drowning was not an accident because he had bruises on his neck."

"Countess, earlier, you'd suggested Benjamin might have organized to meet someone and that's when he met his end."

"Yes, I suspect he might have tried to blackmail Mr. Jameson. Money in exchange for his silence. In the process, he might have mentioned James Clementine's presence in London and that led Mr. Jameson to be on the lookout for him."

Edgar cleared his throat. "My lady, would you like me to delay dinner?"

Evie stood up. "No, Edgar. My apologies for disrupting the schedule. We should go in now."

As she led them through to the dining room, she heard Henrietta murmur, "Didn't I tell you? The killer would just walk in and announce himself."

EPILOGUE

Secret Undertakings

The next morning

*T*oday is the day...
     The thought startled Evie awake. She sprung upright and yelped. In the process, she startled Millicent who had been about to draw the curtains.

"Milady!"

"My apologies. Bad dream."

With her hand pressed against her throat, Millicent looked at her, eyes wide, mouth gaping open. She took a deep swallow. "At least you didn't scream, but the bad dream could be an omen. Do you remember the details?

They might give you a hint and we can stop whatever is about to happen."

Brushing her hand across her eyes, Evie laughed. The wheels were already in motion. "Don't worry, Millicent." She glanced at the window. "The sun is shining. I'm sure today will be a perfect day."

"If you say so, milady. I have a list of tasks all drawn up for today. Once I organize myself, everything should fall in place."

"I'm rather envious of your confidence, Millicent." Evie slipped on her robe and went to stand by the window. "Millicent."

"Yes, milady."

Evie measured her words with care. "If you had to go somewhere, and you were accompanied by someone whom you wished to keep in the dark, what would you do?"

"Distract them, milady, or dangle a carrot."

Evie turned and smiled at her. "That's perfect, Millicent. Thank you. Before I forget, we must write to the Lord Chamberlain and withdraw our application to sponsor Parsody Jane Buchanan." She assumed they would eventually find out what had happened to her.

"I'll work on that straightaway, milady. Just think of it, you nearly sponsored a fake. Your name would have been forever linked to an impostor presented to the monarchs."

"Good heavens, I hadn't thought of it that way. Yes, please, do get to work on the letter straightaway and perhaps send it by special messenger."

"What does that mean?" Millicent asked.

"I'm not sure, it just seemed the right thing to say. Let

me think… Edmonds. Yes, he can drive to St. James's Palace and deliver the missive."

On her way out, Evie eyed the dress Millicent had selected for her and tried not to think how the rest of the day would unfold.

She went down to breakfast and, as expected, found Tom reading the newspaper.

"I'm almost afraid to ask if there is anything of interest. The last few days have been rather hectic, now I wish to enjoy some peace and quiet."

"That sounds ideal." He set the newspaper aside and poured himself another cup of coffee. "And what do we have planned for this morning? A leisurely stroll with no destination in mind? Or will you be practicing your curtsy?"

Sounding as nonchalant as possible, Evie said, "We do have an outing scheduled for today. In fact, we should get ready to leave soon." Before he could ask for details, Evie asked, "I wonder if we'll hear from the detective this morning?"

"It's still early. I'm sure he is up to his eyeballs in paperwork." He checked his watch. "What time are we leaving?"

Evie had already consulted with Edmonds and he had assured her he would get them to their destination by the set time.

"We need to leave by ten."

"That's early for an outing."

"Yes, and… I should go up and change now. I wouldn't want to delay our departure." She finished her breakfast and, standing up, looked at Tom.

"What?"

"Well, you need to change too."

"Change? What's wrong with my suit?" He watched her roll her eyes. "Very well. I won't argue."

A short while later...

"Edgar insisted I needed to wear this suit," Tom said as he made his way down. "Isn't it rather formal?"

"You look splendid." Evie checked the time. "Edmonds is outside waiting for us."

"Why is he driving?"

"I thought it might be nice. Poor Edmonds. Sometimes, I think he feels redundant." Evie mentally checked the contents of her purse. Had she remembered to include the invitation? Yes, she had already checked it twice and remembered telling herself to *leave the gun, take the invitation.*

Outside, Evie greeted Edmonds. He tipped his hat and held the passenger door open for them.

Tom smiled at him. "Sitting in the passenger seat will be quite a novelty."

"Once I finally decide to learn to drive, you will be doing more of that," Evie said as Edmonds got them on their way.

"When are you ever going to find the time, Countess?"

"Tom, anyone would think you're trying to discourage me." Evie kept Tom distracted all the way to the palace.

When they drove through the gates, he frowned. "You

didn't mention anything about going to the palace. Have you been summoned?"

Evie had tried Millicent's idea and had distracted Tom but she couldn't think of a single carrot to dangle.

"Edmonds?"

"Yes, my lady?"

"Have you taken a wrong turn?"

Edmonds, bless him, played along. Either because he didn't wish to contradict Evie or because he knew how Tom felt about this whole business.

"Come to think of it, my lady, I think I may have. Perhaps I should stop to ask for directions."

Out of the corner of her eye, she saw Tom frowning. If he sensed something odd, he didn't say anything.

As swiftly as possible, Edmonds stopped the motor car, they climbed out and Evie led them inside the palace.

At that point, Tom's jaw tensed.

"Countess?"

"Ah, here we are," Evie pointed ahead.

"Lady Woodridge."

Evie smiled as she recognized Sir Augustus Larson, a family friend. "Augustus. How are you this fine morning? It's been too long." After a brief exchange of pleasantries, she made the introductions.

"Mr. Winchester. How do you do?"

Tom remained polite but Evie knew him well enough to read the signs. If he didn't take care, he would grind his back teeth all the way to their roots.

Sir Augustus Larson led them up a grand staircase and Evie maintained a steady flow of conversation all the way to the ballroom.

The ceremony was already under way. Looking

around, Evie saw several dozen people observing the proceedings, while others stood just ahead of them, presumably waiting to have their name called.

Tom stood close enough to her for Evie to notice the moment he tensed. The king, attended by the Yeomen of the Guard, was bestowing an honor on a man, who then bowed his head and retreated.

The Lord Chamberlain called the next recipient. As Evie watched the proceedings, she saw Sir Augustus Larson having a quick word with Tom and knew he was issuing instructions.

After several minutes, the Lord Chamberlain called, "To receive the order of knighthood, Sir Thomas Winchester..."

Shooting Evie a quick glance, which carried a mixture of surprise and rage, Tom stepped forward, walked up to the king, bowed his head, and kneeled on the Investiture stool.

Evie absorbed every second of the ceremony, paying close attention to every detail and committing it all to memory. She knew that, in the next few seconds, she would have a lot of explaining to do. In fact, she suspected she would spend the rest of her life explaining and apologizing for her underhanded tactics.

Newly knighted, Tom approached her, his gaze never wavering from Evie. Taking her by the arm, he led her out and did not stop until they were outside.

"Countess," Tom erupted.

"There's Edmonds, waiting for us," Evie chirped. "We mustn't keep him waiting, Tom." As they climbed in and settled in the back seat, Evie pressed her finger to her lips and signaled toward Edmonds, as if to suggest this was not the most ideal place to air his grievances.

Tom drew down his eyebrows and pressed his lips together.

Looking ahead, Evie worried her bottom lip. There had been something unusual about the proceedings but she couldn't quite put her finger on it.

Several minutes later, Tom pushed out a breath and said in a surprisingly calm tone, "Countess, I hope you realize we will either be asked to leave the country or be thrown in prison for misleading the monarch."

"What?" She hadn't expected to hear that from him.

"Yes, by the way, nicely done, dragging me here and forcing me to finally accept the honor."

"Tom, it had to be done. You couldn't keep postponing it."

"I did that for a very good reason."

"Didn't we discuss this? You don't have to be a British subject to receive an honor. This merely means you are an Honorary Knight. No one will be required to use the title when addressing you."

"And that is the reason why I fear there will be repercussions. There was no mention of an honorary title. This is the real McCoy."

Evie gaped. "That's it! I knew I'd sensed something wrong. Someone must have made a mistake."

"We should return and give this medal back."

"Tom, we can't do that."

He scowled at her. "So, you will have me strutting about, lying to everyone?"

Evie shrugged. "For the time being, no one needs to know. I'll contact Sir Augustus Larson and sort this out.

I'm sure he'll know what to do. The solution is probably as simple as just not using the title."

"You seem to be ill informed," Tom claimed. "The Warrant of Appointment has been signed. This is official."

"How do you know that?"

Tom leaned back and closed his eyes. "I know that because the fellow standing next to the king read it from an official document."

Lifting her chin, Evie said, "In that case, we'll just keep it to ourselves and make discreet enquiries. There must be a way to fix this."

They continued the rest of the journey back to Woodridge House in relative silence, with Tom murmuring about having to leave the country.

When they arrived, Edgar opened the front door. He took Evie's coat and handed it to a footman.

"Where is everyone?" Evie asked.

"In the drawing room, my lady." Edgar led the way to the drawing room and, stepping inside ahead of them, said, "Lady Woodridge and Sir Thomas Winchester."

Tom shot Evie a look that spoke of incredulity. "You were saying?"

How had word spread so quickly? She was about to explain the mistake when she noticed the dowagers and Toodles had company.

"Detective!"

"One moment, please." Henrietta stepped forward and congratulated Tom. Turning to Evie, she said, "As for you, Evangeline…"

Oh, dear.

Henrietta lifted her chin. "Words fail me. You have deprived us of witnessing this momentous occasion."

Evie gulped. The invitation for the investiture had clearly stated they were allowed two guests. She would have had to choose between the dowagers and Toodles. Putting off the difficult decision, she had then forgotten all about it...

Henrietta pursed her lips; a sign Evie recognized only too well.

She was about to be subjected to the silent treatment again.

Giving a firm nod, the Dowager Countess of Woodridge stepped back and began administering her punishment.

Accepting her fate and not daring to look at Sara for fear she might issue the same retribution, Evie turned to the detective. "I hope you've brought us some news."

"I have indeed, my lady. After the extraordinary events of the last couple of days, I felt it only right to inform you of the developments. We have located James Clementine's remaining family. He only had an elderly Uncle. The young man had been his heir. We have also discovered Miss Buchanan's fate. That is, the real Miss Buchanan. Two months ago, she slipped in the bath, hit her head and died. Mr. Jameson had been enjoying her wealth and her death put an end to it all. As they had been living abroad for so long and not mingling in society, he thought no one would know if he found someone to pretend to be Parsody Jane Buchanan. Of course, we now know how that didn't quite work out for him. He will be held responsible for the deaths of James Clementine and Benjamin Hammonds, who had both met the real Parsody."

"And what will happen to the young woman who pretended to be Parsody?"

"There is a matter of deception but her sentence will not be so severe. In the end, Mr. Jameson sealed his fate by befriending you. I'm sure he was not aware of your reputation."

"I wouldn't be so sure about that." Evie remembered what Henrietta had told her about keeping friends close and enemies closer. "He might have tried to hide his nefarious activities in plain sight." In other words, he had gambled and he had lost. "Does Althea know all this?" Evie asked.

The detective's expression hardened.

"Birdie, you can invite her to dinner and tell her all about it. She can join us for the celebration. After all, it's not every day Tom is knighted."

"Yes, well… about that…"

～

A week later, Caro's presentation

Caro murmured, "Sweep my left leg back, bend my right knee… No, that's not right. Wait… yes, it is."

"Caro," Evie whispered. "Our turn is coming up."

"No, it can't be. I'm not ready yet."

"I've already handed them the card. They'll be reading out your name at any moment now." Evie knew she had to do something to encourage Caro, but she could only come up with, "It's now or never."

"Never. Yes, I like the sound of that. Where is it actually written that I have to do this?"

"Caro, everyone's watching." She signaled to one side. "Tom's watching."

Caro searched for him. Evie knew the precise moment she found him because she giggled.

"He looks like he could murder someone. Is he trying to pull down his knee breeches or are his knees knocking together? I must say, Henry was none too pleased about having to wear his knee breeches, but he's enduring it as best he can. Although, he does look a bit stiff standing next to Tom."

To his credit, Tom stopped fidgeting. Lifting his chin, he struck up a pose that could only be described as regal.

"The Countess of Woodridge presenting the Lady Carolina Evans."

Caro stifled a yelp. She then reacted so quickly by taking a step forward, Evie had to hurry to catch up. As they approached the monarchs, they made their curtsy. While Caro did a splendid job of it, Evie nearly stumbled as she rose and noticed the Prince of Wales standing beside his mother.

Wait until I tell Sara, she thought.

Then she remembered the mistake that had been made with Tom's knighthood, an issue which had as yet to be resolved, and did her best to avoid meeting anyone else's gaze.

When they reached the point where they could turn, Caro murmured, "A lady's maid has just made her curtsy in front of the monarchs. I believe we are living in a modern world."

Tom wove his way through the large gathering and

caught up with them. "That went well. Now can we leave?"

"We have to have our photographs taken, Tom."

Nodding, he pointed to a corner. "I'll be standing over there admiring that wall."

"That must be his version of an ostrich hiding its head," Caro whispered.

During their return to Woodridge House, Caro said, "I didn't realize there were going to be so many people lining the streets. Queen Mary has a lovely smile and I believe she gave me a nod of approval. Of course, I'm sure everyone who curtsied before her is saying the same thing. Now I'm glad it's all over and... I'm sorry for all the fuss I made. Everything should settle back to normal now."

Henry and Tom exchanged a look that suggested they might not agree with Caro's prediction.

"At least no one addressed me by my title," Tom said.

Lord Evans laughed. "That's because you avoided talking with anyone. I hope you realize everyone knows."

"What?"

"The Gazette, Tom. The list of honors is always listed." Lord Evans yelped and bent down to rub his ankle.

"Sorry, dearest. My foot slipped," Caro offered.

Evie closed her eyes and thought of the interesting days ahead.

When they arrived, Caro released a long sigh. "I'm almost sorry it's all over now."

"Not quite, Caro."

They stepped out of the motor car and walked up to the front door.

"There is one more thing... but you'll have to close your eyes." Evie took Caro's elbow and guided her inside.

"Where are we going?" Caro asked.

"Are your eyes closed? You promised to keep them closed." Evie guided Caro along the hall, past the library. Up ahead, Henrietta, Sara and Toodles, who had just arrived from the presentation, were all smiles. Evie looked at Edgar and gave him a nod.

Smiling from ear to ear, he made a flourishing gesture with his hand and opened the doors.

"I know this is going to be a lovely surprise but I can't help worrying," Caro admitted.

"Dear Caro, if you don't like what I'm about to show you, then, by all means, tell me."

As they neared the double doors, the dowagers and Toodles hurried inside, presumably to gain a vantage point so they could see Caro's reaction to the surprise.

"Who's there? I heard steps and they were hurried."

"We're nearly there." Evie guided her the rest of the way and they came to a stop in the middle of the room. "You can open your eyes now."

Caro's intake of breath was followed by a yelp. "All this is for me? All those flowers are for me?"

"Yes, of course." Evie cast an appreciative eye at the large ballroom. The chandeliers had undergone a thorough clean and sparkled like diamonds. The red velvet curtains had been drawn and light spilled into the room.

Caro took several tentative steps. "All this is for me," she repeated. "What if no one comes?"

Evie laughed. "At some point, I'm sure, you'll wish people would leave."

A footman entered carrying a tray of champagne glasses.

Before anyone could stop her, Caro took a glass and had a sip. "Oh, it tingles." Caro whirled around. "I'll want the night to go on forever."

***

Printed in Great Britain
by Amazon

22223254R00155